finding TOMORROW

SAVANNAH STEWART

Cover Design: Savvy Designs

Cover Photography: Perrywinkle Photography

Editor: Virginia Tesi Carey

Proofreaders: Virginia Tesi Carey & Traci Kennedy

BOOKS BY SAVANNAH

To my fur-baby, Jack, I will forever miss you.

AFTER

Have you ever had the feeling that the world was moving on without you? That no matter what, you're frozen in place while your entire life becomes a wildfire that burns everything you love to ash?

That's the recurring nightmare I'd been living.

One punch after the other knocked me on my ass. I'd prayed, gotten angry, and tried my damnedest to find solace in the smallest things in hope that my feet would land on steady ground. My chest would fill with a deep burning breath that would provide me with a sense of peace as it expelled from my lungs.

But that breath hadn't come.

As if Mother Nature herself was mocking me, a gust of wind flipped my loose hair across my face, the buzzing nightlife of the city temporarily shielded from sight. Sullen laughter escaped me as I hastily tied my hair at the nape of my neck with the hair tie that rested around my wrist. My forearms laid against my thighs as I leaned forward a bit more, pushing my knees into the brick wall hard enough to cause my flesh to burn. A young woman hurried across the street on her cell phone toward the bar I'd watched almost every night since my life had been turned upside down.

The woman stopped just as she stepped onto the sidewalk. A broad smile most likely spread across her face as a suave looking man in a dark moto jacket wrapped his arms around her waist, lifted her into the air as his mouth met hers, and they spun a couple rotations before sitting her back on her feet. The scene before me blurred as hot tears pushed passed my eyelids and raced furiously down my cheeks, dripping onto my chest. I shoved up from the rickety metal chair.

"Christ," I seethed through gritted teeth as the flesh of my left knee tore open from the rough texture of the brick I'd been pressed against. Yet another round of pain I'd inflicted upon myself, like the universe wasn't doing a good enough job on its own.

The metal chair screeched across the concrete rooftop as I shoved it back far enough to squeeze between it and the makeshift table I'd thrown together from pallet scraps I'd found by the dumpster in the alley beside my building. Being there were only three floors, and I lived on the third, the view from the rooftop to the city below was an easy one to observe. My own personal show almost every night.

Something in my gut forced me to turn around and glance over the edge once more before turning in to drown my sorrows with a bottle of bourbon. A man, in what seemed to be a tailored suit, hurried across the street, much like the woman had before him, a cell phone pressed at his ear. He seemed unraveled. His shirt was untucked on one side, his hair standing wildly as if he'd fingered through the dark locks over and over again. But my eyes didn't stay on him long enough to get a feel of his phone conversation due to a fast-moving yellow blur catching my eye. A car without headlights was barreling around the corner right toward him. My heart flopped as I screamed at the top of my lungs,

"Watch out!" The man glanced up in my direction before his eyes dropped to the car. His phone crashed to the ground as my feet took flight toward the fire escape.

The last thing to cross my mind as I hurried down the shaky stairs was how desperately I needed to get to him.

CHAPTER ONE

I *love my husband, I love my husband, I love my husband.*

The pillow latched down on my head was doing nothing to block out the hellacious snores coming from Liam beside me. I tossed it onto the floor and lifted up to check the time. His alarm would start wailing in about seven minutes, forcing me out of bed for the day.

Any other time his snoring wouldn't wake me, but for some reason I was hyperaware to everything going on, his snores, the clinking of the ceiling fan that's gone off balance, and the headlights shining through the curtains every time a vehicle passed by.

Insomnia had claimed me as its newest victim.

Not wasting another second tossing and turning, I slipped from the bed and padded into the bathroom, not bothering to turn on the light until the door was closed. Liam needed every ounce of sleep he could get, and I didn't want to be the reason to wake him before need be.

"Oh, Terra..." I stared at the mirror in horror. Dark circles lived beneath my eyes from lack of sleep, my hair had seen better days, and my skin was far too pale for my normal self.

I'd been slacking on taking care of myself since I'd decided to ditch my nine to five to embark on the journey of owning my own business. Liam warned me it would be tiring, although I already knew that up front from spending six years watching him build his empire from the ground up. One sunny afternoon when I was home with the stomach bug, he'd come barging in from work early, stressed from dealing with his shitty boss and fellow coworkers, and tossed the idea of trading stocks at me. I'd never been one to drown someone's dreams, so I agreed if it was something he wanted to give a try he should go for it. Six years later and we were sitting pretty comfortably, thanks to him being brave enough to take a risk.

I ran a brush through my wild hair and placed rejuvenating eye patches on the darkness making its home beneath my eyes, hoping they'd make me look a little more human. Midway through brushing my teeth, Liam's alarm roared from our bedroom. I hated the sound of that thing, its angry noise to startle someone awake. I preferred the radio myself, but I hadn't used an alarm in quite some time, thanks to my internal clock.

"Hey." His sleep filled voice came from the doorway.

I rinsed my mouth out before turning to him. "Good morning." A grin easily spread across my face.

He scratched his head and yawned. "Been up long?" Liam squeezed my shoulders as he passed me to turn on the shower.

My lungs deflated with a sigh. "Unfortunately, yes. For some reason my mind was going a million miles a minute last night."

His eyebrows furrowed. "About what?" He continued to undress.

"Absolutely nothing, and everything at the same time."

Liam chuckled.

I crossed my arms over my chest and leaned back against the sink. "Are you laughing at me, Mr. Anders?" One eyebrow rose in question as my eyes roamed his bare flesh. My husband had a body that most women gawked at. Lean muscle, strong shoulders, and a booty that I couldn't achieve with a thousand squats a day, made up a portion of my man. He was completely gorgeous, and one hundred percent mine.

"What if I was?" His teasing tone had me smiling from ear-to-ear as I watched him step into the shower, pausing with the glass door held open.

I grabbed the hem of my cotton tank top and pulled it from my body. "It's not nice to laugh at people, you know." The material slipped from my fingers and dropped to the floor.

Liam's Adam's apple bobbed, frozen in place holding the shower door open. "Maybe I need to laugh some more." His almond colored eyes darkened.

"Is that so?" My bottom lip tucked between my teeth. I slipped my hands into the waistband of my pajama shorts and pushed them to the floor, stepping out of them on my way to the shower stall.

"You're killing me, Terra," Liam groaned as undeniable want swam in his eyes.

I stepped over the threshold of the shower and closed the door behind me. "How about you let me love you instead?" My lips were merely centimeters from his as I smoothed my hands around his lean waist, ran my fingertips up his muscular back, and pressed my naked self against him.

"I wouldn't want to shower any other way, but first..." Liam peeled the eye patches from beneath my eyes and dangled them between us.

Hysterical laughter erupted between us as I took the eye patches from him. "I forgot I had those on." I sat them beside the shampoo bottle for the time being.

"You looked cute." He chuckled as he pulled my body back to his.

"No adult woman wants to hear she's *cute*." I playfully pushed his shoulder.

The corners of his mouth tipped upward. "How about," he

drug a finger down the valley between my breasts, "you look remarkably sexy."

My arms snaked around his neck and rested against his shoulders. "Eye patches and all." I giggled.

"You'd be sexy in a paper bag." His thumbs skated across the underside of my breasts.

"Pretty sure I've worn one recently." Cracking a joke at my lack of making myself presentable didn't go unnoticed. The frown that pulled his lips down made me sigh.

Liam leaned over to grab the body wash I used and squeezed a nice helping into his hand. "You know what I'm going to say." He paused as his fingers massaged knots from my tense back. "I make more than enough money to keep us living comfortably. You don't have to stress yourself out like this."

I knew he meant well, but the thought of not working didn't sit well with me. He'd offered time and time again that I could get into the trading business with him, but I needed something that was mine. A career I was proud of, not something to pass the time. I'd been lucky enough to quit a job that I only kept because it paid decently. I needed to make use of the free time to find my passion. What that was, I wasn't sure yet.

"You're right." I kissed his wet lips and squeezed his shampoo and conditioner combo into my palm. "I need to stop stressing about figuring out the future and find what sets my soul on fire. Whatever passion that drives me, you know?" I tiptoed and massaged the combo against his scalp.

Liam locked an arm around my waist, water pelted from his head onto my bare chest. "I want you to be happy, baby, that's all."

"I know you do, and I love you even more for that."

How I'd gotten so lucky to find a man like Liam, I'd never know. His heart overflowed with love and admiration for all those around him. He'd never turn his back on someone in need, and I was constantly in awe of him. It was rare that you found a beautiful man who had a kind soul to go with his looks, but fate had given him to me one unexpected rainy night, when I'd broken down on the side of the road. When his beautiful face peered at me through my car window, I never imagined ten years later we'd share a home, along with the same last name.

After our shower, Liam had gone into the office to get some work done, while I spent the morning cleaning house. When lunch rolled around I took it upon myself to surprise him with an array of cheese, crackers, salami, and olives on a platter. "Hungry?" I stepped into Liam's office. A giant smile relaxed the creases of heavy thinking away that had been on display when I first passed the threshold.

"You're a godsend." He leaned back in the chair as I sat the tray on the desk and kissed him deeply. His hand held the back of my head to prolong the kiss, sending the butterflies deep in my core fluttering into chaos. "Mmm... maybe I should have you for lunch instead." His heady words were spoken between hot kisses.

"I wouldn't complain," I breathlessly managed as I turned the chair and slipped onto his lap.

Just as we were getting hot and heavy a ding came from his laptop. "Uh, I'm sorry, baby." Liam frowned. "Stock indicator for an upcoming trade."

I shook my head. "There's no need to apologize." I kissed him once more. "I know you're working. Just wanted to bring you something to eat." My lips lingered a moment longer than before. This time I stood from his lap and headed for the bookcase in the back corner of the room.

I couldn't tell you the last time I'd read a book, or even had time to do so. Heck, I didn't even own an e-Reader, if that told you anything. All my friends had them, even ranted and raved about how convenient they were, and the pricing of the books they read, but I never took a dive into that world. Given that I had more time on my hands, and a journey of finding my passion ahead of me, I picked a book at random from the shelf and took a seat in the plush chair beside the bookcase.

A couple pages in and I couldn't help that my attention was caught by my husband. His hair was in disarray from fingering through it as he worked. I watched him overtop the book as he typed away, staring intently at the computer screen. A smile tipped one side of my mouth as the thoughts of the amount of love my heart housed for him. Life before the two of us seemed like a faraway alternate reality that never actually existed, but it had. I thought I was happy back then, casually dating, but never finding the guy who knocked me off my feet. All of those crash and burn relationships were simply building me up for the man I'd been destined to be with, and boy does he still knock me off my feet.

"Son of a bitch," Liam mumbled.

"Everything okay?"

He slammed his hand against the desk before turning to face me. "Sorry, I forgot you're in here." The other hand went through his hair and an exhausted puff of air passed his lips. "Things can get a little intense in here while trading stocks."

"Really?"

"Yeah." He nodded. "In a rapid second you can lose quite a bit of money—which I just did, actually." A humorless laugh deflated Liam.

"Oh." I nibbled my bottom lip, not knowing what to say.

A shaky grin replaced his frown. "No worries, I'll make up for it this afternoon."

Liam looked exhausted. Even though he'd been sleeping soundly for weeks, it seemed as if he wasn't fully resting. I hadn't noticed just how drained he seemed to be. "You okay?" I closed the book and sat it on my lap.

"Just tired." He combed his hair with his fingers once again. A tell-tale sign that stress was getting the best of him.

"I have an idea." A mega-watt smile adorned my face as I pushed up from the chair. Liam raised an eyebrow in question as he awaited my response. "Do you work all day?"

"I don't have to..." He narrowed his eyes. "What are you concocting in that head of yours?" I rummaged through the drawer beside where he sat, knowing the last time I'd seen what I was looking for, it was in there. "What in the world are you doing?" Liam scooted back a bit to give me room.

"Ah, ha!" I jerked the certificate from the drawer, holding it up for him to see. "We've had this couples massage voucher since Christmas, I think it's time we use it."

He rolled his head around his neck and closed his eyes for a brief moment. "You know what?" He powered the computer off. "Let's see if they have availability for today. It's been a while since we've been able to enjoy some us time with no distractions. The stocks will be there tomorrow, and I'd like to have some time with my beautiful wife." Liam wrapped his arms around my waist and pulled my body against his. Our lips molded together without hesitation, his hands smoothed up my spine as mine gripped his strong back.

"I love the sound of that." I stepped from his grasp and went to retrieve my phone.

* * *

My limbs were languid as I flopped down on the couch. Liam fell beside me and pulled my legs onto his lap. His hands smoothed up my bare shin. "Why don't we get couples massages more often? It makes you feel like a new person afterwards. No stress clouding your mind, no tension built up in your body, just the simple want of taking a nap."

I gushed with laughter.

Liam was right though. I always felt like a new person after having a massage, and it was something the both us desperately needed.

"You know, I could take a nap myself."

He slowly grinned. "You probably need one after the sleepless night you had."

A heavy exhale left me. "Isn't that the truth, and you know I'm not one to nap."

"Then let's take advantage of this opportunity." He moved my legs and lifted from the couch, extending a hand for me to take. Once I was on my feet, Liam swept me into his arms. Laughter bubbled up my throat and echoed through our silent house as he carried me into our bedroom, pulled the blanket back, and laid me beneath it.

Discarding my dress, my eyes roamed Liam's body as he stripped down to his boxers before snuggling in beside me. The warmth of his skin against mine had me snuggling into him as close as possible. With one leg hooked over his and my head resting against his chest, I found myself easily falling asleep.

"Terra?" Liam's raspy voice pulled me back to awareness.

"Hmm?"

"I love you, and whatever path you choose for your career, I'll be there cheering you on." He kissed the top of my head and pulled me even tighter against his side.

"My love for you is more than words can express." I placed my hand against his chest right above his heart and gently kissed his skin.

Sleep found me quicker than it had in quite some time.

CHAPTER TWO

Stirring awake, I arched my back and slid my hand across Liam's chest. The warmth that had put me to sleep wasn't as prominent. *I must've left the air on.* With the warm nights coming to a close and fall rolling in, I constantly had to switch the thermostat from heat to air and back again.

My eyes fluttered open to find the setting sun beaming through the window, painting orange and pink hues onto our plain white walls. *I really need to make this house a home now that I have the time.* Liam was fast asleep with his mouth slightly parted. I could spend all eternity staring at him. His thick eyelashes were much darker than his sandy hair and his plump lips beckoned me to kiss them. Men always got the better lashes and perfect lips, it wasn't fair.

I leaned over and pressed my lips against his bottom one, softly tickling his side. "Liam," I gently shook him, "wake up sleepyhead. We've been napping for hours."

"Uh…" he groaned, rolling toward me.

"You okay?" I smoothed a hand up his forehead, pushing his hair back just a bit to check for a fever.

Squinting, his throat bobbed as he swallowed. "Worst headache of my life." His words were barely audible.

I lifted from the bed and slipped my dress over my head. "How about I get you some water and medicine? Maybe that'll help."

Liam shot upright. "Think I'm gonna be sick." He swung his legs over the edge of the bed and attempted to stand but his knees buckled. His hands shot out in an attempt to grab onto something, knocking everything off the nightstand.

"Liam!" I ran with my arms outstretched, making it to him just in time to help guide his body to the floor. "Baby, are you okay?" My heart frantically slammed in my chest as I watched his eyes roll back in his head, his mouth slack and his body go rigid. "You're having a seizure, it's going to be okay. You're going to be okay."

Oh God...Oh God...Oh God...

I reached for his cell phone, but when he fell he'd knocked it out of sight, leaving me unable to call for help.

Was he going to be okay?

Emotions sat thick in my throat as I watched the man who owned my heart jerk, gasp for a breath, and fall limp in my arms. "Liam..." Tears filled my eyes so hastily they shot down my cheeks at a rapid pace. "No, no, no..." I rocked him against me, not knowing what to do. *Look for a pulse, do CPR!* My mind screamed and I jumped into action. His pulse hammered harder than my own, and then just stopped.

"One, two, three, four...." I counted out compressions between hiccupped cries. *This can't be happening...*

My hands shook as I reached for his wrist to check his pulse again, but there was nothing.

No beat.

No slight tick of his skin.

Nothing.

"God, don't do this to me...I love you, Liam. Don't leave me." I reached for his neck, to check there, yet again coming up empty.

"Oh, Liam…I'm so sorry…" I collapsed onto his chest, my body shaking violently from my sobs, willing his heart to start beating beneath my face, but the stillness remained. My eyes searched the floor for one of our phones, but neither could be found. I needed help. Liam couldn't be gone…that wasn't a possibility.

I lifted from the floor and took off for the front door, flinging it open. "Someone help! Please! Somebody help me!" My desperate sobs pulling the attention of neighbors.

A man I'd seen numerous times came running. "What's going on?" He gripped my arms, but all I could do was cry and point into the house.

"My—my husband! Bedroom!" I managed to choke out before he took off through the door.

His face was replaced by a woman's attempting to console me, her words were a foggy ensemble I couldn't quite make out. The thumping of my heart roared in my ears, my mouth was dry, and my eyes burned from all the tears.

My hearing focused on a man rambling off my address. I turned my head to find him on his cell phone.

What's happening?

I pulled from the woman's hold and barreled back into the house. As I hit the threshold of our bedroom I watched the man doing CPR on my husband. The coloring of his skin had changed, but the man was still going, pumping his palms into his chest before breathing into his mouth.

Sirens blared off in the distance, growing louder with each passing second. "Paramedics are here," the woman I hadn't realized was directly behind me called out.

Everything seemed to blur as paramedics rushed past me, one stopping to ask questions. "Are you his wife?"

"Ye—yeah?" My arms wrapped tightly around myself.

His eyes were soft with understanding. "Can you run through what happened for me?"

I nodded. "We woke up from a nap and he said his head was

hurting…the worst headache of his life…I got up to get him some water and medicine when he thought he was going to be sick. Liam pushed from the bed and collapsed trying to get to the bathroom—" My voice thickened as even more tears rushed my eyes. The EMT placed a hand on my arm. "I—I couldn't find either of our phones to call for help…I tried CPR, but—" A sob cut my sentence short.

The EMT working on Liam cleared his throat and silently spoke. "Time of death, nineteen forty-eight."

* * *

The keys hitting the counter echoed through the empty kitchen. My eyes dropped to the pair of boots Liam wore when he mowed the grass, sitting just inside the door in the mudroom, green staining the soles. The ache in my chest intensified. Leaning over, I gripped the counter with one hand, the other wrinkling my dress from the death grip I had at my heart. *Breathe, just breathe, Terra.* I tried to will the tears away, but they won in the end, silently rolling down my swollen cheeks, dripping onto the bare flesh just above the collar of my dress.

"Do you want me to sta—Oh, Terra." Hysterics hit me full force as Laura held me against her chest. I gripped the back of her shirt, my body convulsing from the quiet sobs ripping through me.

A few steady breaths and I stepped from her arms. Laura meant well, I knew that, but I didn't want my unraveling to take place with others around. I needed to do that alone. "You don't have to stay."

"Terra." Her bright blue eyes softened with sympathy. I couldn't stand seeing that look in regard to myself, especially coming from those closest to me.

"I'm serious." I turned my back to her. "You don't have to stay, I'll be fine. Liam will be cremated after the autopsy, and…" My bottom lip trembled as the millionth onset of tears made their appearance. How someone could produce so many tears, I never knew. I sucked my lip between my teeth and inhaled deeply through my nose.

Laura touched my arms, slowly turning me toward her. "I can't even begin to imagine what you're going through, so don't worry about saying anything more." Her hands smoothed up and down my biceps. "Call me no matter the time. I mean that, Terra. I'm here for you, Mark is here for you. We love you, don't you dare think otherwise."

She let go of my arms as I nodded. "I love you guys, too." My chin quivered as the words hung in the air. Laura's eyes dropped to my hands. I wrung them together, one of my nervous habits.

"Well." She paused, her eyes lifting back to mine. Laura didn't want to leave, that was obvious, but she would never push me to let her stay either. She lifted her purse from the counter and tossed it onto her shoulder. "Eleven minutes is all it takes for me to be here."

Sniffling, I wiped my nose. "I know."

Laura backed away until she bumped the door, hesitation etched on her face. "I really don't want to leave you alone…"

My shoulders slumped as I exhaled. "I know, and I love you even more for that."

A small smile tipped Laura's lips. "I love you too, Terra." Tears brimmed her eyes as I watched her leave, waited for her car door to slam, and the acceleration of her vehicle to fade before I crumbled to the floor in a heaping mess.

Time ticked away as I lost every ounce of resistance I had left. My head throbbed, my eyes stung, and my chest felt like someone had hollowed it out, but I managed to push myself up from the floor. I wasn't sure how much time had passed since Laura had left, but knew it was a while, since the sun was rising, bringing beautiful colors and happiness along with it.

I officially loathed that giant burning orb.

How could it still rise when my life had been swallowed by darkness?

The only light on in the house was the one above the kitchen sink. Cold loneliness filled the place I called home. The sight of a stock trading book left open on the sofa, with a bookmark stuck between the pages, filled me with heartache. I twirled my wedding band as I braved the storm and stepped into our bedroom, which was still in shambles. Bypassing the mess, I tossed myself onto the mattress—Liam's side to be exact—his scent enveloping me as if he'd just slipped from bed. "Why did you have to go?" My voice cracked.

I closed my eyes and breathed in deeply. My face buried into Liam's pillow, I reached for the comforter and pulled it over my head. Never leaving the bed was the only option that made sense to me. It was the last place he'd been, the last place we'd shared before...

A vibration rattled against the foot of the bed over and over, stopping for a brief moment before starting up again. I scooted to the edge and hung my head over. Liam's cell phone stared back at me. It had been within arm's length the entire time. The screen flashed from an incoming call. I didn't bother seeing who was calling or answering for that matter. Instead, I rolled over and pretended the world no longer existed.

If only life was that easy.

Annoyance at the damn thing grew the more it rang. I jerked the covers back and retrieved the burden beneath the bed, not bothering to read the number flashing on the screen. A scream ripped from my lungs as I launched the cell phone across the room. It shattered against the wall as another gut-wrenching wail tore from within me. My knees slammed into the carpet as I toppled over, and the palms of my hands caught the brunt of my weight, my breaths quick and short—my throat burning from the ache closing it off.

I. Can't. Breathe.

Pressure raged in my chest as my heartbeat erratically spiked, my head in a haze as the world closed in on me. I curled into a ball on the floor, trying my damnedest to calm myself, but failing miserably. "God, please..." I gasped. "I. Can't. Do. This," I choked out between breaths.

With my eyes shut, I wrapped my arms around my head and clutched the back of my skull. *Please, I beg you...please let this pass...* Inhaling a giant breath, I tossed my head back and broke out into sobs. Every inch of my being ached from heartache. How was a person supposed to deal with such an intense feeling? Let alone heal?

I shot up from the floor and ran into the kitchen, yanking open the cabinets until I found what I was searching for; a bottle of Scotch. The exact bottle of Scotch that we'd brought home from our honeymoon in Scotland to use as a celebratory drink. Sadly, we'd never gotten around to cracking it open when good things had come our way over the years.

Tears streamed down my face as I frantically opened the bottle and turned it up. Chugging the amber liquid as fast as my throat would allow, small streams raced from the corners of my mouth and dripped onto my chest. The burning would usually make me cough, but my heart was so shattered that nothing could cause me more pain than I was already in.

I slammed the bottle onto the counter as I gasped for a breath, liquor was thick in the air around me. I'd never been one to drink excessively, but I had a feeling everything I once knew about myself was going to change. Gripping the counter for support, I hung my head between my shoulders and tried to slow my breathing, but nothing was helping.

My mind was swimming in a fog.

My heart was dying an agonizing death.

And my soul...my soul was torn down the middle the moment Liam took his last breath.

With the bottle clutched in my hand, I stepped onto the back patio and flopped into the bed swing, sloshing a bit of Scotch onto the cushion, a scowl firm on my face as I stared into the sky. The beauty of the day made me angry as I took swigs from the bottle every so often.

A gentle breeze rolled across my face, whipping my wild hair as memories of the happiness I shared with Liam flooded in. Silent tears made an appearance, this time they weren't brewed from sadness of his loss, but bittersweet heartache of what we once shared. A chuckle rolled through my body like a foreign object at the thought of his boyish grin every time he did something silly. I closed my eyes and rested my head back against the plush cushion as I chugged a nice helping of the Scotch before snuggling the bottle against my side. A heavy sigh expelled from my lungs as a calming sensation washed over me for the first time since my world had been knocked off its axis.

CHAPTER THREE

I flipped my cell phone face down on the table and silenced the call. Nothing about speaking with Liam's mother was appealing at the moment. Don't get me wrong, I loved my in-laws with all my heart, but over the past six months since his death it's been hard to hear their voices. Even replying to their emails pulled a stitch out of my fragile heart. I wasn't sure that avoiding the people who loved me was the right way to go about the journey of healing, but who had a handbook on that kind of stuff?

I sure as hell didn't.

So, I did the one thing I'd learned to do best...I ran.

A few months after losing the love of my life, I'd put our home on the market. I couldn't bear being alone within those walls. His presence was too strong. It constantly felt like he was still there, which some would call a blessing. I, however, called it torture.

It didn't take very long, just a few weeks actually, for the house to be sold. A young couple, embarking on their journey into marital bliss, bought it. Their smiling faces chipped away at my heart the day I signed the paperwork. I remembered being that happy—loving the life I lived—not so much anymore. I was in a constant nightmare that I couldn't wake from, and the only option for me was to find a way to adapt.

I sold the majority of our belongings, only holding onto the sentimental items that meant the most to me. No, I wasn't trying to forget Liam, or the life we had shared. But hanging on to everything that reminded me of him was housing me in a state of depression. It was as if time was moving on around me, yet I was standing still without the capability to move even an inch. I needed so desperately to move far more than an inch.

With very few ties left binding me to Ann Arbor, I allowed my heart to make the decision of leaving it behind. As crazy as it sounds, I packed the remainder of my belongings into my vehicle and allowed the road to lead me to my next destination. The unknown always frightened me, but in that moment on the open road it did the opposite. It gave a sense of adventure, a sense of finding what was meant to be next for me, and the next chapter of my life ended up being Philadelphia, Pennsylvania.

My nails tapped against the coffee mug as I stared out the large glass pane windows, the chair across from me the perfect height to rest my crossed ankles on. Magnolia had quickly become the spot I found peace. A quaint coffee shop resting in the corner of a large brick building that had seen many years of wear. I loved the history Philly housed.

I caught sight of my still closed laptop resting on the wooden table. I'd yet managed to open the damn thing. My mind wasn't focusing like it had been the past few months. Today, it was filled with heavy thoughts and heartache that hadn't haunted me so intensely lately. Which most likely was caused by Janet's, my mother in-law, recent email and persistent calling.

She'd begged me to answer her calls. To give her the time of day, because I was the only thing they had to hold onto from the last years of Liam's life, but I couldn't bring myself to be their comforting blanket. The pain was too severe for me to be able to help them deal with losing him. Hell, I couldn't even be that person for myself, so how could they expect that of me?

Death caused a ripple effect. Those left behind had to figure out a way to cope with the aftermath, and his parents were struggling just like myself. None of us were the balm to soothe the ache in the other's chest. We were more like the knife twisting slightly deeper into the chest cavity. Guilt was a heavy burden within me, but I couldn't seem to put those feelings to bed.

Burning filled my eyes as tears washed to the surface. I let out a heavy sigh and shook my head, trying my damnedest to clear my thoughts. "This is exactly why I push people away." I hastily collected my things, gulped down the remainder of my coffee, and headed toward the door. My hand shoved the door open as I tilted my face toward the sun and closed my eyes, slamming into someone in the process, and sending my belongings tumbling to the ground. "I am so sorry!"

"Excuse me is more like it." The man was irritated as he bent down and helped retrieve my items.

Our eyes connected as he handed me a handful of pens. His thick dark hair fell forward, covering a portion of his forehead. "It's not like I meant to slam into you," I huffed, snatching the pens from his grasp.

"Who needs that many pens anyway?" He stood, dusting himself off. The navy-blue suit he wore showcased his hazel eyes. I cursed myself for even noticing. "Are you going to answer me, or not?" The man was unbelievably smug. I wanted to smack the sourpuss attitude from his mouth, but instead I stood staring in bewilderment.

Is he for real? "Maybe if you tried being an inkling nicer I'd answer your stupid ass question."

His staccato laugh was anything but friendly as he ran a hand through his disheveled hair. "You're welcome by the way." His eyes narrowed as he moved past me.

I spun. "Excuse me?"

He glanced over his shoulder. "It's about time you excused yourself." The man disappeared into Magnolia's, leaving me on the sidewalk in a flustered, pissed off state.

My cell phone stirred to life, with Janet's name flashing across the screen once again. "Great!" I tossed my hands into the air before powering my phone off and stuffing it into my bag. "I've had enough of this day." The declaration was louder than I'd anticipated, and a few patrons turning to see what the fuss was about. Their attention made me want to crawl in a hole until the coast was clear, but instead I kept on trucking it down the sidewalk. I was even more thankful that my apartment building was a few blocks away from my *once* favorite spot.

* * *

No matter how hard I tried to shake the encounter with Mr. Stick-up-his-ass, I couldn't. My blood had been boiling ever since, and apparently, I was taking my anger out on the boiling pasta from the rate I was stirring it.

"Shit." I snatched a potholder and quickly dumped the once noodles into the colander. They almost disintegrated as I pushed them around with the wooden spoon. "There's no coming back from that..." A heavy sigh left me as I dumped the mush into the trashcan. My eyes found the stack of menus on the island, and like instinct, I went directly to them. "Pizza, pizza, Chinese, Mexican, more pizza..." I tossed the stack onto the counter and dropped my head back against my neck. Like most people, I could eat my weight in pizza, but it seemed that I'd been living off of that yummy goodness. A girl needed something more every now and then.

The last thing I wanted to do was make myself presentable and go on an adventure to hunt down some food. Especially with the mood I was in, but the options before me didn't sound very appealing. Glancing down at my attire I grimaced. Leggings that were once black and an oversized Led Zeppelin shirt rounded out my outfit...if you wanted to call it that. I chuckled and slipped my feet into a pair of Chuck Taylors before tying a knot in my shirt at the hip. "This is the best it's getting." Not bothering with my still turned off cell phone, I grabbed my keys from the counter.

The sun was beginning to set, which meant the bar next to my building would be hopping within the next couple hours. As I reached the door, the aroma of greasy delicious bar food caused my stomach to howl. "Settle down now," I patted my belly, "I'll give you what you want." I slipped inside, not bothering to check the name of the place, and leaned myself against the U-shaped bar. Patrons filled the medium size joint already, but the drunks hadn't made their appearance yet. Those people came out in droves once the sun could no longer show its true colors, as I'd seen for far too many nights from the rooftop of my building.

"What can I get you?" A slender blonde a few inches taller than myself laid a circular napkin before me.

"Oh, I'm not drinking." I slid the napkin toward her. "Just wanted to see a menu perhaps?"

Her pointed stare, from over bright red glasses that looked like they'd travelled from the fifties, made me squirm. "That's a first." She chomped her gum, popping it every so often.

"What is?"

"Someone like you," her eyes drug down my body before focusing on mine again, "coming in here at this hour just to order food."

My head snapped back. "Seriously?"

"I kid you not." She extended a menu. "Everything on the right side the kitchen will still make."

I exhaled. "Okay, thank you." With a tight lip nod, she left me and headed to the opposite end of the bar where customers awaited.

Having five choices of food was apparently too much for my

brain to handle. I kept bouncing between the grilled chicken sandwich and a juicy bacon burger. Getting both would probably be frowned upon. The thought made me laugh for some reason. My body jarred and my eyes lifted from the menu to see who in the hell had just about dislocated my shoulder. A woman swaying from too many drinks frowned at me. I grabbed her arms to keep her from falling down and helped her onto the stool beside me.

"Sorry." Her eyes half closed as she grinned and extended her hand. "I'm Becca."

Doing my best not to erupt with laughter, I took her hand and gave it a shake. "Nice to meet you, Becca. I'm Terra."

She shook her head, almost falling forward. Quickly, I turned her body and she lowered her head against her crossed arms on the bar. The girl was a damn mess.

"Becca!" A shaggy haired guy came barreling up to the bar.

"I take it you know her?" I raised an eyebrow.

"Yeah." He pushed a hand through his heavy hair. "She's my sister."

"Well, you might want to take your sister home. She's on the verge of passing out."

His boyish grin made me smile. "She's a handful on a good day…today hasn't been one of those." By the end of his statement, his smile had disappeared. I knew all too well how life could knock you off your feet.

I laid my hand on his resting on the bar. "Give her time, and show her love. She'll make it through whatever she's facing."

His touch was gentle as he helped his sister to her feet, scooped her into his arms, and began to walk away. Stopping after a few steps, he glanced back at me over his shoulder. "Thank you. Those words were exactly what I needed to hear."

A closed lip smile tilted my lips. Words had failed me, but the man didn't expect anything else. I watched him carry his inebriated sister to his car parked at the curb and secure her into the passenger seat. Loving someone who's fighting demons was hard.

I only knew that from trying to love myself again. Guilt stabbed at my heart from the way I'd pushed Liam's parents out of my life, as well as the friends we had together. I'd quickly secluded myself for the past six months, but the thought of interacting with those people suffocated me. Everything about that horrible day would come rushing back, forcing me to relive the pain of losing him. There was no way I was strong enough to endure that...not yet at least.

"Decided on what you want?"

I lifted my eyes to find deep brown ones staring at me through those red outlandish spectacles. "Yeah, I'll take the grilled chicken sandwich and the bacon burger." I slid the menu across the bar.

"Ah, must be having a date night in." She tapped her pen against the notepad in her hand.

"No, it's just me. I couldn't decide between the two, so I chose them both." I shrugged.

Her musical laughter filled the space between us. "I like you..." She shook her head while grinning and disappeared into the kitchen.

Not sure how long it would take for my food, I slipped onto the stool Becca had occupied and caught sight of a large tin sign across the room that read, *Side Street Drafts,* in white rusty letters. Much like Magnolia's, this place had likely been around for quite some time. The stories seasoned buildings could tell. "I really need to get out of my apartment more often and take in what Philadelphia has to offer," I spoke aloud to myself. My eyes roamed the room. Antique wooden tables filled a good portion, with chairs to match. Singular lightbulbs hung from exposed beams, with chipped brick walls that stretched from floor to ceiling. It was a beautiful work of art that had taken time to age to perfection, much like a nice bourbon.

"Ma'am!" I called out to the bartender.

With a pointed stare overtop the red frames, she moseyed

down to where I was seated. "Never. I repeat, NEVER call me ma'am."

I raised my hands in surrender. "My apologies."

She huffed, "Your food will be out in a minute." She turned to walk away.

"That's not what I wanted." She turned midstride and raised an eyebrow. "Can I get a bourbon on the rocks?"

"So, you do like alcohol." She flopped a circular napkin before me and pulled a glass from the beneath the bar.

"I stopped drinking for a while." My eyes dropped to my bare ring finger.

"Oh, no..." She shook her head. "I'm not going to be the reason you fall off the wagon." Her hands were planted firmly on her hips.

"It's nothing like that." My sigh was heavy at the thought of explaining why I hadn't had a drink in a while.

"Care to explain?"

"I thought bartenders hated hearing people's life stories?" I wringed my hands together.

She full on belly laughed. "You know...I usually don't, but for some reason right now I do." Her hands dropped from her hips and hung loosely at her sides.

"I appreciate that." I paused, sucked in a deep breath, and let it out slowly. "In a nutshell, my husband passed away six months ago, I went on a bender to numb the pain, and then uprooted my life." Explaining the death of someone close to you was a hard conversation to have. People didn't know how to respond to such heartbreaking truths, myself included.

She cleared her throat. "Starting over can be therapeutic." Her response wasn't one I expected. It wasn't the usual apology for the loss, or sad smile. It was pure support in moving forward with things.

"I like you." I grinned, mocking her previous statement.

We snickered.

"I'm Gabby by the way." She filled my glass with the honey-hued liquid I hadn't had in quite some time.

"Terra."

"Order up!" a man called from the window on the opposite side of the bar.

Gabby held her index finger in the air and I nodded. She carried a plastic bag with two to-go containers inside. "Here's your food." She sat it on the counter beside me. I took a large gulp of the bourbon, but the glass was still decently full. "No rush. I'll be down there if you need anything. Also, if you'd rather eat here than at home, that's fine too."

I didn't respond as she headed back down the bar to wait on others. I was surprised how my end had been pretty scarce with people trying to get drink orders. Then again, there wasn't a large amount of space between the stools and the front window. Not wanting to sit there and look like a pig, I downed the remainder of the glass and took my bag from the bar top. "Thanks, Gabby!" I extended a hand into the air as I headed for the door.

"Come back anytime. I'll be here." She waved in return and popped the top off a couple beer bottles.

I stepped into the night's air and inhaled deeply. Chatter buzzed around me and a smile appeared, firm and genuine on my lips. I hadn't felt such happiness in far too long. Who knew that small talk with a stranger, and giving advice on how to help someone cope would do that? Funny thing is, I didn't even realize I had advice to give.

The walk back to my apartment was nicer than any I'd taken in months. A small portion of the heavy weight of life had chipped away and fallen to the ground. One step at a time is all it took for me to find my footing again. I'd stumbled on numerous occasions, fallen on my face even, but one thing was for sure; I was learning to get back up again. I needed to learn to be thankful for the now, for being able to live another day. Liam's life was cut short at the drop of a dime. Nothing was guaranteed.

I sat the food on the counter and stepped over to the window that overlooked the street I'd just walked down. This time was different than my other gazes out of that window, because this time I took in the beauty of what was around me. Philadelphia was now my home, and I needed to start acting like it.

CHAPTER FOUR

One thing that seemed to be the norm for Philly was that the sun appeared to be shining quite often. Or at least it had since I'd taken up residence in the city. The walk to Magnolia's was a nice start to the morning. It got my blood pumping just enough to wake me up more than just rolling out of bed and driving to an office. So, when I actually got my cup of coffee, my body had a good kick-start.

I slipped in line behind a group of teenage girls who were giggling at God knows what. Most likely high school gossip, or which boys they thought were the cutest. As much as my life had changed, I didn't miss those days. Mainly because I was the nerd in school. Thick glasses, a slight gap between my front teeth, and a strawberry shaped birthmark on the left side of my neck just below my ear. All the things I was insecure about are the exact things I grew to love about myself over the years. Well, minus the glasses…I traded those in for some good old contacts as soon as I could, and years later settled on Lasik surgery.

The bell above the door dinged and I turned to see who had come in. Not that I was expecting anyone, mainly out of habit. A man in dark slacks and a crisp white button down stood tall a couple people behind me. My encounter with Mr. Stick-up-his-ass came to mind. Thankfully it wasn't him, but he did look similar to the man. Out of all the mornings I'd setup shop in Magnolia's, I'd never noticed how many businessmen frequented the spot. Maybe because I'd been stuck in my own bubble for the majority of the time, or maybe I'd become hyperaware of those around me. Either way, it piqued my curiosity as to what this part of the city had to offer.

I ordered my usual black coffee with a side of honey and took a seat at the table in the front of the joint, right up against the windows, tucked against the corner of the room. Safe and secure in my private little oasis. I kicked my feet up in the chair across from me and opened my laptop. Today had to be a productive day. I'd wasted half a week staring out the window due to my thoughts being a jumbled mess. Thankfully I'd awoken with a different mindset this morning.

Being a freelance writer was a career choice that came out of nowhere for me. I loved writing throughout school, but as the years passed by, the less I had the chance to write. Life got in the way and my ambitions changed. On my quest to find what set my soul on fire again, I ran across a blog post about freelance writing. The more research I did, the more intrigued I became. So, I signed up online with a company I'd never heard of and a few weeks later my first job bid was sitting in my inbox. The rest kind of fell into place. One thing I couldn't pass up was being able to work from wherever I wanted. Being stuck in an office setting wasn't for me. I'd tried it on numerous occasions and failed miserably.

Two weeks was all it took for me to spiral into a drunken state of almost no return. But late one afternoon I woke up on the bathroom floor, face down in my own vomit, and decided it was time to get my act together. So, I cleansed my body, literally, and began doing the same figuratively with journal entries. It all started around two in the morning. I'd tossed and turned for hours, trying to mentally talk myself into sleeping but my mind wouldn't shut off. I'd gotten up and padded into the kitchen for a glass of water when I caught sight of an old journal I used to keep track of bills in. I flipped it open to a blank page and retrieved a pen. Taking a seat at the counter, I began to write. That night I spent a good three hours pouring my heart and soul into that journal. Writing out the anger, the heartache, and the memories I so desperately wished I could relive. When my eyes became heavy, I carried the journal into the spare bedroom—where I'd been sleeping before I sold the house—and climbed back into bed. I'd fallen asleep that night with the notebook and pen tucked beside me.

"Penny for your thoughts?"

I nearly jumped from my skin as Gabby slipped into the seat across from me, pushing my feet to the floor in the process, and tossed a penny on the table.

"Jesus..." My hand covered my heart. "You scared the ever-loving shit out of me."

She held her palms up and snickered. "I would apologize, but that was priceless."

I gave her the finger and took a deep breath to calm my racing heart. "For some reason, I'm not surprised that you aren't apologizing...and a legit penny," I held it between my first finger and thumb, "really?" One of my eyebrows rose in question.

My statement only made her laugh even harder. "Theatrics always make moments better." She linked her fingers together and rested her hands against the tabletop.

"This," I waved my hand toward her, "version of you is quite a bit upbeat compared to the hard exterior you had at the bar the other night."

She shrugged. "Like I said...theatrics."

I shook my head and opened the document I had been working on. An advertising spread for a new line of dry shampoo. Snore, I know, but it was good for resume purposes. Any free-lance work helped.

"You still haven't answered my question." My eyes rose overtop the laptop screen. Gabby sat with her hands still clasped and resting on the table, a shit-eating grin on display.

"What question?"

She faked a yawn. "You really need to pay attention better."

A staccato laugh escaped me. *Was this chick serious?* I closed my laptop and sat up straighter. "Care to ask it again?" The annoyance in my tone was a bit thicker than I'd meant for it to be.

Gabby's face went void of any emotion, and I questioned if I'd crossed a line, hoping I actually hadn't. She seemed like someone I could be friends with, even if she was a bit in your face at times. I opened my mouth to apologize for sounding so harsh when she erupted with laughter, tossing her head back and cackling into the air as she slapped a hand down on the wooden table. "You should've seen the look on your face." Her laughter bubbled through the air filling everyone in Magnolia's ears. Gazes swung toward the two of us, making me want to shrink into a tiny ball and roll away as quickly as possible. I wasn't one to enjoy much attention, especially from a group of people I didn't know. But apparently Gabby was oblivious to it, or she honestly didn't give two shits.

"Dude," I whisper yelled.

"What?" Her eyes came back to mine as her laughter slowly died.

"Everyone's staring." I shrunk in my chair.

Gabby's eyebrows drew together. "Let them stare." She waved a dismissive hand in the air. An exuberated sigh deflated my chest as I slid a bit further down in the chair. "Why do you care?" She leaned her forearms on the table.

"I—I don't know…I'm not a fan of attention."

"Seriously?"

I nodded.

"Don't let insecurities run your life, Terra. Who cares if

someone stares? At least you're having fun in the moment." She shrugged and hopped up from her seat.

My internal alarm blared, afraid of what Gabby was about to do, but to my surprise she simply got in line to order.

Opening my laptop, I took a steady breath and let it out slowly. She'd rattled my calm with her unexpected visit and off the wall antics. I cracked my knuckles and looked over the information in the email I'd been provided for the dry shampoo job. It was pretty cut and dry, far less in depth than other jobs I'd already tackled. So, I could easily complete it within a couple hours at the most. That is, if I put my mind into it.

My fingers began to fly over the keyboard as I typed away what I felt was a nice marketing promo. I wasn't sure how long it had been since Gabby had vacated her seat, but the shadow of her sitting back down caught my eye. I didn't bother lifting them to see what she had gotten, instead I kept plugging away. I was in the groove and nothing was going to interrupt that.

"Fancy meeting you here...again."

That fucking voice.

The hairs on my arms stood at attention. Hoping my ears were playing a trick on me, I glanced over my computer screen. Sure enough, Mr. Stick-up-his-ass himself was perched in the chair Gabby had vacated. My eyes narrowed as I took in his smug grin, all perfectly straight white teeth shining bright against his olive skin. The sudden urge to toss my coffee at him reared its head. I griped the mug with one hand and silently talked myself out of doing so.

"Do I need to take out a restraining order?" I cocked an eyebrow as I tilted the screen of my laptop down just a smidge.

Deep laughter expelled from his chest as a lopsided smile settled on his mouth. "You're witty."

"And you're an asshole, but that's none of my business."

He nodded. "I deserve that."

"What do you want?" I let out a puff of air.

He ran a hand through his thick hair. "Nothing really." Leaning back in the chair he rested his elbow on the top. "Saw you sitting here all enthralled in whatever you're doing and thought I'd say hi."

"Goodbye sounds quite a bit better." Something about the nameless man got under my skin. Maybe because of our first encounter, or maybe because of the way he carried himself. I wasn't sure which, but either way he rubbed me the wrong way.

Amusement danced in his eyes as he ran a hand over his mouth, my gaze following the motion. A silent sigh passed my lips and I mentally smacked myself. *What the hell are you doing, Terra?* Even though he didn't seem as uptight as our first encounter, he was under my skin like a splinter that needed extracting.

"Up." Gabby snapped her fingers.

Mr. Stick-up-his-ass diverted his eyes toward where she stood. A sly grin morphed on his face as his eyebrows rose. "Yet another snarky woman." He chuckled.

"Yeah, and this snarky woman wants her seat back." Gabby took a pull from the fruity drink in her hand.

He rose to his feet and stepped aside for her to sit. "My apologies." Still grinning, he brought his attention back to me. "I'm sure I'll see you around."

"I hope not." I leveled him with my gaze.

My statement only made him smile even wider. I wanted so badly to knock the amusement off his perfectly sculpted face, but that's frowned upon. He shook his head as he left Magnolia's without so much as a drink in tow.

Had he shown up just to see me? Who was I kidding? He must've forgotten to order something after he saw me.

"You know that hunk of deliciousness?" Gabby eyed me as she took a long pull from her drink.

Like a ton of bricks, it hit me. I didn't know his name. Granted, I had made one up for him, but it would've been kind of nice to put an actual name with his smug as hell self.

"I really don't know."

Gabby narrowed her eyes. "Come on now! I'm not going to steal him away or anything."

My humorless laugh vibrated from my chest. "First, he isn't mine for anyone to steal. Second, I honest to God haven't a clue what his name is. We ran into each other outside of here one day and he acted like a total ass bag. I thought it was you that sat down, not him. And why in the hell am I justifying anything to you right now? We barely know one another, and I really should be working instead of having this odd as hell conversation."

"You done?" She took another pull from her drink.

I stared at the plastic cup clutched in her hands. *Was that thing bottomless or something?*

"Yeah." My body deflated from the large breath I let out.

Gabby sat her cup on the table and leaned back in the chair. Her eyes turned toward the window as a group of teenagers loudly passed by. It was evident that she was thinking about something. What, I wasn't sure, but I was sure she'd most likely be sharing it any moment.

"I know you're probably thinking what in the hell is wrong with this girl? Well, I'm trying to find my footing again just like yourself. In a different way though. I divorced someone I'd spent the majority of my life with and decided to buy a bar."

"You own *Side Street Drafts?*"

"I do." She smiled as her eyes came back to mine. "What I'm getting at is...when you told me about your husband I knew we were experiencing similar things. How life changes so quickly, and all you can do is roll with what's coming. I need a friend as much as you do, and I think we could be that for each other. I'm sorry if I overstep at times, which I'm sure I already have," we both laughed, "and I'm not asking about that guy to push you toward him. Just curious is all." Gabby reached across the table and picked up my cell phone. Without questioning her, I allowed her to go about whatever business she was doing with it. Once she was done, she sat it on the table where it had previously laid and gave me a small closed lip smile. "I put my number in your contacts in case you want someone to lean on while you're figuring out life."

Gabby lifted from the chair with her drink in hand and gave me a wink before leaving me sitting at the table, baffled at how the day had already unfolded. I flipped my phone over and the screen lit up with my contacts still open. A round of full belly laughter immediately escaped me as I focused on the name she'd put her number under.

Forever Stalking You, Gabby.

CHAPTER FIVE

S omething about washing my face at night helped put me to
sleep. I used to skip a skincare routine at night. I felt it was
pointless at a younger age, even though we all know that isn't the
case. Everything about my life had changed and taking care of my
body was officially a priority.

I patted my face dry and applied nightly serums before flipping off the bathroom light and tucking myself into bed. The past
few nights had been restless ones. I'd woken up every other hour
with my mind roaming from my childhood to the memories I'd
shared with Liam, like I'd opened Pandora's Box and couldn't get
the lid back closed. But I didn't give up trying to get as much sleep
as possible until the sun began to peek through my curtains.

My journal laid on the sheet beside me with a pen tucked into
the spine. I debated flipping it open and scribbling down my
thoughts for the day, but I was actually tired for once. Instead, I
rolled onto my stomach, tucked my arm beneath the pillow, and
closed my eyes, hoping and praying I'd float off into a slumber
that I wouldn't wake from until mid-morning.

The whisk was covered in chocolate icing as I pulled it from the bowl.
Some threatened to fall on the counter, but I quickly swiped it with my

finger and plunged the deliciousness into my mouth. A moan fell from my lips as I took in the rich flavor I'd created with this batch of home-made goodness.

Liam's going to love it.

His birthday was upon us, and even though he wasn't a fan of making a big to-do of it, I couldn't let the day pass without letting him know just how much I adored him. Even though it was disappointing that his parents weren't going to make it into town, that wasn't going to ruin the day.

I continued about in the kitchen, putting the double chocolate fudge cake together as the chicken potpie baked in the oven. Liam never had homemade potpie until we started dating. Mine quickly became his favorite dish, so every year on his birthday I made it a staple for our night together.

The cake sat beautifully on the white ceramic table with a clear glass cover so anyone who walked into the kitchen could see its beauty. I took a seat at the bar and gazed at it while I waited for the potpie to finish cooking, my stomach grumbled from the delicious aroma floating through the air.

I laid my arms on the counter and rested my head against them. Taking advantage of the silence before our friends arrived, I closed my eyes. I could feel myself slowly slipping into a half-asleep, half-awake state when hands came down against my shoulders. I lurched upright, almost knocking my arm into the cake table.

"That cake looks amazing." Liam placed a loving kiss against my cheek as he massaged my tired shoulders.

"I didn't hear you come in." I steadied my uneven breaths and pressed my lips to his.

"Sorry if I startled you." He rounded the counter and turned on the light inside the oven. Liam gasped and spun back to face me. His eyes wide with excitement. "Is that a homemade chicken potpie in there?"

I nodded, biting my lip to keep from smiling like a Cheshire cat. "You're the only person I know that gets more excited over regular food than dessert."

Liam turned my stool so that he could step between my legs. *"That's because I'm one of a kind, baby."*

Giggles bubbled up my throat as he gently rubbed my arms. *"You're definitely one of a kind."* I leaned forward enough to capture his mouth with my own. His tongue swiped across the seam of my lips and I granted him access. The temperature in the kitchen spiked as our tongues danced in a sensual rhythm, our hands roamed one another's bodies, and a low groan rumbled Liam's chest. That sound was the sexiest thing I ever heard.

The timer blared on the oven, causing the two of us to separate. *"Duty calls."* I slipped from the stool but Liam stopped me from moving any further as he wrapped his arms around my midriff and pulled me flush against him. *"The best decision I ever made was asking you on a date, and the second-best decision was the day I asked you to marry me."*

My cheeks burned from the smile still planted firmly on my face. *"And the third will be moving out of my way so I can get that potpie out of the oven before it burns."* Liam chuckled, placed a gentle kiss against my forehead, and moved to the side.

With oven mitts covering my hands, I reached into the oven and brushed the top of my arm against the inside. I yelped as part of my skin burned like an inferno, dropping the chicken potpie onto the door. Tears pricked my eyes as I stared at my once masterpiece, crumbled into a messy soup spilling onto the inside glass.

"Shit!"

"Don't cry, baby, I'll clean it up." Liam tenderly moved me to the side, turned off the stove, and grabbed the trashcan.

My bottom lip quivered. *"I ruined your birthday dinner."* I covered my mouth with my hand to try and stifle the sob threatening to escape.

Liam paused cleaning up the mess and lifted his eyes to mine, a frown pulling the corners of his mouth. *"It's fine, Terra, it really is."*

"It's your birthday tradition..." Hot tears rolled down my cheeks.

His eyes softened as he swiped his thumbs across my face to stop the round of tears from going any further. *"We can make a new tradition."* The soothing tone of his voice was like a balm against my achy heart.

"I wanted it to be perfect."

Liam cleared the remainder of the mess from the oven and removed the mitts from my hands before taking them in his own. "Perfect is over-rated, sweetheart. I'll settle for a chaotic intense roller-coaster ride as long as it's with you."

I shot up in bed, my hand flying to my chest which was covered in a thin sheen of sweat, the erratic beating of my heart easily felt with my palm. I tried to swallow the lump in my throat, but the dryness made me cough. Kicking the covers off, I ran into the kitchen and snatched a glass from the cabinet beside the sink. I flipped the faucet on at record speed, filled the glass, and downed the entire thing before repeating it a second time. My hands gripped the counter as I leaned forward, hanging my head between my arms. Inhaling deeply, I let each breath out slowly until I felt that I had a good grip on the panic attack that reared its ugly head.

"So much for a good night's sleep." I padded back into the bedroom, retrieved my journal from the bed, and wrapped the robe that had been hanging on my bedroom door tightly around my body.

I slipped my feet into the plush warmth of the slippers I'd left beside the couch and headed to the roof. My sanity needed cleansing, and the only two things I'd found peace in quickly was writing in my journal and the calming air on the rooftop.

Being on the top floor of the complex made the venture a short one. The building manager frowned upon anyone going to the roof, but the security alarm on the door hadn't worked since I moved in. There was no telling how long it had been disabled without him knowing, but I wasn't about to tell him either.

The heavy metal door moaned as I shoved it open. The cool night air wrapped around my body, making me secure my robe a little tighter. A heavy breath fell from my lips as I crossed the concrete roof and flopped down in the rinky-dink chair I'd claimed as mine.

The nightlife below was scarce, which made me wonder what time of the morning it was. I hadn't bothered looking as I raced out of the house in a fury. Not that it actually mattered. My body was quickly becoming accustomed to lack of sleep. I suppose the longer you do it, the easier it was to get up and get moving. I enjoyed my rest, had far too much of it at times even, but it seemed my peaceful slumbers were full of memories. Ones I never wanted to forget, but also didn't want to relive every time my eyes closed.

They say time heals everything, but I'm not so sure of that.

I'm sure when they said time, they meant years upon years, but I still wasn't so sure about that. Six months seemed like forever in certain circumstances, while in others it seemed like yesterday. Wounds heal at their own pace. Not when you need them to, or want them to, but when they're ready.

There was no telling when my wounds would be ready to heal.

I propped my feet up on the brick ledge of the roof and flipped the journal open in my lap. The pen tapped against the blank page as I tried to decide where to start. So much was jumbled in my head from my dream, it was hard to make heads or tails of my thoughts. I took a steady breath and closed my eyes, feeling the gentle breeze envelop me. The calm after the storm in my case.

Slowly opening my eyes, I tilted my head toward the sky and smiled at the vast stars shining bright. I hadn't seen so many in the sky at the same time in forever. The beauty of their twinkling selves, giving hope to those who made wishes upon them. I remembered doing so as a child. That wonder faded the older I got. Another innocent outlook on life taken away by the heartaches dealt.

With the pen firm in my grasp, I began to write. This time it wasn't about the loss of Liam. No, this time it was about the loss of wonder...of dreaming of what's to come. The innocent outlook we have as a child—as long as you grew up in a good home—that gets squashed as the years pass by. Prime examples being the tall-tales of certain holidays and events that happen to you; Santa, the Tooth Fairy, the Easter Bunny, and so on. All ploys to make children believe in the wonder of life. Hell, I believed it all myself.

It's nice to have something to hold onto like that—something to believe in—but when the rug is pulled out from beneath your feet with the truth of the matter, it's the first gut punch lesson of true life.

My pen rolled over the pages as the sun began to rise, its beautiful colors bringing about the dawn of a new day. I paused and watched the sunrise, something I hadn't done in many years, the warmth rolling up my face as the giant orb filled a small portion of the sky. A single tear rolled down my cheek as a closed lip smile rose almost as slowly as the sun had on my face. Being in a fog of grief made it hard to appreciate the life I had. The life that Liam would have given anything to continue to live. The thought of how selfish I'd been crossed my mind at least a dozen times a day. Deep down though, I knew there was nothing selfish about grieving...even the dark thoughts that came with it.

A car horn blared, startling me bad enough to toss my journal from my lap. My breath caught as I watched it fall just beside the ledge of the roof. Thankfully, it didn't topple over. I bent over and quickly retrieved it, clutching it tight against my chest. My nerves were shot, and my chest housed that familiar ache that made itself at home the majority of the time.

Living was hard.

So. Damn. Hard.

A familiar voice floated from the street below, but I couldn't quite make out what was being said. I leaned onto the ledge with my arms crossed against the brick and spotted Gabby giving someone ten kinds of hell. She was a woman with an undeniable amount of character, not simply one kind of character either. I chuckled as she tossed her hands in the air before settling two middle fingers directly in front of her at the man storming off.

"Hey!" I called out, not sure if she would be able to hear me or not. Gabby's head whipped from side-to-side. "Up here!"

She dropped her head against her neck, placing a hand over her eyes to shield them from the beaming sun. "Terra?"

"Yeah!" I grinned from ear-to-ear.

"What the hell are you doing up there?" Her head tilted to the side.

"I live in the building."

She nodded.

"Are you naked?"

I rolled my eyes, but obviously she couldn't see that. "No, I'm in a robe, thank you!"

"Oh!"

"Who was that guy?"

"Some asshole who doesn't know how to park! I hate to run, but come see me later at *Side Street!*"

I laughed. "Sure thing!"

Even though a friendship with Gabby was the last thing I was looking for, just the few interactions I'd had with her were enough to let me know it was healthy to have someone like her in my life. As much as I wanted to push her away and be my usual lonesome self, I wasn't going to allow myself to do that any longer.

* * *

Hitting send on the email for the dry shampoo job was like a breath of fresh air. It had taken me almost double the time to complete than another job that was twice its size, most likely due to the hectic days I'd been having. Running into Gabby, as well as Mr. Stick-up-his-ass on multiple occasions, had thrown me for a loop. Although, I now found myself willingly headed to *Side Street Drafts* for a few drinks.

I hadn't gone out at night for drinks in a very long time,

mainly because the nightlife was always buzzing with booze, music, and laughter. I'd only enjoyed those things with Liam. We'd gotten together early in our lives and spent the majority of our firsts with one another. So, learning to take those steps without him hadn't been the easiest.

Music and chatter filled the air as I stepped inside *Side Street Drafts*. Gabby, along with a short brunette, manned the bar. I waved as her eyes connected with mine and a giant smile spread across her face. Those same red glasses she wore the first night I'd met her, perched on her nose. The thought hit me, the other day she wasn't wearing them. I made a mental note to ask her if they were prescription or just a part of her bar ensemble.

"Bourbon on the rocks." She slid me a glass half full.

"A girl after my own heart." I raised the glass and took a swig, that familiar burn warming my throat as it washed down.

I slipped against the wall to the only open spot at the bar. There was no stool to sit on, but that was okay. I'd done my fair share of sitting with my laptop the majority of the day, I needed to stand. A familiar song pumped through the speakers, causing me to sway and bob my head to the beat while I slowly drank my bourbon. It felt good to be in a normal setting, interacting with strangers, and socially drinking. Getting out was the medicine my soul had needed.

Gabby made it to my end once again. "It's packed in here." I loudly spoke so she could hear me overtop the music.

"This is a normal crowd, wait until closer to midnight." She wiped her forehead with a bandana.

"I don't know how you do it." I drank the remainder of my glass and extended it to her.

"It's one of those jobs where you get used to it, and eventually it either makes you bitter or you grow to love it. The fast pace and being myself is the best part...however, I do own the place. That's the toughest part." I watched as she hastily poured me another round and perfectly slid it across the bar into my hand.

A giggle bubbled up my throat as I shook my head. "You're good at this job."

"I know." She winked and took off to the other end.

One song turned into another as I stood there people watching. Most of the crowd looked to be in their thirties and forties, but I'm sure the occasional twenty-something group was intertwined. Growing older made it hard to tell people's age. Once you hit that thirty mark, everyone younger than you looked like babies or far older than they were, and vice versa with those older than you. I'd always said I never wanted to experience dating again, mainly because of how society had changed, but I was headed back into the pool eventually. Without much choice at that. I mean, I guess I could be single for the rest of my life. That was an option, right?

"Hey," a voice came from beside me before the man stepped into my line of sight. "Aren't you the girl who helped my sister out?"

I nodded with a closed lip grin. "I am."

The shaggy haired guy surprised me by pulling me into his chest and hugging me tightly. "Thank you again for helping her, and for the advice. It's actually given me a different outlook on her drinking." He let me go and ran a hand through his messy hair. "Becca has been through a lot. I'm not going to dive into any of it, because it's her story to tell, but dealing with someone who's fighting demons is hard. Actually," he humorlessly laughed, "hard doesn't even begin to describe it." He cleared his throat as I linked my hand with his and gave it a gentle squeeze.

My heart squeezed in my chest from the pain he was attempting to choke back, but I knew he was hurting. That was evident in the way he spoke about the situation. "You're a good brother..."

"Oh, sorry." He smiled. "I never gave you my name or got yours actually. I'm Nicholas."

"Well, Nicholas. She's lucky to have you on her side."

A faint blush crept across his cheeks "Thanks."

"I'm Terra." I took a step back, sensing the conversation could come across in the wrong way, which was the last thing I wanted to happen.

"Nice to officially meet you, Terra. Can I buy you a drink?" Nicholas stared down at me with the most infectious smile.

I raised my glass from the bar and smiled back. "Thank you, but I already have one."

He slipped his hands into his pockets. "Maybe another time then."

I took a sip, watching him over the rim of the glass. "I'm sure I'll see you around."

He nodded. "I hope so."

To say I was thankful that one of his buddies called out for him from the dance floor would be an understatement. My eyebrows rose and I smiled as he took one last glance in my direction before disappearing into the crowd. I hadn't realized how badly my palms were sweating until he was gone. I placed my glass back on the bar and wiped them on a napkin before leaning over the bar top and tossing it into the trash.

"You okay?" Gabby slid into view.

"Yeah," I sighed.

"That's a heavy sigh for a positive word." She eyed me.

I shrugged. "That's just me."

"I beg to differ, but okay." She motioned toward my close to empty glass. "Another?"

I shook my head. "Beer this time. Anything light."

Without a word she slid the cooler open and grabbed a beer from it, popped the top and handed it to me like she was born to bartend. She could handle three or four customers at a time without screwing up a single order. There was no way in hell I could juggle orders like that.

"You working all night?"

Gabby slid a round of some fruity looking shots to three girls and turned her head toward me. "Depends. If Shelia shows her ass up I'll take a few hours off. If not, I'll be behind here 'til closing."

"Gotta' love half ass workers," the brunette who was also bartending added. "I'm Jess." She wiped her hand on a towel hanging from her front pocket and extended it to me.

I gave her hand a shake. "Terra."

"Ah, so you're the newbie in town Gabby was telling me about."

"I suppose so."

"What brought you to Philly?" She leaned her heavily tattooed arms against the bar.

Gabby clasped a hand on Jess' shoulder. "No time for chitchatting. A bachelorette party just squeezed in at the other end of the bar."

"Nice to meet you, Terra."

"You too."

"Sorry about that." A sad smile barely tipped the corners of Gabby's mouth.

I waved her off as I took a pull from my beer. "Don't worry about it. That's the number one question I get asked. I can't run from it."

Jess called out to Gabby for some backup as the far end of the bar filled with more people. "Holler if you need a refill."

I held the bottle in the air and nodded.

The eighties music soon faded to newer songs I'd heard on the radio. A younger crowd filled the dance floor. I watched as bodies molded together and drinks rose in the air. My eyes landed on Becca swaying with her back pressed against a tall guy who looked like he'd stepped out of a Calvin Klein catalog. It was obvious she was inebriated from the lack of keeping her rhythm to the song. I've seen bad dancers before, but she was on a completely different level than that.

My eyes scanned the room looking for Nicholas. He was tall enough to notice, but it seemed the crowd was packed full of men around the same height. I sunk back against the wall and continued my visual search of him, but still came up empty-handed. Giving up, I turned to glance out the windows when my eyes caught sight of Nicholas coming through the door, fury blazed on his face as his eyes latched onto his drunken sister and her dancing partner.

Without thinking, I took off in his direction, hoping to bypass him before he reached Becca. I shoved through the heavy crowd the best I could, apologizing as I went. Nicholas was a couple people from reaching his sister when I grabbed his forearm. His furious eyes dropped to mine, calming just a fraction.

"Let's dance." I pulled him in a different direction than where his sister was and didn't give him a chance to deny me as I began to move in front of him, my hips swaying to the euphoric beat of the bass pulsing through the building.

A lopsided smile showcased his boyish beauty as he placed a hand on my hip, his fingertips moving against the slice of flesh between my jeans and cinched waist length top.

What the hell are you doing, Terra? my mind screamed as realization came crashing down that no man had touched any part of my body, besides my hands, other than Liam. I took a shaky breath, hoping Nicholas didn't notice how uncomfortable I'd become. It wasn't anything to do with him, it was me, and I didn't want to give the guy a complex if I could avoid it.

This was yet another step I needed to take in life, even if it made me feel like I was doing something wrong. As if the situation could get any worse, the song ended and a slower love song took its place. My heart slammed like a wrecking ball within my chest as Nicholas pulled me close, linking one of our hands together as he began to move us to the sweet rhythm of the song. My breaths were short and fast as my throat thickened like it was closing off. A panic attack was rearing its ugly head right there on the dance floor.

"I'm sorry..." I choked out before sprinting toward the bathrooms.

I pushed the door open praying one of the stalls was empty since there was no line. My blurred eyes focused on a line of urinals and two empty stalls. I'd gone in the men's, but there was no time to rectify the situation as I rounded into one of the stalls on a gag.

My knees slammed against the floor and my body lurched forward as the contents of my stomach rolled up my throat and splashed into the toilet. Tears shot down my face as the second, and then third round of vomit made an appearance. I wasn't sure how long I'd been sitting there, puking my guts out when a warm hand gently touched my shoulder.

"Terra?" Nicholas' tender voice filled the stall. I squeezed my eyes shut, not wanting him to see me like that...not wanting anyone to see me like that. "Do you need me to call someone for you?"

I shook my head as a strangled sob escaped me. My body was exhausted as I slouched back against the cold wall of the stall and palmed my face. But before I could protest, Nicholas scooped me into his arms and I instinctively curled into his chest. "I don't know what you want me to do, but I can't let you stay on that nasty floor." His niceness made me cry even harder as he carried me from the bathroom.

"Terra?" Gabby's worried voice forced me to lift me head. "What happened?" She looked from me to Nicholas.

"I need to go home." I moved my legs so that he'd place me on the floor.

"Shelia's here, I'll go with you."

"No." I held my hand up, my body flooded with embarrassment. "I mean, thank you for the offer, but I'm okay." With my eyes focused on my feet I hurried away from the two of them, wishing like hell I could turn back time and never leave the comfort of my apartment.

CHAPTER SIX

Have you ever had the feeling that the world was moving on without you? That no matter what, you're frozen in place while your entire life becomes a wildfire that burns everything you love to ash?

That's the recurring nightmare I'd been living.

One punch after the other knocked me on my ass. I'd prayed, gotten angry, and tried my damnedest to find solace in the smallest things in hopes that my feet would land on steady ground. My chest would fill with a deep burning breath that would provide me with a sense of peace as it expelled from my lungs.

But that breath hadn't come.

As if Mother Nature herself was mocking me, a gust of wind flipped my loose hair across my face, the buzzing nightlife of the city temporarily shielded from sight. Sullen laughter escaped me as I hastily tied my hair at the nape of my neck with the hair tie that had been resting around my wrist. My forearms laid against my thighs as I leaned forward a bit more, pushing my knees into the brick wall hard enough to cause my flesh to burn. A young woman hurried across the street on her cell phone toward *Side*

Street Drafts. I'd watched that place from the rooftop almost every night since my life had been turned upside down.

The woman stopped just as she stepped onto the sidewalk, a broad smile most likely spread across her face as a suave looking man in a dark moto jacket wrapped his arms around her waist, lifted her into the air as his mouth met hers, and they spun a couple rotations before he sat her back on her feet. The scene before me blurred as hot tears pushed past my eyelids and raced furiously down my cheeks, dripping onto my chest. I shoved up from the rickety metal chair. "Christ," I seethed through gritted teeth as the flesh of my left knee tore open from the rough texture of the brick I'd been pressed against. Yet another round of pain I'd inflicted upon myself, like the universe wasn't doing a good enough job on its own.

The metal chair screeched across the concrete rooftop as I shoved it back far enough to squeeze between it and the makeshift table I'd thrown together from pallet scraps I'd found by the dumpster in the alley beside my building. Living on the top floor made the view from the rooftop to the city below an easy one to observe. My own personal show almost every night.

Something in my gut forced me to turn around and glance over the edge once more before turning in to drown my sorrows with a bottle of bourbon. A man in what seemed to be a tailored suit hurried across the street, much like the woman had before him, a cell phone pressed at his ear. He seemed unraveled. His shirt untucked on one side, his hair standing wildly as if he'd fingered through the dark locks over and over again. But my eyes didn't stay on him long enough to get a feel of his phone conversation due to a fast-moving yellow blur catching my eye. A car without headlights was barreling around the corner right toward him. My heart flopped as I screamed at the top of my lungs, "Watch out!" The man glanced up in my direction before his eyes dropped to the car. His phone crashed to the ground as my feet took flight toward the fire escape.

I hurried down the shaky stairs, desperate to know if he was okay. The last few steps I skipped, jumping to the sidewalk below. My shoes slapped against the concrete. I watched as the man toppled to the ground, the yellow Volkswagen barely missing him. "Turn your fucking lights on, jackass!" my voice roared as I stepped from the sidewalk to check the man out.

He lifted from the ground, bracing his hands against the road. "Holy shit..." His words whispered in disbelief.

"Are you okay?" I leaned before him. His eyes slowly lifted to mine. I blinked a couple times before a very audible gasp left me without warning. "Mr. Stick-up-his ass?" The nickname I'd secretly given him fell from my lips before I could stop it.

His eyebrows furrowed. "What did you call me?"

Heat rushed my face as I fumbled with what to say, my mind failing me miserably. A bulb of blood rolled down his temple. "You're bleeding." He touched the side of his head and glanced at his crimson covered fingers. "We really need to get out of the road and check your wounds."

"I'm okay." He slowly lifted to his feet as the once small observing crowd grew. After a couple steps he swayed to the right, almost sending himself tumbling to the ground. My eyes landed on his untucked shirt, which was once crisp white. Spots of blood speckled down the front from more injuries than those visible to the eye.

I quickly grabbed his arm and hooked it around my shoulders, allowing him to put a large portion of his weight onto me. "You've bled through your shirt." He attempted to look down. "Don't. You'll topple us over."

Silence hung between us as we entered my building and stepped into the elevator. He moved from my hold and leaned against the wall farthest from where I stood. In the light, scrapes and shallow bruising were visible on the side of his face where the blood had dripped down from his head. "Was that you on the roof?" His hazel eyes lifted to mine.

"Yeah." The elevator dinged and the doors slid open. Thankfully my apartment was only a couple doors down.

Closing the distance between us, I reached for his arm to hook it back around my shoulders, but he moved away. "I can do it." My hands shot up in surrender.

"Okay, this way." I turned out of the elevator and headed directly toward my apartment, not bothering to glance back to see if he was following or not. Would I still have helped him out if I'd known it was *him*, yes. Being a good person doesn't always mean helping those you like, it involves helping those that are difficult to deal with as well.

I held the door open to allow him to enter. He slowly limped past me, my eyes dropping to his midnight blue slacks. An oblong area was darker than the rest, most likely from another injury. "We really should take you to the hospital."

"No." His voice boomed as the door clicked shut behind me, sending a chill across my arms. My reaction must've been on display because his eyes softened as he leaned against the wall. "I'm sorry. I just—can we see the damage before we decide?"

"Sure." I flipped the light on in the bathroom and lowered the toilet seat cover then stepped aside so he could sit down. The bathroom was even smaller with his large frame in it. My throat tightened as I realized he was going to have to disrobe the majority of his clothes for us to tell how bad his chest and leg were. Standing to my full height, I backed up against the wall.

"What?" His eyebrows pulled tight in the center as he eyed me.

My hands covered my face as I inhaled deeply. The bathroom felt as if it was closing in on me. Why had I brought him back to my apartment instead of taking him directly to the hospital? I'd officially lost my fucking mind.

"Are you okay?" To my surprise, his tone wasn't smug. Instead, it was laced with genuine concern.

I lowered my hands and focused on him sitting on the closed toilet seat, leaning his weight against the counter. "Yeah." I shook my hands out. "You're going to have to take your shirt and slacks off."

His eyebrows rose as a giant smile settled on his lips. "Damn, you're forward."

Laughter bubbled up my throat as warmth flooded my cheeks. "Don't even..." I tried to suppress the smile making its appearance on my own face, but knew I was failing miserably. A chuckle vibrated deep in his chest as he slowly rose to his feet and began to unbutton his shirt. My eyes fixated on each button as it slipped through the eyelet. I swallowed, thickness closing my throat. "Wait!" I reached out and covered his hands with mine. "What's your name?"

Gazing down at me he stilled. "Drew."

Drew. The sound of his name bounced around in my head. It fit him well. Manly was the main word that described the name Drew, which was most likely short for Andrew. Although, I didn't bother to ask.

His attention dropped from mine as he finished unbuttoning his shirt and laid it over the shower curtain rod. I quickly looked away as he dropped his slacks and sat back down. "Your turn?"

My eyes skirted to his. "What?"

Amusement danced across his perfect rectangular face. "It's your turn to give me your name." The tension in my body eased. Drew had a way of insinuating one meaning with his words, even if he meant another.

"Terra." I retrieved the first aid kit from below the sink and sat it on the counter beside him. His chest was scraped up pretty badly, but nothing that required stitches. The only thing I could do was clean the area and apply ointment.

"So, Terra..." Drew trailed off as he hissed from the stinging of the cleansing pad smoothing across his wounds.

"Yeah." I didn't bother looking up, knowing that most likely the conversation he was attempting to embark on wasn't going to be one I'd want to be involved in.

"What brought you to Philly?"

That dreaded question.

Why did it seem everyone I met asked the same question? No one honestly cared, did they? Maybe I wanted a fresh start on life, got a job promotion where I had to move, or even had family in the area. But it felt as if everyone knew I had a heartbreaking reason I didn't want to constantly talk about.

"Who says I'm not from here?" I applied the ointment and scoped out his thigh. The flesh was scraped quite a bit worse than his chest, but yet again, no stitches would be required. A ping of disappointment hit me as the hopes of having to take him to the hospital vanished, knowing his head wound wasn't much to worry about since it stopped bleeding almost as soon as it started. He'd need to stay up for hours on end in case of a concussion, but that was something he could do from the comfort of his own home once I got him in a cab.

"Your accent does." *Crap.*

"Oh, yeah…that."

His bellowing laughter filled the room and I found myself chuckling all the same. There was something about him that was infectious, even if he'd rubbed me the wrong way on our first few encounters.

"Well, are you going to tell me your story, Terra?"

The lump in my throat grew as I ran through exactly what *my story* was in my head. It wasn't one I wanted to share, especially with another man in the bathroom of my apartment. A man I didn't know from another stranger on the street.

What the hell had I been thinking bringing him here?

"I'm almost done with your leg, then I'll check your head and we can get you a cab home."

Thanks to my evasion of answering Drew's question, the silence that filled the bathroom was deafening. I couldn't bring myself to share my life story with him, at least not anytime soon.

What do you mean anytime soon? It's not like you're going to see him again.

"You do that a lot you know."

My eyes lifted to his hazel orbs. "Do what?"

He pulled each glove from my hand and dropped them into the trashcan. "Get inside your own head." His eyes searched mine. "Your face plays the story out without giving away any details. It's fascinating and yet maddening at the same time."

"Glad I can be your emotional roller-coaster." I opened the shower curtain and took a seat on the edge of the tub.

"There's those snarky comments I've come to enjoy." A lopsided grin tipped one corner of his mouth.

I diverted my eyes to the first aid kit and lifted from my seat. Waiting a minute to check the cut on his head was for the best. Drew was causing my heart to flutter with each look, my hands to shake with each word spoken, and my throat to constrict as if I'd die at any moment. I hadn't felt such intensity toward a person besides Liam. And I shouldn't have been feeling it so soon for another man.

I latched one section of the first aid kit I wouldn't be using and Drew's hand closed around the top of mine. "Did I say something wrong?" My eyes turned to his. The intensity within the swirls of browns and greens was like a siren singing beautifully to the sailors at sea.

"No," I shook my head, "it's just..." Stepping back a few steps I took a giant breath and slowly expelled it from my lungs before bringing my eyes back to his. "I moved here to get away from the heartache of my previous life." The truth had been given, even if it wasn't a clear painted picture as to what that heartache entailed.

"Unfortunately, love can be like war where both parties are casualties." He dressed and sat back down. That statement couldn't have rung truer. No matter what scenario of heartache you were in, love was a lot like war. No one survives in the end.

Those left behind are plagued with despair until it's their time to perish, as twisted as that sounds.

Putting on a fresh pair of gloves, I lightly pushed his thick hair back from his forehead. A two-inch-long cut went diagonally into his hairline above the ear. Yet another wound that needed to be cleaned and left alone. A spot I thought was a scab was actually a tiny piece of cement stuck in the wound. I tiptoed and reached behind Drew, careful not to bump against him as I searched for tweezers in the cabinet above the toilet.

They were just out of my reach, resting in a glass on the second shelf. I stretched a smidge further on my tiptoes when my balance teetered, sending me falling forward onto Drew. His hands gripped my hips, stopping me before my chest could smash against his face. I shivered as his fingertips curled into the exposed flesh between my clothes. The warmth of his hands caused a second shiver to roll through me. I quickly snatched the tweezers from the glass and lowered onto my feet. His face tilted up just slightly so he could look me in my eyes.

Unsaid words hung in the air as one of his hands slid gently up my side as he gauged my reaction through hooded eyes. My mouth went slack as he pulled me between his open thighs and lifted just enough to bring his lips to mine. For a brief moment, my eyes fluttered closed and I took in the feel of my lips against another's. The dampness of his plump mouth pressed against mine, but the moment was short lived as an image of Liam flashed behind my eyelids. Shoving backwards, I gasped before quickly exiting the bathroom. I slammed against the wall as I turned into the living room, sending a picture crashing to the floor.

"Terra!" Drew called after me as I hit the front door running, not bothering to grab anything on my pursuit out of the apartment.

My shoes slapped the stairs as I climbed to the rooftop, the only place I could quickly get away to. Tears filled my eyes as I crashed into the chair, trying my best not to topple over onto the concrete. Heavy uneven breaths filled my lungs as I gripped the brick ledge.

"What did you do?" I frantically huffed. One hand curled around the collar of my shirt, the material feeling as if it was cutting off my breathing. My knees buckled, scraping down the brick wall, crashing against the concrete as sobs ripped through my body. With my forehead resting against the brick ledge, I cried harder than I'd cried since I'd left Ann Arbor. "So damn stupid."

"Terra..." A gentle hand touched my shoulder.

I jerked away, flipping onto my bottom and resting my back against the brick. "Don't."

There was a sadness swimming in Drew's eyes that made my heart ache even more. "I'm not going to hurt you." He held his hands up. "I'm sorry for what I did back there. I shouldn't have kissed you."

I shook my head back and forth, unable to speak through the emotions barreling down on me.

"Let me get you back to your apartment and I'll leave." He extended his hands palms up for me to take.

My bottom lip quivered with my teeth pushed tightly into it. Embarrassment and anguish pounded away at any composure I thought I had. Not only did I allow another man to kiss me, but I'd made a complete emotional fool of myself in front of him. "I'll be fine." With my hand on the wall, I pulled myself upright. "You don't have to worry about me."

"I'm not leaving until you're back in your apartment." Drew's eyes were pinned to mine as I slipped onto the ledge with my bottom. He took two giant steps forward and yanked me into his chest.

I gasped from the sudden movement as his arms tightened around my much smaller frame. Realization hit me on a chill. "Did you think I was going to jump?" My words were spoken between labored breaths.

"I wasn't sure what you were about to do, but I knew I couldn't let you do anything I wouldn't be able to live with later."

His statement made me cry even harder. It reminded me so much of Liam, and how he'd do whatever it took to make sure I was safe. Even if I didn't realize I was putting myself in danger, he always had a grip on any situation at hand.

I stepped from Drew's arms and wrapped mine around myself. "I wasn't going to...jump, you know." My burning eyes dropped to my feet as I kicked concrete pieces around.

"Look at me, Terra." The conviction in his tone had my eyes lifting to his. "I've lost people in my life, those circumstances were out of my control, but I'll be damned if it'll happen again without me being able to say I fucking did something. Maybe you weren't about to jump, but accidents happen, and that's an accident I was making damn sure wouldn't take place. Now let me get you back to your apartment and I'll head home." He motioned for me to go first.

With my arms wrapped tightly around my midriff, I didn't say a word as I passed him and headed back down the stairs. Entering my apartment, I waited for Drew to come in before shutting the front door. His limp was a bit more prominent than before. Guilt washed over me, because he'd most likely hurt himself even more by chasing my crazy ass to the rooftop. "I really am sorry," I mumbled.

Drew leaned against the wall. "There's no need to apologize."

"But there is. I'm not crazy, I swear." A humorless laugh escaped me. "It's just—" I took a deep breath.

He closed the distance between us and cupped my face, turning my head up enough so he could see directly into my eyes. "Don't feel obligated to tell me a story you aren't ready to tell." His lips brushed against my forehead and my eyes closed. A moment later his hands left my face and the clicking of the front door closing filled the room.

My eyes shot open and I searched the room. Drew had left without giving me a chance to explain.

CHAPTER SEVEN

Two weeks had passed since I'd made a complete hysterical ass out of myself the night Drew had been at my apartment. The entire night unfolded like a train wreck. I'd saved him from being ran down by a Volkswagen Beetle, cleaned the majority of his wounds, gotten kissed, and ran to the rooftop to fall apart in a heaping mess of emotions. Only to be saved by Drew, who thought I was going to jump, or fall, to my immediate death below. Whose life was that dramatic?

Apparently, mine.

"You're kidding, right?" Gabby bellowed with laughter across the table from me.

"No," I growled through gritted teeth. "I couldn't make this shit up even if I wanted to."

"Oh, my...that's too good!" She continued to cackle like a hyena.

I rolled my eyes and leaned back against the wall at my favorite end of the bar. "It's not that funny." My tone was sharp as a knife.

"Here." Gabby sat a plate of food before me on the bar. "Eat, you'll be less hangry." She patted my hand and I jerked it away from her reach.

I opened my mouth to hit her with some snarky ass comment, but my mind blanked as the aroma of whatever deliciousness she'd placed before me overtook my senses. I turned to find a grilled chicken sandwich and waffle fries awaiting me. The roar of my gut made me groan. "As much as I'd love to throw that plate of food at you, I'd hate to waste it."

"Good girl." Gabby sat a glass of pop down with a giant smile on her face.

My eyes narrowed as I took a drink. She was really laying it on thick, knowing how badly she'd annoyed the hell out of me. If anyone had watched me eat, they would've thought I hadn't had a meal in years. Which wasn't the case at all. I'd skipped breakfast, and almost skipped lunch, from my lack of paying attention to the time. When a girl—like myself—misses a meal, things can get a little intense.

"Forgive me yet?" Gabby took my dish, raising an eyebrow as she awaited my response.

"Ask me again after you refill my glass."

She nodded. "Fair enough." She headed toward the kitchen with my dishes.

I leaned back against the wall and placed my feet on the stool beside me. *Side Street Drafts* was pretty scarce on a Wednesday right after the lunch crowd. But a few familiar faces lingered around, people I'd come to recognize from becoming a frequent customer myself.

"A refill, my dear." Gabby sat a chilled mug full of pop on the bar this time around.

My eyes grew and I perked up a bit. "I've always wanted Coca Cola in a chilled mug." I clapped my hands together with excitement.

"You really need to get out more."

I swatted at the air. "Hush." The cool glass pressed against my lips as I took a nice slow drink. "Ahh…" I sighed, over exaggerating just how good it was.

Gabby shook her head. "So, what are you going to do about *Drew?*"

"Absolutely nothing." I crossed my arms and laid them on the bar.

She tossed a hand towel onto her shoulder. "What do you mean, absolutely nothing?"

"Exactly what I said."

Gabby leaned against the bar and crossed her arms over her very on display chest. "Yeah, the two of you had an intense night of *what the fuck* moments, but that doesn't mean you can't go down that avenue of dating."

My hand quickly rose to stop her. "Dating? Are you kidding me? I couldn't even make it through an unexpected kiss without going off the deep end. Who's to say he would even consider being around me again? And lastly, I only have his first name, nothing else. No phone number, address, last name, or place of business."

"Have you tried searching him on Facebook?"

My eyes narrowed and my mouth thinned. "Did you not hear what I just said? I don't know his last name."

"Just try Drew, or Andrew. See what pops up around here." She shrugged.

"I don't have time for internet stalking." I tossed some cash on the bar and collected my purse.

"Where are you going?"

"Home," I replied over my shoulder as I made my way to the door.

* * *

My sneakers slapped against the pavement at a steady rhythm as I picked up the pace. Running was a love of mine in high school. I'd ran Cross Country, and even won medals during that time. But like everything else, the urge to run faded away as life became more hectic.

Fairmount Park had quickly become one of my favorite spots, along with a handful of the other parks around Philadelphia. The peaceful setting, and large amounts of acreage to explore made it the top spot for runners, bikers, and everyday get-togethers. But today, I found myself running off the stress of the past week. I clicked on one of my upbeat playlists and drowned out my surroundings. It was only me, pulse thumping tunes, and the great outdoors.

Have you ever gotten lost within a song? Or maybe, ten plus songs? Well, apparently that's what happens when you drown out the world with music. I glanced around, realizing I'd ran farther than I'd ever gone in Fairmount Park before. My feet were burning as badly as my lungs as I bent at the hips, rested my hands on my thighs, and tried to settle my body back to a steady functioning pace.

Two men ran past me, going the opposite direction and waved. People, for the most part, were nice in Philly. That made adapting to my surroundings a hell of a lot easier, even if I rarely ventured from the few blocks surrounding where I lived. I pulled up the route I'd taken on my phone and realized just how far I'd gone past my normal turnaround point. "Shit, that's going to be a long walk back." I blew out a puff of air.

The afternoon sun blazed hot and bright above me. I took a steady breath and started the trek back to my vehicle. It's crazy how changing your lifestyle can make you feel better. Running, writing, and being around mostly happy people helped rid my mind a little bit of the depression and anxiety that afflicted me. Don't get me wrong, both still reared their ugly heads without permission when they wanted to. There was no fully stopping that. However, those encounters seemed to be less frequent. As also, the intensity was at a lower rate most of the time.

I was kicking myself in the ass for not bringing along more water, but carrying one bottle was enough baggage when you didn't have a backpack with you. Usually, that one bottle of water would last the majority of my run, but today that wasn't the case. Forty-five minutes later and the main entrance of the park came into view. "Thank you, Jesus," I huffed as my feet continued to carry me forward. I knew that as soon as I sat down, it would be a while before I'd want to get back up. Which meant the ride home was one to be thankful for rather than complaining about the traffic.

My car beeped as I pressed the unlock button on the fob. I'd never been so thankful in my life to see my Audi. It'd always been just a car to me, but today it was a godsend. I opened the back-door and tossed the few belongings I'd carried with me onto the seat before discarding my shoes and socks. I'd worn them bad boys long enough, flip flops were my next priority. Closing the backdoor I faintly heard someone calling my name. I didn't even bother looking around to see if they were actually trying to get my attention because hardly anyone in Philadelphia knew I existed. Not to mention, Terra was a common name, even if my spelling was different than most.

Cranking the engine, I retrieved my cell phone from the storage compartment to see if I'd missed anyone. A pang of guilt rolled through me as I stared at my father in-law's name beside the missed call icon. Clearing it from the screen, I sat the phone on my thigh so I could remove my iPod from my arm. I wasn't like the usual people who ran with their phone attached to them. Yeah, I probably should for safety purposes, but I didn't want the distractions of calls, texts, or any other form of being gotten hold of. Fairmount Park was my solace away from all the noise.

I jerked the Velcro a bit harder than I'd anticipated on my arm band, sending my cell phone sliding off my lap and onto the floor-board. "Great," I huffed as I leaned forward, searching the floor with my hand, hoping I wouldn't have to move the steering wheel to retrieve the phone. It was in the perfect spot, and nothing irked me more than someone messing with the placement of my seat or steering wheel.

Pounding on my window caused me to jerk upright, my heart matching the rapid beat of the unknown person's hand against the glass. A quick scream erupted from my lungs as I whipped my head in the direction of the noise. The person standing on the other side wasn't who I expected. Not that I actually expected it to be someone I knew. A fellow park enjoyer who maybe saw me drop something or needed directions maybe. Definitely not Drew.

With my hand over my heart I rolled the window down. "Give a girl a heart attack, why don't you," I managed to say through heavy breaths.

"Sorry." He chuckled, showing his pearly whites. Thankfully, he was wearing dark tinted aviators to hide those intense hazel eyes. "I thought you saw me and were trying to make an escape before I could catch you."

"No."

"You didn't hear me call your name?"

I leaned forward to reach for my phone once again. "That was you? I thought someone was calling after another Terra. Hardly anyone here knows me."

"What are you doing?" He leaned in the window, placing his face in my personal space.

My eyes dropped to his mouth, as if I needed my hormones to overtake my sanity. The corners of his lips tipped up slightly and I pulled my attention away from him. Drew was going to be the death of me if I allowed it, I could feel it deep in my bones. The last thing I needed in life was someone to come in like a hurricane and knock me on my ass. I'd been thrown off kilter on far too many occasions. Couldn't I settle for a little peace and normalcy for once? Who was I kidding, peace and normalcy was doubtful.

Evading his question, I continued to rummage around the floor. *How the hell does a phone vanish?* I huffed as the driver's door swung open. My eyebrows furrowed as I stared dumbstruck at Drew. "What the heck are you doing?"

He dropped down to see into the floorboard. "Trying to help you out." His arm brushed against my calf as he reached under the seat. "Looking for this?" He lifted my cell phone into the air.

"Give me that." I tried to snatch it from him, but he moved too far for me to reach. "Let's see what kind of dirt I can find in here." His wide smile began to fade. I knew exactly what had caused it too.

"About that picture." I slipped from the seat and jerked my phone from his grasp, this time he was more than willing to hand it over.

"No explanation needed." He shoved his sunglasses into his hair as the sun tucked behind a row of clouds. "I hadn't noticed your ring before." His eyes zeroed in on the silver band adorning my ring finger.

"I don't always wear it." I twisted the band.

"You might want to do that so you aren't misleading people." Drew lowered his shades onto his eyes. "I should be going." He motioned over his shoulder. "Running a little behind on the day, thought I'd say hello." That was his attempt to run away from the elephant between us.

"Hey!" I called after him as he took off in a nice jog. He was literally running away from me. "Now I know how he felt chasing after me," I grumbled, turned the car off, snatched my keys, and took off after him. The man had some speed, and my legs already hated me from putting them through the wringer earlier. "Drew, stop!" I cried out as loud as I possibly could, and to my surprise he indeed stopped.

My chest heaved as I caught up to him, placing a hand on his bicep so he'd turn to face me. "You always that winded after running a short distance?" His question was one of concern instead of sarcasm.

"No," I huffed, bending at the waist to catch my breath. "I'd been on the trails for too damn long earlier." I waved a dismissive hand. Why I was out of breath wasn't the issue, the photo was.

"Give me a chance to explain the photo."

"You really don't have to, Terra. You're married, I get that. If you weren't still together you wouldn't have your wedding photo as your screensaver. I misread what was going on between us the other night, and I apologize for kissing you. If I'd known you're a married woman, I wouldn't have done—"

"Drew, if you don't shut your mouth and let me talk I'm going to hurt you." He pulled his sunglasses from his face, his mouth open as if he was going to speak, but he swiftly closed it without a word, shock blatantly rested on his face from my interruption. I ran a hand through my thick ponytail, wishing we weren't standing in Fairmount Park, but life likes to throw curveballs.

"My husband died a little over six months ago," I blurted out, feeling that dull ache throbbing within my chest. Drew's mouth fell open as sadness filled his hazel eyes. That same look that I tried my damnedest to avoid.

"Terra..."

"Don't." I held up my hand. With my eyes shut I tried to gain composure once again. Having a breakdown in Fairmount Park wasn't on my bucket list. After a few steady breaths, I opened my eyes, unshed tears blurred my vision. "It was unexpected and absolutely devastating." The words barely passed through the thick emotions clogging my throat.

Before I could register what he was doing, his arms wrapped firmly around my body. He held me against his chest and rubbed soothingly up and down my back. The realization of how badly I needed a hug hit me as I stood enveloped in his embrace. My shaky hands lifted to rest against his back. Laughter and conversation of other park goers filled the air as we stood with silence between us, and for a brief moment I allowed myself to be at ease. I let my guard down and soaked in the warmth of another human trying to console me.

Drew wasn't someone with a major stick up his ass, my first impression of him was wrong. There was a lot more to the man that a part of me desperately wanted to learn about, but could I allow myself to do that?

"You know," Drew's voice was soft at my ear. "I've never been one to jump to conclusions, and if I'd thought through everything you've told me, I could've put two-and-two together. The heartache comment that brought you to Philly, the photo, and the missing wedding band the other times I've seen you. I'm an asshole for thinking you were anything other than a grieving widow."

Grieving widow.

Those two words were like a punch to the gut. I know he didn't mean anything by them, because honestly, they were the truth. I was classified as a grieving widow, but that was the first time I'd heard them said aloud. My throat bobbed as I swallowed the thick emotions overtaking me. I knew I needed to get away from the impeding heartache barreling down on me, away from Fairmount Park, and away from *Drew*.

Something about him evoked too many emotions. It was as if I couldn't control my own emotional response. I'd gone through an array of feelings the few times we'd been around one another, and I wasn't sure if that was a good or bad thing.

"I need to get home," I spoke against his chest.

Drew dropped his arms and took a step back; his eyes were glassy as I glanced into them for the briefest of moments. I tucked my bottom lip into my mouth and harshly bit down, hoping seeing his unshed tears wouldn't bring on more of my own. His overflow of emotions hit me hard in the chest.

He cleared his throat and scrubbed his hands over his face. "I'm usually not this big of a fuck up." His humorless laugh made me smile. I knew all too well how he was feeling because I felt the same when it came to him. That everything I said or did was a giant clusterfuck. When it came to how disastrous we both felt, we were on the same page.

"I should probably say the same." I pretended to kick a rock that wasn't even there.

"How about we start over? Get a coffee maybe? Pretend the majority of what's happened, didn't actually happen." He scrunched his face, anxiously awaiting my response.

As good as it sounded, who could pretend things didn't happen that actually did? I'd never tried it, but the thought alone made it hard to believe it could be done. "I don't think that's a good idea."

Drew's face blanked, he wasn't expecting that for my answer. I'd be lying if I said I didn't feel a smidge like an asshole for saying no, but I knew getting close to someone so soon—especially someone like him—wouldn't be good for my wellbeing.

"It's not you—"

"Don't even give me that it's not you, it's me, bullshit." He tucked his hands into the front pockets of his jeans.

Was he really running in jeans?

It was the first time I took in his full appearance. White V-neck shirt that showcased his olive skin, and dark wash jeans that rested perfectly on his hips. He looked like a different man than the GQ version of himself. And yet, both were unbelievably attractive.

"Okay." My sad smile barely registered as I tiptoed to hug him around his neck. "Maybe in another life we could've been something," I whispered before I let go and hurried to my vehicle, hoping like hell he'd let me go this time.

As I drove off, I glanced in the rearview mirror at Drew fading away.

CHAPTER EIGHT

"I'm going to yank that doorbell from the wall," I growled and rolled out of bed. Whoever was ringing the damn thing was more than persistent.

After the first few chimes I thought they'd give up and leave. That wasn't the case. Most likely a neighbor's child selling something for school, or a delivery of some sort. Whichever the case, I was going to give them the third degree for not giving up and letting me sleep. I slipped on my cotton robe and secured it at the waist, not wanting to give my uninvited guest a peepshow.

The sun beamed through the kitchen window, cascading a rainbow onto the living room floor. I hadn't realized it was that late in the morning. For once, I'd slept longer than a few hours without waking up. My mind, body, and soul were still very exhausted, and the annoyance pulsing through me from that damn doorbell continued to grow as I stubbed my toe on the entry table. "Seriously!" A strangled cry fell from my lips.

Stomping my injured foot, I made quick movements of unlocking all three locks on the door and ripped it open. "Don't you realize some people are still—"

"Good morning to you too." Drew took a step back as he eyed me.

Suddenly, I was kicking myself for not looking better when answering the door. My hair was in disarray, my face most likely displayed red marks from my pillowcase, and I'm not even going to mention the robe situation. "What are you doing here?"

"Wanted to see if you'd like to go to breakfast." That beautiful smile of his made its appearance.

"Drew…" My heart slammed wildly and I paused.

He rocked back on his heels. "All I'm asking is for breakfast. The two of us can be friends, right?" His head cocked to the side.

It's just breakfast.

I gripped the door with one hand, the other resting firmly on my hip. "Get in here before I change my mind."

Drew's laughter filled the hall outside my door before he stepped over the threshold. "Give me a few minutes to look like a human," I rattled off as I headed for my bedroom.

"You look fine to me." I quickly turned, knowing damn-good-and-well he was joking. But the look on his face was anything but comical. The man was serious. "You could put on a trash bag and look good."

I wiggled my index finger back and forth. "Although I appreciate the compliment, that kind of conversation isn't in the friend code."

Trying his best not to grin, Drew nodded. "I'm a little rusty."

I shook my head and slipped into my bedroom. Being a glutton for punishment had never been my thing, until Drew.

* * *

"Here are your menus." A lovely older woman extended a laminated sheet to the both of us.

"Thank you." I smiled.

"I'll give you two a few minutes." She winked and slid her pen behind her ear.

My eyes roamed the tiny diner. It was adorable, exposed brick walls with black and white photos of the city throughout the years as decor. A hole in the wall place that only the regulars would know about. Philadelphia had loads of character. Like a melting pot filled with different hues of paint, yet none of them clashing together, only blending. I was starting to love it, even if the reason I lived in the city wasn't a pleasant one.

"In that pretty little head of yours again?"

My attention drifted back to Drew. "Just admiring the place."

"Liberty has been around for as long as I can remember."

"So, you've grown up here?"

"For the most part." He ran a hand over his mouth.

"Ready to order?" the waitress interrupted.

"We'll both have the special." He took the menu from me and handed them to her.

Surprise hit me. I'd never in my life had someone order food for me while I was present, and Drew had done just that. It was an odd feeling, thinking someone might know what you like before you do, but I was open to see if he did.

"What's that look for?"

"What look?"

"The one on your face right now."

I shrugged. "Nothing really."

"Oh, it's something." His chuckle was music to my ears, bringing a smile forward.

My eyes lifted to the ceiling as a horrible attempt to avoid his questioning. The casual flirting was growing with each sentence that passed between us. Being friends already seemed to be a heavy task we might not accomplish.

"There you go again..."

"Will you stop?" I tossed the balled-up paper from my straw at his face, the lightweight material missing by a good foot.

He crossed his arms and leaned on the tabletop. "I'm just trying to get to know you better is all."

"Start with something simple then. Like, my favorite color or favorite movie."

"Well, what's the answer to both of those?"

I nibbled my bottom lip. "Green, and *P.S. I Love You.* But, my favorite movie changes quite often."

"That's a good one."

"You've seen it?"

"Who hasn't?"

"Only the majority of the male population."

Drew pressed his fist against his mouth, stifling a laugh. "I beg to differ."

My head shook. "If you've honestly seen it, you're the only single guy I know that would've watched it without coercion."

His smile slowly faded. "Who said I was alone when I watched it?" His question was void of amusement.

I'd hit a nerve. One I hadn't intentionally meant to hit.

"I just...assumed."

A sly grin tilted his lips. "You know what they say about assuming..." A knowing look passed between us.

I erupted with full belly laughter. "Yeah, yeah." I waved a dismissive hand in the air.

"We'll continue this conversation momentarily," Drew rambled as the waitress made her appearance with our food in tow.

My eyes widened as she sat two plates of gooey deliciousness on the table. The aroma of cinnamon and vanilla filled my senses, causing me to inhale deeply. "Mmm," I moaned, knowing what awaited me on that plate would be an orgasm for my taste buds.

"Anything else I can get ya?" She smiled widely, awaiting our response.

Drew shook his head since he'd already dived in. "No, ma'am. This looks to be plenty."

"Enjoy."

The napkin blanketed as I shook it out and placed it on my lap. Lifting my fork, ready to inhale a giant bite, I glanced up to find Drew staring at me. "What?" My eyebrows dipped in the center as my fork stayed suspended in the air.

"Surprised of how big a bite you have on that fork is all."

My head dropped back on my neck as I let out a groan. "Hush your mouth."

"Carry on." He motioned for me to take the bite, and I did.

"Cinnamon roll?"

He nodded with a giant smile.

"Best. Thing. Ever," I spoke around a mouthful of food.

"Didn't your mother teach you manners?"

I swallowed and aimed my fork at him. "I'll stab you." My eyes narrowed.

His hands shot up, sending his fork clattering against the plate. "Down, girl. I was only kidding."

"How'd you know cinnamon rolls were my favorite?" I eyed him as I slipped another bite into my mouth.

"I didn't. Just hoped you liked them as much as I do."

"Good thing I'm not allergic to let's say...cinnamon."

"That's a good thing, because it would probably be a deal breaker."

I laughed. "An allergy would be a deal breaker?"

He shrugged. "Guess we'll never know."

"Hope you don't have any cats then, because I'm highly allergic."

"Planning on coming to my place, are you?"

Heat flooded my cheeks as I shoved another bite of food in my mouth. There was no easy way to answer his question. Either say no and make him feel like shit, or say yes and seem as if I wanted to see his place. I'd put my foot in my mouth.

"You really need to stop overthinking things."

"I wasn't."

"And stop lying."

I feigned shock. "How dare you call an upstanding woman, such as myself, a liar."

"If the shoe fits."

I shook my head and turned my attention back to my plate. Conversation with Drew felt natural, like I didn't have to try to seem smart or funny. His personality was magnetic, it pulled me in and allowed me to put out the same witty banter. Life itself was dark enough at times, so to be able to surround myself with someone that brightened the darkness was a blessing.

Taking the last bite, I pushed my plate to the end of the table. Drew sat back with his linked hands resting on his stomach. He looked comfortable, at ease with the life around him. I'd been like that almost every day with Liam, but the darkness took over after his death. I craved that kind of contentment. Maybe one day I would have it.

"Ready?" I hooked my purse across my body.

"Yeah." Drew pulled his wallet out and tossed a lump of cash on the table. I knew our meals couldn't have cost as much as he'd put down. A smile tipped the corners of my mouth. The man was a good tipper, which meant he genuinely cared about people.

We stepped into the blazing mid-morning sun. People hustled down the street to get to their destination, cars honked as someone sat during the green light a second too long. The intensity of city life wasn't new to me, but it did hit my anxiety pretty hard at times. Something I never had to deal with before.

"You okay?" Drew looked down at me through his aviators.

I half grinned. "I'm not going to break, you know."

His hand linked with mine. "I can't help asking."

My eyes dropped to our hands perfectly fitting together between us. A part of me wanted to jerk mine from his hold and run in the opposite direction, because friends didn't hold hands. But the other part of me wanted to grip his hand even tighter and beg him to never let go. That familiar stinging stirred deep in my eyes, and I willed it away. I'd done more than my fair share of crying in front of him, and we'd only been friends for a very short minute. It was surprising he hadn't run for the hills and never looked back. Instead, he'd ran in my direction and refused to allow me not to acknowledge him. This time, I was going to allow myself to feel the warmth of a hand linked with my own. To pretend that my life hadn't been uprooted, that I wasn't the same Terra who lived back in Ann Arbor, but a completely different version of myself. Is that how people moved on after the death of a significant other? I wasn't sure.

With such heavy topics rolling through my mind, I hadn't realized we were to his vehicle until the car beeped. Drew opened the passenger door and I slipped inside. My eyes stayed fixated on him as he rounded the front and climbed into the driver's seat with ease. His dark hair and morning scruff perfectly encased his beautiful face. He was the type of man that broke your heart by simply looking at him.

"Why are you single?" I blurted out, wishing like hell I could retract the words as soon as they hung in the air between us.

Drew's head turned in my direction, his mouth slack like he was at a loss for words. "Umm..." Trepidation wrapped around the bland word he managed to say. "That's a story for another day." He cleared his throat and cranked the engine.

As badly as I wanted to press the issue, I knew it wasn't the time. Drew was evasive when it came to personal questions. I'd learned that quickly. If he wasn't ready to talk about it, there would be no conversation. He'd sweep it under the rug and pretend it hadn't been asked. But why would that simple question be one he didn't want to answer? There was no way he was seeing someone, because he'd gotten bent out of shape when he thought I was a married woman whose husband was alive and well. My life had become an open book to him, yet his was secured firmly with a padlock.

We sped down the busy street in silence, no conversation or music to fill the awkwardness. I absolutely hated it. My leg bounced with nerves as we took a right and I realized we weren't headed back in the direction of my apartment. "Where are we going?" My eyes scanned over his profile.

"I need to run by my house."

"Like I said, you better not have a cat." I crossed my arms over my chest and slouched in the leather seat.

He chuckled. "I guess you'll have to see when we get there."

"I'm not coming in."

The light turned red and we came to a stop, his head turning in my direction, that meg-watt smile that caused flutters in my gut on full display. "The hell you aren't. I've seen yours, it's only fair that you see mine." Somehow his grin grew even larger, knowing exactly how that comment came across.

I shook my head and pulled my sunglasses onto my eyes from their resting spot atop my head. "Maybe I don't want to see yours."

My snarky remark pulled the loudest laugh I'd heard from him yet. "Oh, pretty girl, you definitely do." Heat engulfed me.

Checkmate.

Winning remark goes to Drew.

I wasn't familiar with the part of town we were in, mainly because everything screamed expensive. No, I wasn't hurting in the finance department, not even close, but I didn't splurge on lavish things anymore either. An expensive taste was something of the past, it wasn't what made life great.

We pulled into a parking garage that went underground, the dim lighting forcing both of us to remove our sunglasses. His hazel eyes cut to mine for a split second. "What?"

"Just wanted to look at you is all." He continued down the spiral drive before slipping into a parking spot designated for nineteen-fifty-two.

Killing the engine, we both exited the vehicle. I glanced around, not understanding the way the parking garage was laid out. "Why would they put the higher-level parking spots on the lower level of parking?"

"There are businesses on the first few floors, guess they thought it was a good idea to put parking underground for the residents." He clicked the lock button on the key fob.

"You've never really thought about it, have you?"

"Not for a second." Our laughter echoed against the concrete walls. "Elevators are this way." Drew extended his hand for me to take, and surprisingly I went for it without pause.

A shaky breath left my lungs as we headed for the elevators. The parking garage was rather empty, meaning the majority of the apartments were either vacant or the residents all worked the same shift.

Crossing the threshold into the elevator I was in awe. They looked brand-new, but the building couldn't have been. It wasn't a part of the city that had been under construction, at least not in the past few years. I'd done my fair share of research before moving to Philadelphia, just to have some kind of expectation of what I was getting myself into, and this part of town I'd scanned over. Even though I knew I didn't want to live in it, mainly because of the price tag, I did admire its beauty, but construction hadn't come up in my research.

The ride to the nineteenth floor was a quick and smooth one. The doors slid open and I followed closely beside Drew. My mind was hyper aware of our hands still being linked. The pulse in my hand thumped rapidly with each step we took, like a beacon reminding me that hand holding wasn't in the friend code, but I couldn't bring myself to let go.

The carpet was a deep burgundy like wine with charcoal grey walls. Plain, yet sleek at the same time, with bronze new-age chandeliers hanging every eight feet or so from the ceiling. I was beginning to wonder if Drew's career choice was legal, with as fancy as the building was. We passed at least ten doors before we took a left and curled around a backward S shaped hall. A single black door was directly ahead of us, the only door in sight. My eyes landed on a metal rectangular sheet hanging to the left that read nineteen-fifty-two.

We'd arrived at his place.

Drew typed in a long passcode on the keypad attached to the door handle and a faint beep followed by a click. He pushed the door open and held it for me to go in first, dropping my hand in the process. I sighed, partially thankful he let go of my hand and partially in awe of the foyer.

The door opened up to a circular foyer with a high ceiling. An archway on the other side led into the very spacious and open floor plan. The kitchen and living room were on full display. Sleek elephant gray countertops stretched in a U with charcoal cabinets showcasing the back wall. A pale gray rug covered the seating area with a single couch facing large windows that showcased a gorgeous view of the city. What surprised me was the lack of a television.

"This place is…" I spun around, taking in every inch before focusing on Drew who was leaning against the arched doorway, "breathtaking."

"When they re-vamped the building about six—no, seven years ago, future residents had a say-so in what their place would look like. A good buddy of mine was working on the project and mentioned there were a few penthouses left with a lower than average price tag, it seemed like a no brainer to me. I was in the market for a new home at the time, so I jumped on it."

"So, you helped design this." I spun around again, this time with my arms spread wide.

"I did." The pride in his smile was so stunning, it literally made my heart ache.

"Wow," I beamed with astonishment as I walked over to the large windows, mesmerized by the view.

Why hadn't I purchased a place in this part of town?

"The view is even better at night." Drew's voice was low at my ear, sending a shiver down my spine. His hands smoothed up and down my biceps. "Are you cold?"

Our eyes connected over my shoulder. "No." Turning slowly in the space between him and the window, my mind was void of the possible consequences of being in such close proximity.

"Terra..." Drew gently rubbed the back of his hand across my cheek, my eyes closed as I relished in the feel of his flesh against mine.

You don't realize how much you crave another's touch until you no longer have it. The simplest brush of fingertips, arms firmly around your body, or the back of a hand smoothing across your face. Every single encounter felt refreshing, and I wasn't so sure it would feel like that with just anyone. The magnetic pull Drew had on me was unlike any other. Different than Liam's, yet all the same. Don't get me wrong, Liam's love was beautiful and one of a kind. The love of my life, if I had to guess. But the feeling Drew was evoking made me pause and appreciate its raw passion, so intense and earth shaking.

There wasn't a single word in the dictionary that could explain the depths of emotion I felt being around him. It terrified me, yet intrigued me as well. How could someone I'd just met cause such severe feelings to stir within me? I wanted to hate myself for thinking such. Liam didn't deserve that—our marriage didn't deserve it either, but I couldn't deny how my heart felt. It reminded me of climbing to the highest peak on a roller-coaster, only to fall at such a rapid pace that it caused your stomach to bottom out and your breath to catch in your lungs. Terrifying, yet thrilling all at the same time.

His fingers skirted around to the nape of my neck and rested there, pulling me back into the moment. My eyelids lifted, his face so close to my own. Drew was intoxicating, even in the simplest moments. "This is more than a friendly standoff." My voice was barely above a whisper.

"Don't I know it." His eyes dropped to my lips and lifted back to mine once again.

I slipped from his hold and put a good amount of distance between us. "Drew." My brain was unable to form a proper sentence to explain what I was feeling without sounding like a complete fool.

"I get it." His hazel eyes full of sorrow.

"Do you?" My tone was harsh, unexpected even to myself.

Drew's hands shot through his hair. "I want to be friends with you, Terra, but for some reason, it's so damn hard to keep my hands off of you. You draw me in like a fix does an addict. I can't explain it..." His humorless laugh filled the room. "I'm not sure I even want to explain it."

Very rarely have I had moments of full blown bravery that I didn't second guess, but when those moments hit there were no stopping my actions. "Then don't." Drew's eyes pierced me where I stood, as if he was searching for confirmation to make a move.

Reality slapped me hard as I began to twist the wedding band sitting on my ring finger. Not so long ago my husband was alive. Now I was standing in Drew's place, a man who was still very much a stranger to me, wishing he'd kiss me senseless. "Is the car unlocked?"

Confusion washed across his face. "No."

"Can I have the keys?" He nodded and motioned toward the counter. I snatched them up and headed for the entrance, stopping as I reached the archway. I pivoted enough to see Drew. "I think it's best if I wait in the car."

"But you didn't get the grand tour."

"Some other time." A smile barely registered. I had to get out of there before I did something I would later regret.

CHAPTER NINE

He dropped me off just outside my apartment, not bothering with parking. I'm sure Drew would've parked if I'd invited him in, but things became awkward at his place and I needed some time away from the intense feelings he stirred up.

Out of the corner of my eye I noticed Gabby headed in my direction from *Side Street Drafts*. She was one of the last people I wanted to see. I hurried inside and took the stairs two at a time, trying to outrun her if she was indeed coming my way. Exhaustion washed over me and the urge to take a warm bath settled in my mind. The day had been a hectic one I needed a break from.

When I reached the top of the stairs I peeked over the railing to see if anyone was following me. The coast was clear. Hurrying past the elevator, I noticed it wasn't in use either. Maybe she wasn't on her way to visit. Relief released the tension in my shoulders. I felt bad for avoiding her.

I locked the door behind me and tossed my belongings on the coffee table. The day had been one I wouldn't soon forget. Hell, the majority of the days since I'd moved to Philly were ones for the books. I'd moved in search of a fresh start that wouldn't be as stressful as staying in Ann Arbor, yet I was handed a different kind of chaos in return. The grass wasn't always greener on the other side. Such a cliché slogan that couldn't ring truer for me.

I flipped the Bluetooth on for my phone and waited for the robotic female voice to say it was connected to the speaker in the bathroom before clicking on some slow jams. Relaxation was going to be mine, one way or another. I dumped a hefty amount of lavender bath salt in the bottom of the tub and turned the faucet to hot. I wouldn't mind if my first layer of skin was scalded, the hotter the better.

Quickly discarding my clothes, I left them on the floor as I stepped into the rising water, thankful I'd found an apartment with a bathtub long enough for me to lay in. My mind drifted to the first home I'd rented with Liam. The tub was too short for me to stretch out in, let alone him. My knees had to stay bent for my upper body to sink into the water. I really loathed that bathtub but loved that house. It was the first place we shared together.

Sadness rolled through me as I sunk deeper into the warmth. Why I'd allowed my mind to go to Liam when I'd had such a trying day was beyond me. Although it wasn't like I could turn off the memories of him, only allowing them to seep into my thoughts when I wanted them to. Maybe in a perfect world.

I definitely wasn't living in a perfect world.

A heavy sigh deflated my lungs as Sarah McLachlan's "I Will Remember You" filled the room. "You've got to be kidding me." I wanted to sink beneath the water and never emerge. But that would've been the selfish choice. Liam didn't get the option of living, I shouldn't allow the thoughts of dying on my own terms fill my head.

Even though the song was heartbreaking, I sang along. Tears rapidly filled my eyes and rolled down my cheeks, mixing with the faint purple water. The lyrics were like an arrow straight through the heart, raw and passionate. Words written about remembering a loved one who left this Earth. Death was something you couldn't outrun. No matter the lifestyle you chose, the end would always be there. Some sooner than others. Death always won.

The ache in my chest was too much to bear as I rolled onto my side and silently cried. My body shook with each heavy soundless sob that ripped through me. I missed Liam more than I could explain, and yet I was easily falling for another man. That couldn't be a rational love, could it? I didn't feel that he was a rebound. Drew felt the same, that's what scared me the most. If the feelings I had were a one-way train I could easily alter the route, but with his train coming head on there was no other choice but to collide. I inhaled a few shaky breaths and tried to smother out the heavy weighing emotions.

If someone told me a year ago I'd end up an emotional mess ninety percent of my days I would've told them they were crazy. I had never cried very often, until life decided mine needed to be turned upside down. How did people survive losing all of their family in a freak accident? There's no way I could. I've had people tell me you learn to adapt, to live again once your heart is ready to begin the healing process. But when did the healing process start? Day one, or day one thousand? I know it's different for each individual, but the route to get there was far too exhausting.

Figuring out what you wanted out of life sometimes made it hard to actually live. Especially if you're one of those people, like myself, who constantly second guessed everything. I'd been that way before I met Liam, but being with him had put a lid on my second guessing...at least for the most part...and allowed me to live without regrets. Since he'd been gone, I'd fallen back down the rabbit hole.

Second guessing had come back like second nature. Bringing back the outlook of whether or not something was good enough —if I was good enough—and the not wanting to become complacent with certain aspects of life. My theory was, how could someone commit to a lifetime in one certain job? Burnout happens, as well as interests changing. Jobs were like moments.

You find the one that inspires you, and once that feeling is gone, you move on to the next.

The change in topic helped to calm me. The tears had subsided, and the water was turning cold. Even a warm bath wasn't relaxing anymore. I pulled the plug and sat there until the tub was empty. Lifting the towel from the floor, I wrapped it around my body and padded into the kitchen. There was a nice merlot waiting for me on the counter. I retrieved a wineglass and popped the cork on the bottle. Nothing was better than a fresh glass of wine. Tonight's glass was going to be a double, maybe even a triple.

With my glass and wine bottle in tow, I headed back to my room, flipping the bathroom light out as I passed. I placed my glass and the bottle on the nightstand and quickly slipped into a silk nightgown. One I hadn't worn in many years. The material felt nice against my bare flesh. "Now I remember why I loved sleeping in this." My hands smoothed across the silk covering my stomach. I flipped the comforter back and climbed into bed, grasping my wineglass in one hand and the television remote in the other. Numerous hours of *The Office* awaited me once I pressed play. I finished my first glass and gave up refilling it, settling on using the bottle instead. I stacked pillows behind my upper back so I could sit comfortably while I watched. I needed bundles of laughs, and *The Office* was one guilty pleasure that never failed me.

* * *

I stirred awake, the crashing of my cell phone hitting the floor pulling me from the dreamless sleep I'd fallen into. Temporary delirium swam within my head as I blinked a few times to settle my foggy brain. The room dark as night, even the television had turned itself off after sitting idle for so long. *How long had I been asleep?* The empty wine bottle sat on the floor beside the bed, where I'd placed it before falling asleep. I was careful not to kick it over as I lowered my feet to the chilled wood floor. My phone had slid under the bed, which meant I had to get on my stomach to retrieve it, or I could simply leave it be. It wasn't like I needed it for much. Ninety percent of the people who called me I avoided, and those I'd recently become acquainted with didn't have my number anyway.

My fingertips curled against the side of the phone case just enough for me to yank it to me. The phone slid into my chest and I pushed up from the floor. I tossed it onto the bed and took the empty wine bottle and glass into the kitchen, knowing if I left it on the floor I'd only end up hurting myself in the morning. I yelped as lightning lit up the apartment. My heart thundering almost as loudly as the crack of the next round of lightning flashing in the night's sky. I gripped the wine bottle tighter, thankful I hadn't thrown it to the floor out of fright. I placed the wineglass in the sink and tossed the empty bottle into the trash. My mouth craving a cold beverage. I'd had far too much wine for one night, so I settled on a large bottle of vitamin water before heading back to bed.

I slipped beneath the covers and turned on my side facing the window. Lightning and thunder went about their usual song and dance as I checked my phone to see what made it tumble to the floor. Four missed calls from Janet stared back at me. All about thirty minutes apart, and two voicemails ready for my listening ear. I checked the time and noticed her last call was a good three hours prior. I sighed with relief. My finger hovered over the screen, wanting to swipe left and press delete on both messages, but guilt reared its head before I mustered up enough courage to do it. Instead, I pressed play on the first.

Terra, it's me...Janet. I really wish you'd call me back. This is hard for us too, you know. All I want is to spend some time with you. To know that you're okay and where you are now. Just...just please let me know you're okay.

As the message ended I quickly deleted it, afraid to listen to the last one she'd left. I felt bad pushing my in-laws away, but I honest to God didn't know if I'd be strong enough to endure having a relationship with either of them. The wounds were too raw for me to constantly be picking at them, and that's what I'd be doing if I had them in my life so soon. Maybe I'd send her an email, letting her know what I'd been up to and that everything was fine. It would be an outlet to speak with her without actually speaking with her. The entire situation was a hard pill to swallow. I missed them almost as much as I missed Liam, but I just couldn't...

I let out a heavy breath and hit play on the second message.

Terra, dammit. She was crying. *This is ridiculous. We love you! Liam wouldn't want you to close us out of your life. He wouldn't want you all alone trying to mourn the loss of him. You need your family and friends. I spoke with Laura yesterday, and was surprised to find she hadn't heard from you since you sold the house. You're better than this, Terra, so much better.*

She was right. I'd ran away from everything...everyone. I pulled the top drawer open on the nightstand and dipped my hand inside. The smooth surface instantly filled my palm as I wrapped my fingers around its ceramic shape and lifted it from the drawer. The deep red heart held a portion of Liam's ashes. The rest laid in Lake Michigan. He loved it there, so I wasn't surprised when he'd mentioned doing that if he passed before me. I rubbed my hand across the top and closed my eyes.

"Do you ever think about your arrangements after you die?" Liam stared out at the horizon.

"What do you mean?" His question threw me off guard. We'd never talked about dying much.

"Whether or not you want to be buried or cremated. Have you ever thought about it?" His gaze drifted to me as the warm breeze moved his longer than usual hair over his forehead.

I sat in silence as I thought about the question. "Not really. I guess dying seems far off when in reality it can happen at the snap of your fingers."

"Right." He pulled me into his side. His lips found my forehead and I snuggled closer into him. "Everyone wants to believe their life will be a span of many years, but you never know. Something can happen at any moment."

"Well, have you thought about it?"

"Yeah," he nodded, "when I die have me cremated. Bring my ashes out on the boat and spread them here in the lake."

"Really?"

"Absolutely. Lake Michigan is one of my favorite places. That's all I need."

"Would it be weird if I wanted to keep a portion of you?"

Liam erupted with laughter. I, however, didn't find the topic very funny at all. "It's just ashes, Terra. It won't necessarily be me anymore."

"But it will be you..." I sucked my bottom lip between my teeth. All the talk about death made me emotional. Liam realized that.

His lips pressed softly against mine as he lifted the sunglasses from my eyes. "You do what gives you comfort. But who's to say I'll die first?" He grinned.

I playfully slapped his chest and snuggled into him. "I really hope I go first, I don't know how I'll survive without you."

"And I don't know how I'd survive without you." Admiration swam in his coffee colored eyes.

"Hopefully we will have many more years before we have to think about any of that." I laid my head against his chest as the boat swayed with the light current of the water.

"I hope so, too, baby." Liam held me tight as his eyes drifted back to the water ahead.

Being on the lake was serene and beautiful at the same time. It was the place we could go to clear our heads and cleanse our souls of the everyday hustle and bustle of life. Just the two of us with the sound of the water lapping against the boat as we moved across the lake. We waited *all winter for the days when we could get out on the water, and those days seemed to fly by more and more as the years passed by.*

My throat tightened as I held the ceramic heart against my chest. Never in my wildest dreams could I have known that merely eight months after we had that conversation I'd lose him. Each memory that flashed before my eyes since his passing was like a knife twisting deeper into the chamber that held my fragile heart. I was beginning to realize that losing someone never got easier. You learned to live without them, but the memories and anniversary always came, bringing with it a mixture of happiness and sorrow. Every *first* without them bringing a similar grief as the day they left. A revolving door that kept on turning.

I cherished the memories, but I needed the time to come where I didn't want to scream and cry as I relived them. I wanted to be able to smile without tears as I reminisced the good and bad times we had. Six months wasn't long enough for that to happen though...at least not for me.

Life was a fickle thing we all took for granted at times.

Placing the ceramic heart safely in the drawer, I rolled onto my back. The ceiling above was an off-white with popcorn texture covering it, the constant lightning gave me enough light to see it. I don't know why, but something about it soothed me. The longer I stared, the closer I felt myself drifting toward sleep again. "I need to find something to pour myself into. Or maybe I could get a dog. I've always heard they help with depression." The thought of a fur ball curled up beside me in bed, running through the park after a Frisbee, and making messes throughout the apartment had me smiling.

That was it, I needed a companion. Which didn't necessarily mean I needed another man in my life; a dog would do just fine. Unconditional love without worrying about if they'll leave or break my heart in the end. As I closed my eyes to find sleep, for the first time in a long-time, happiness danced behind my eyelids.

CHAPTER TEN

Sirens blaring sent me into a frantic state of getting out of bed. "What the hell is going on?" I cried out, snatching my cell phone and slipping my feet into the slippers beside my bed.

The fire alarm.

I ran into the hallway and grabbed my robe from the back of the bathroom door as I quickly passed. The building must've caught fire. My heart thundered as I snatched my purse from the counter and hurried out the front door. Neighbors poured down the steps in a frenzy to get outside.

"What's going on?" an elderly man questioned as he took the stairs as fast as his feeble body allowed him to.

"I—I'm not sure." A woman carrying an infant hurried past.

"Sir, let me help you." A teenage boy stepped up and draped the elderly man's arm over his shoulders as he wrapped one around his waist to support the man's weight.

I couldn't help the smile that stretched my face from the self-less act of the boy. Society needed more teenagers like him. Hell, the world needed more people like him period, not just teenagers.

It didn't take long to reach the ground floor and exit the building. Thankfully all three floors weren't to capacity with occupants. Fire trucks lined the street as police officers designated what area we needed to move to. Everything was fast paced and kept under control as I kept a death grip on my robe to keep it firmly closed, wishing like hell I'd slept in my normal pajamas instead of the tiny silk nightgown.

"Excuse me." I tapped a female officer on the shoulder.

She turned. "Yes?"

"Do you know what happened? Is the building on fire, did lightning strike it?" I rambled, the anxiety of losing everything I owned if the building was indeed on fire weighing heavy on my thoughts.

"As of right now, we're unsure. The fire department is checking each floor to see. We will let you know as soon as we know."

"Thank you." I stepped back into the crowd.

The waiting game was the worst part of high anxiety situations. The seconds seemed like minutes, the minutes seemed like hours, and the hours seemed like eternity. I faced the road and tried steady breathing, a technique I'd read about online. Just normal in and out slow breaths to help calm your nerves. It worked every now and then, hopefully it would be my current saving grace.

"Terra?"

"Gabby? What are you doing here?" She stood a few feet away, looking as exhausted as I felt.

"I stay here on occasions."

"Really?" I closed some of the distance between us.

"My girlfriend, Izzy, has an apartment here. Have you heard what's going on?"

I nodded, not knowing what to say about Gabby having a girl-friend. She'd never mentioned dating anyone, let alone Izzy's name before. I wondered if the relationship was new, or if she simply hadn't divulged that much information to me thinking I'd be one to judge her sexual preference.

"Where's Izzy? I'd love to meet her."

Gabby's face lit up at the sound of her name. "She's around here somewhere. Always helping to make sure people are okay."

"Is she an officer?" I wondered if the woman I had spoken with was her.

Gabby shook her head. "She's a nurse. Had just gotten off shift, actually. That's why you haven't seen her at *Side Street*. She's usually working, but her schedule is about to change."

"Ah, makes sense."

"Yeah." A blush crept across her cheeks, something I'd never seen from Gabby before. "We're pretty new. Testing out the waters of staying with her since it's close to the bar, her idea to be exact."

"How nice."

"Yes and no. Her place is quite a bit smaller than mine, but she lives closer to both of our jobs than I do."

"Well, we might just have to find a happy medium then, huh?" A beautiful raven-haired petite woman stepped into our conversation with a wide smile lighting up her porcelain skin.

"You must be Izzy." I extended my hand, which she bypassed and pulled me into a quick hug.

"And you must be Terra." Happiness radiated off of Izzy in swarms. I was amazed by it, especially with her career in nursing. There was nothing easy about that job.

"How'd you know?"

"Gabby told me a little about you. Blonde, killer legs, and freckles across the bridge of your nose and cheeks. Had to be you." She laughed.

"Killer legs?" I glanced down at my bare legs. "I'd say they could be better."

Gabby and Izzy bellowed with laughter, but I wasn't joking. I guess all the running in Fairmount Park was paying off.

"Did you find out anything?" Gabby leaned into Izzy.

"I know they cleared the roof, third, and second floor. No word on the first yet."

A sigh of relief passed through me. If the first floor had been on fire they probably would've noticed when entering the building, so hopefully it was only a fluke.

A crack of thunder roared causing a few unexpected screams and voices to fill the air, hoping the storms would hold off. "How much longer?" a mother with fussy twins called out.

"We're asking everyone to remain calm," an officer held his hands up and announced.

"It'll be hard to remain calm if another storm comes through and we're stuck outside," a man who seemed to be the father of the twins countered.

"Excuse me!" Gabby called out. "I own *Side Street Drafts*." She motioned toward the bar. "Why don't we all take shelter there until we've been cleared to return inside?" The crowd rattled off thank yous as they made their way toward the bar.

I followed Gabby and Izzy down the sidewalk and helped usher people inside. Gabby had a good heart for offering her business as shelter to everyone. "I love you even more for doing this." After the last family walked inside, Izzy pulled Gabby into a passionate kiss, one that you kept for the most private of times. I diverted my eyes from their intimate moment and caught site of a familiar dark vehicle pulling up to the curb.

Drew emerged from the driver's seat in a pair of sweats and a plain shirt. "Everyone okay?" His hand shot through his messy hair as his eyes focused on me.

"I think so. How'd you know..."

"I heard the call over the radio and wanted to make sure you were safe."

His words made me want to run over and wrap my body around his. "Radio?" I hugged myself tightly, doing my best to avoid doing just that, aware that I was barely clothed beneath my knee length robe.

"Police scanner."

"Oh, okay." I noticed Gabby and Izzy had gone inside, leaving me on the sidewalk with Drew.

"It's something my father and I used to listen to for hours during my childhood. Kind of stuck with me after he passed."

"That's good of you to keep the tradition alive."

My eyes focused on Drew's tongue as he moistened his lips. Fireworks shot off in my chest. "It's the small things you hold onto that keep the memories alive."

His statement couldn't have been truer. Little fractions of those you love and have lost are the parts that help you remember what you had. The love, the traditions, and the trinkets; each holding a giant piece of the puzzle that was the two of your lives molded together. My eyes lifted to the sky as I tilted my head back. A few stars peeked between the storm clouds. "Even during the darkest of times, you can find beauty."

"What did you say?" Drew stepped to my side, facing the same direction as me, and looked up to the sky.

"I hadn't realized I said it aloud."

"Say it again."

"Even during the darkest of times, you can find beauty." I repeated the statement loud enough for only the two of us to hear.

His head turned toward me. "Beautiful statement from a beautiful girl."

I turned my face and gazed into his eyes, my mouth slack as his statement hung in the air between us, the depth of admiration in those hazel orbs piercing me straight through the heart. Why was I running from him? Drew could very well be the man to help me piece together my shattered soul. I lifted my hand and cupped his cheek, the stubble rubbing against my palm as he turned his face into it. "Thank you for seeing if I was okay." My voice was barely above a whisper.

Drew's hand touched my hip and pulled me in closer. "I genuinely care about you, whether you believe that or not."

"You barely know me."

"Then let me get to know you already."

Blocking out everything but that moment, I lifted enough to press my lips to his. Drew paused, most likely waiting to see how I would react, given I had pushed him away on many occasions. My tongue smoothed against the seam of his lips and a brief second passed before he granted me access. His hands slipped down my side and came to rest on my hips as he drew me in even closer. His hot mouth molded with my own, sending my heart into an erratic state. We were two people succumbing to the moment we'd been running from.

Thunder cracked. Drew gently pulled his head back. "We should probably get inside."

I lowered my face against his chest and circled my arms around his narrow waist. "So many people in there." The mumbled words were just shy of an admittance that I'd love to have been alone with him for little a bit longer.

Laughter vibrated his chest as he freed my hair from its messy binding atop my head. "Yes, there are." His husky words were enough to let me know he wished the same.

"If you're a resident of the complex, you can go home now. The building's been cleared." One of the officers working the scene spoke as he passed by to enter *Side Street Drafts*.

A knowing look passed between us. "Want to come up?"

"Do you think I'll get towed if I leave my car parked at the curb?"

His answer let me know he wanted to. "I doubt the owner of the bar would do that, I've heard she's pretty lenient." Drew's hand slide into mine.

A smile tugged at my lips as we walked hand-in-hand to the building's entrance. Emergency personnel were beginning to clear out as the voices of other residents spilled onto the street behind us. With the building being empty, the wait for the elevator was nonexistent, and the ride to the third floor was quick. Not a single word was spoken between us until we reached the front door of my apartment.

"Are you sure you want me to come in?" Drew stared down at me as I twisted the doorknob. "Why is your apartment unlocked?" He unexpectedly changed the subject.

"I wasn't exactly in the state of mind to ensure it was locked when I ran out thinking the building was on fire. Managing to grab a robe was a miracle in itself." I clutched the plush collar as I stepped inside.

Drew shut the door and faced me, his eyes dropping down to my chest before lifting back to mine, desire staring back at me. I glanced down, not realizing I had opened my robe when I tugged on its collar. The entire upper half of my nightgown was exposed, even the peaks of my breasts were plain as day through the silky material. My hands shot to the robe, trying to quickly cover myself but he stopped me. "If I'd known *that* was beneath your robe…" His unfinished statement hung in the air as Drew's fingertips skimmed across my collarbone, leaving a chill in their wake.

I closed my eyes and took in the feel of his hands gilding beneath the robe, heating my flesh as he shoved it off my shoulders. My body temperature dropped as it slid from my body onto the floor, causing every inch of my skin to pucker with goose bumps. If my nipples weren't on display before, they sure as hell were after that. Instinct within me screamed to cover my chest with my arms, but I didn't listen. I wanted Drew to see me, every inch if that's where this was going, I couldn't deny that.

Taking a step forward, my arms circled his neck as I pulled his mouth to mine. His hand gripped my waist, one snaking around to my back and smoothing up my spine, not stopping until it threaded into my hair at the nape. A moan fell from my lips as the kiss deepened, intensifying the heat overtaking my very being. My legs bumped the arm of the couch, almost sending me toppling backward, but Drew's firm hold kept me upright. "I'm sorry." His apology was spoken through labored breaths.

"For what?"

"For that." He let go and took a few steps back, putting distance between us.

My hands hung loosely at my sides as I stared at him, not wanting to comprehend why he was apologizing for kissing me the way he had, but there was no running from it. "Don't apologize," I took a step forward, trying to bring us closer again, "do it again." A lopsided grin tipped the corner of my mouth.

Drew's heavy sigh filled the room. "It's really late, and I don't want to push this too far." He motioned between us.

Why did I even try...?

"It's fine." I waved a hand around and stepped behind the counter. A huff escaped me before I could stop it as I pulled a vitamin water from the refrigerator, twisted the top off, and chugged a nice helping. Drew stood there watching me with one eyebrow raised and a smirk settled on his delicious lips that I so desperately wanted to slap right off. "Something amusing?"

"Definitely." His smirked transformed into a full-blown smile.

"What?" The bottle knocked against the counter so hard water toppled from it.

"You're super sexy when you're upset."

My eyebrows drew together. "I'm not upset." I took another giant swig of vitamin water.

"Oh, yes you are." He started to round the counter when my phone sprang to life from the bedroom.

I lifted my index finger in the air. "Hold that thought." My feet slapped against the cool floor as I hurried down the hall to retrieve it. The caller identity was known before I glanced at the screen. Janet must've tied one on to be constantly calling me at such late hours, which wasn't like her unless she'd traveled down memory lane.

Not bothering to silence the ringer, I carried it back into the kitchen and tossed it on the counter. "Not going to answer that?" I shook my head and continued with the vitamin water. "Late night caller, must be a booty call." That slap worthy smirk danced across his face.

I scoffed, "Not quite."

"Hey," Drew raised his palms, "I'm not knocking anyone for getting some action."

"I tried to get some action, but was hastily denied," I blurted out. My eyes widened as I mentally slapped myself, wishing so desperately I could rewind that moment and keep my mouth shut.

Many emotions rolled through Drew's eyes as he bit his lip. Why was he fighting the obvious attraction? I knew why I'd second guessed myself far too many times. If I was being honest with myself, I'd admit that I was terrified to do much more than kiss. A part of me felt awful for doing that, like I was betraying Liam, and in a way, I was. But you can't move forward if you're stuck in the past.

Or at least that was the line I'd fed myself anyway.

"It was actually my mother-in-law...well, I guess ex-mother-in-law...I mean—"

Drew held his hand up to stop me. "I get it." He leaned across the counter to retrieve my phone. Anxiety hit me like a ton of bricks as I watched him stare at the screen. What was he doing? I swallowed the last of the vitamin water and tossed the bottle into the trash. "There," he slid my phone toward me. "My number is in there now. I'm heading home but would love to see you more often than just random occasions."

My teeth dug into my bottom lip, trying to suppress the grin wanting to make its appearance. "I think we can make that happen."

Drew palmed my shoulders. "Good." A smile curved his lips as he pulled me into an embrace. He kissed me and stepped away. "The ball's in your court now."

"Okay."

With a wink, Drew left.

My heart thundered like a herd of horses galloping through a field as I gripped the counter and hung my head. "Steady breaths..." I guided myself to try and calm down. "In...and out." I repeated the steps a handful of times, happy when my heart rate slowed. Had I honestly attempted to jump Drew? My laughter filled the apartment as I flopped onto the couch. "You've lost your damn mind, Terra." I cackled, tears pricking my eyes from laughing so hard. Those same tears quickly morphed into sad ones.

Laughter transformed into sobs as I clutched a pillow to my chest and buried my face. "Liam, I'm so sorry..." Saying his name out loud intensified the pain, wishing so badly I could go back in time and tell my past self to ensure Liam sees a doctor, even if he felt fine. That it could possibly save his life. But, sadly that was only an option in fiction novels and television shows, not real life.

Turning onto my side the sobs slowed into silent tears. Exhaustion overtook my limbs and I began to drift off, hoping the sleep that was coming would be a restful one.

CHAPTER ELEVEN

The only thing that seemed to be going my way since I'd woken up on the couch with a crick in my neck was the fact that the sun was shining and humidity was low. Magnolia's was out of my favorite smoothie for the warmer days, so I'd settled on some horrid looking green thing that actually didn't taste half bad. The animal shelter was closed, which made no sense whatsoever. Why would a place who wanted to help put animals in their forever homes be closed on a weekday? Didn't seem like a good way to ensure said animals would get homes, but maybe that was my inner child rearing its head from being told "not today."

I sat my bag on the ground and pulled the blanket from within, fanning it out over a nice little section of real estate on the grass just to the left of the infamous LOVE statue, giving myself the perfect view of the fountain and tourists having their self-made photoshoots with the piece of history. Personally, I didn't want a photo with the damn thing. The word itself made me snarl. My love had been shattered, ripped from me without a choice. The thought alone caused tears to well in my eyes, but I pushed them away as I made myself comfortable and pulled my laptop out. I needed to get some work done.

Flipping onto my stomach, I laid my laptop before me, and bent my legs at the knees. Something about lying on my tummy made me concentrate better. As far back as I could remember it was my go-to position when I did homework, read a book, played video games, and so-on. I'm not sure why, but I always assumed maybe I was a belly baby. My email was overflowing with messages, a good portion from none other than Janet, my mother in-law. I knew I needed to read them, and maybe someday I would, but this time I avoided them all together and hit the create button. There was no better time than the present time to jump in head first and let her know how I was doing.

Janet,

Sorry it has taken me so long to reach out. I've been dealing with a lot, as you are too, I'm sure. Everything with me is decent. The move to Philadelphia was a big change, but I'm adjusting pretty well. Made some new friends and started working again. I'm sorry if I've hurt you by avoiding your calls and emails. It's just been...I don't want to say hard because that's unbelievably cliché, and you know how much I loathe clichés. But, everything to do with Liam is like a rip at my heart all over again. I know time will help me heal—help us heal, and I hope you understand where I'm coming from since I know things have been far from easy for you all as well. Life just isn't the same, even though I wish it could be. Just wanted to let you know that I'm as okay as I can be given the situation at hand, but tomorrow is a new day. Hopefully one of the new days we will be able to have a coffee and enjoy the day together again.

All my love, Terra

With the mouse hovering over the send button, I tapped the touch pad before I could change my mind and dropped my head onto my arms, hoping my email didn't cause her more grief, but knowing deep down it most likely would. Having her constantly calling and emailing was doing just that to me, causing more grief. There needed to be a happy medium, one that could stand between us until I was ready for more. Was that selfish of me? Most likely so, but my wellbeing was the number one priority in my life. No one else was going to take care of me. I mouthed a silent prayer of forgiveness and exhaled the giant breath I was holding. Now that I'd reached out to Janet, it was time to accomplish one of the new jobs sitting in my inbox.

Clouds moved in front of the sun, providing the perfect amount of afternoon shade in Love Park. I closed my laptop and rolled onto my back taking a minute for myself and stared up at the sky to see what shapes or figures the afternoon clouds impersonated, a game I loved to play as a child. Something about it was calming. One could've easily passed for a stack of books, while another mimicked the upper half of a dolphin. A closed lip grin spread across my face as my eyelids grew heavy.

Liam rolled us so that I was beneath him, his hips fit perfectly between my thighs as he rocked steady and fast. My mouth was slack as I moaned out the bliss he was giving me. Every thrust, kiss, lick, and suck against my flesh pushed me closer and closer to that euphoric feeling only he evoked within me. No one before him compared. Not even in the slightest way.

"Oh..." I gasped, my hips bucking upward as he rubbed against my sweet spot.

Liam cupped my face, kissing me so deeply I almost fell over the edge. "What did I do to deserve you..." Liam breathlessly spoke against my mouth.

I nipped at his bottom lip and gripped his backside. "I could ask the same."

A deep groan rumbled his chest as he picked up the pace. Nothing but labored breaths filled our bedroom. "I'm. Going. To..." My words were lost as white spots danced behind my eyelids.

"Let it go, baby, let it go." His husky voice was hot at my ear, that

extra little push to shove me over the edge. I cried out with glory, my
body quivering as Liam continued to ride me in search of his own
release.

As the pulsing in my core slowed, my eyes lifted to his. Familiar
desire filled hazel eyes stared back at me, that gorgeous slow grin tipping
one side of his mouth upward. "Terra..." The husky way my name fell
from his lips as Drew moaned his release.

I shot up from the blanket, my heart erratically skipping in its
cage. "What. The. Hell." One hand covered my chest as the other
dug through my bag for a bottle of water. Discarding the top at
record speed, I turned it upward, squeezing the plastic container,
filling the air around me with its loud crinkling, not taking a
single breath until every drop emptied down my throat.

Liam had turned into Drew.

Quick staccato breaths left my lungs, making it hard to grasp a
nice steady flow of air. The aching in my chest from the image
burned straight through me. The internal battle I was facing took
over my entire thought process, even while sleeping. I didn't want
to replace Liam, but that's what I'd be doing if I moved on,
wouldn't I? Some would say no, while some would say yes. But in
reality, when you move on from one person to another, you're
replacing the person before them, whether that relationship
ended due to death or a breakup. It was just about one in
the same.

Out of the corner of my eye I caught sight of my laptop, still
open waiting for me to actually work, but my mind was else-
where. There was no way I could concentrate until I figured some
shit out. I desperately needed to learn how to balance everything
going on in my life. The thought of seeing a therapist crossed my
mind, but even the thought made me uncomfortable. I'd never
been one to pour my heart and soul out to others, especially to a
stranger who in return would tell me how to handle my life, or
what medication they believed I needed to have a grip on reality.

Don't get me wrong, there has been a lot of good come from people seeing therapists, but I couldn't bring myself to schedule an appointment.

I'd always been the type of woman who had control of her emotions. A woman who had a handle on what life threw at her. No longer being that woman was devastating. Learning to become a new person after the old you had been obliviated was a daunting task. The amazing thing about the human brain was that with time, it would learn to ease the heartache and pain that came with traumas. It blocked out the way those instances made you feel, dulling the horrific need to escape the happy thoughts associated with the person, place, or thing involved. The sadness would always linger, but the heart clenching grief would fade. I did my best to tell myself that, even on the days when it seemed as if all of the *"it will get better"* mantras were bullshit.

Today was one of those days.

"Breathe, Terra. Just breathe." My face tilted toward the sky as my breathing slowed. Panic attacks were the worst. They snuck up on you when you least expected them. Never felt the same. Never happened at the same time of day, or the same day of the week. Never brought on by a certain instant. Totally unexpected and draining both mentally and physically.

I'd been dealing with self-diagnosed anxiety going on seven months. I couldn't imagine living with it my entire life. People who've had to battle anxiety their entire life deserved a medal. I'm not sure I would've been strong enough myself to deal with it for so long. As my pulse came down, I did my best at pushing away the remnants of the dream. Focusing on a single task was the only way to accomplish that, so I clicked an email for a new project and dove into reading what the client was looking for.

Twenty minutes and loads of information later, I lifted my eyes from the screen to give myself a break. The park was buzzing with people young and old. One of the nice things about living in a big city was finding little gems of places to take in the beauty of your surroundings, enjoy people watching, and do whatever your heart desired. I'd tried cooping myself up inside to work, but that only seemed to suck the life out of me. My soul craved different surroundings like Magnolia's, Gabby's bar, the numerous parks around Philadelphia. Each place provided a separate atmosphere than the one back at my apartment. Not that my apartment had a crappy atmosphere, it simply didn't fuel the creative portion of my soul.

A smile broke out across my face as I took in a curly haired blonde infant laughing hysterically at something her mother had said. The mother daughter duo was absolutely adorable. Something I'd dreamt for myself on many occasions. I was even further away from having that than ever. The tiny head of curls took off, her chubby legs carrying her toward the fountain as her mother laughed and followed not far behind. The happiness beaming on both of their faces was enough for me to enjoy watching them together. Her mother lifted her onto the ledge of the fountain, allowing her to splash around in the water with her hands. The girl's face lit up. She was having the time of her life making memories with her mom, and she was too young to realize it. That moment would most likely be a memory she remembered the older she got, one that's forever tied to her mother, one I hoped she would still find happiness in after she's gone.

A heavy sigh passed my lips, hating that my mind took a turn for the darker parts of life. But that was me nowadays. The storm cloud that barreled between you and the sun. I'd been consumed by the darkest parts of heartache and devastation. Even though I had more than a decent life to live, it was a feeling I couldn't shake. Like the eye of the storm was about to swallow me whole and all I could do was float in the abyss until it consumed me.

"Do you mind?" My head whipped to the side. A man most likely in his mid-fifties stared down at me. His army green shorts were quite a bit shorter than what your average male wore, with an unbuttoned navy and white striped shirt.

"I'm sorry."

"Do you mind if I set up shop here beside you?" His friendly demeanor lightened my mood.

"By all means." I motioned toward the ground, wondering why he wanted to sit so close to me.

My eyes scanned the area. I hadn't realized how busy the park had gotten. Beautiful weather tends to bring people out of hibernation, and the weather couldn't have been any more beautiful. I watched the man fan out his small blanket, my eyes catching a glimpse of a book tucked beneath his arm, piquing my interest in what author he'd chosen. You could tell a lot about someone by the shows they watched, music they listened to, and books they read. If they even did all three, as most of society didn't anymore. Which was a pretty depressing thought.

I caught a glimpse of the spine. The only information I could see was Stephen King's name. He'd chosen well. The literary God of thrillers and suspense. "Like to read?" The man held the book in the air grinning.

"It's one of those hobbies I put down for too long and am just picking back up."

He nodded. "I've learned as I've gotten older that putting off things until "tomorrow" only hurts yourself. That's how we lose our hobbies, forget important things, and even neglect taking in the beauty around us. Society is so fast-paced that we're forgetting what makes life great."

He hit the nail on the head. "I couldn't agree more."

His laughter floated through the air. "Honestly?" My eyebrows drew together, confused as to what he meant. He motioned toward my laptop and cell phone lying beside where I sat. "Looks like you're doing a fine job of keeping up with technology."

He had a point, and for a moment I felt self-conscious about bringing my laptop to the park. "Work." I shrugged. "I'd much rather be out here indulging in the sun than cooped up at home."

"Okay, you get a few points there." The man laid on his back, flipped the paperback open to the spot he'd bookmarked, and slipped one arm behind his head.

I took in my surroundings, the majority of the people around me weren't engulfed in electronics. They were enjoying the day, a book, and even each other. Placing my laptop back in the bag, my eyes dropped to my cell phone. Loneliness reared its head, an emotion I'd grown too familiar of in the past months. A few touches of the screen and *his* name stared back at me, "Drew Cabot," speaking loud enough for only my own ears. Prior to looking at his contact in my phone, I hadn't known his last name.

Three days had passed since the night of the building evacuation. Three long ass days of me second guessing every move I'd made and didn't make of course. I'd yet to call or text Drew, even when I so desperately wanted to. But sitting on my blanket, watching all the happy people around me, I craved to have that again.

Happiness.

My fingers flew over the screen as I asked Drew if he wanted to grab a late lunch, the time being well past noon. The pitter patter of my heart increased slowly with each second that passed without a response. Delivered switched to read just below my message, letting me know he'd seen it. Nerves were getting the best of me as I chewed on my thumbnail. The conversation bubble popped up as three dots danced in the center.

Where and when?

You tell me what works best for you. I'm not as familiar with Philly.

Where are you coming from, home?

No, Love Park.

Please no sarcastic comment.

Ah, nice day for it.

I suppose.

I'll text you the directions. See you in twenty?

Perfect.

Like a giddy schoolgirl I shot up from the blanket and quickly collected my things. Maybe the day was looking up after all.

* * *

It didn't take me long to realize where his directions were leading me. Liberty Diner. If the rest of their menu was anything like the breakfast I'd tried, it was going to be absolutely delicious.

The bell above the door chimed as I stepped inside. Drew's smiling face was the first I saw from a booth directly in my line of vision. I gave him a small wave as I headed in his direction and slid into the vacated side.

"Hey, you."

"Hi." I couldn't help the smile causing my cheeks to burn.

"I was surprised to hear from you." His linked hands rested on the table.

"Really?"

He nodded.

"What can I get you to drink?" A voluptuous brunette, most likely under the age of twenty-one, popped her gum as she awaited my response.

"Water, please."

"And you?" Her eyes scanned Drew's torso, appreciation swimming in her baby blues, yet he was oblivious to it all.

"Water as well." He gave her a grin before turning his attention back to me.

"What made you think I wouldn't contact you?" My bottom lip tucked between my teeth as I nibbled away.

He shrugged. "I've learned to never expect anything, that way if instances don't turn out, you aren't as letdown in the end."

"You and your wise words."

He waved a dismissive hand. "Just well-read is all."

"I need to read what you've been reading then. Because my life is a clusterfuck."

"A girl with a dirty mouth…" His eyes heated, but the waitress broke up the growing tension by setting our waters on the table.

"Ready to order?" Her eyes planted on Drew's profile.

"You ready?" His question was aimed at me.

"I haven't had a chance to really look over the menu."

"Mind if I?"

"Sure." Of course, I was going to let him order for me again. He was familiar with Liberty Diner, didn't fail me with his breakfast choice the other morning, and enjoyed doing it. Those were three wins in my book.

"She'll have this," he pointed to the menu, "and I'll have this." I watched as his finger slid to the other side. Drew had the menu tilted to where I couldn't even get a glimpse of where his finger sat.

The shithead.

Our waitress laid her hand on his shoulder and took the menu with her other. "I'll put that right in."

His demeanor morphed from friendly to stiff. "Thank you."

Once she was out of earshot I leaned my forearms onto the table. "What's wrong?"

He shook his head and took a pull from the straw. "It's nothing."

"Oh, it's something." He wasn't getting off that easy. Drew was the master of evading questions, and I was growing tired of it. "Now spill."

"Just a pet peeve of mine."

"Which is…"

"Females who overdo it." Surprise painted my face that he'd actually spoken up for once.

Resting my chin in my hand I tilted my head. "Tell me more."

Drew rolled his shoulders and popped his neck, as if he was

getting ready to take someone on. "Women don't have to try that hard to be noticed by men. It's a given, we're men." I chuckled because he was right. "But nothing irks me more than a woman overly flirting. Acting fake as hell in an attempt to grab the attention of someone who obviously isn't interested." *Did that mean he wasn't interested in the waitress?* "In my eyes, there's nothing sexier than a woman who doesn't even realize the magnitude of her beauty. One that goes about her life in her own way, not trying to grab the attention of those around her." He shook his head, those hazel eyes twinkling as they bored into mine. "That's a woman I'd want by my side."

All of a sudden, I had the urge to fan myself, but nothing on the table would've made good use for that. Instead, I gulped down a nice helping of water as my eyes stayed locked with his.

"Your food should be out in a few minutes." The waitress winked at Drew as she passed our table, chomping on her gum like a feeding cow.

"She totally just winked at you," I chuckled.

"Did she?" His eyebrows dipped low as he scrunched his face in distaste.

I couldn't help the laughter that bubbled up my throat. "Yeah, she totally did."

He dropped his head onto his arms and huffed before lifting to full height again. "Today's youth needs some lessons in flirting."

"You just made yourself sound old as hell."

"Maybe I am old as hell."

I cocked an eyebrow. "I highly doubt that."

"Looks can be deceiving." He shyly grinned. There was no way he was much older than myself, if that, and I was pushing thirty-five. "Go ahead, ask my age. I know you're dying to. Men don't get all bent out of shape over a number like most women do."

"Okay, *old man*, how old are you then?"

"Forty-two."

Surprise!

Not what I was expecting at all. "You're not much older than me, so I take offense to the old as hell comment."

His laughter was music to my ears, filling the room, and grabbing the attention of those around us, our waitress included. In reality, he could be her father. But I can't say that I blame her for drooling.

"There's no way you're a day over twenty-five."

"Flattery at its finest."

The waitress slid our plates on the table. "Here you go." She smiled at Drew, not bothering to acknowledge my existence yet again.

"Don't you think?" He beamed as he pulled the young woman into our conversation, while I hastily shook my head behind her back.

"Don't I think what?" Her lust filled gaze drank him in.

"That this beautiful woman I'm with couldn't be a day over twenty-five." Drew motioned toward me.

I wanted so badly to snicker as every ounce of happiness drained from her face. She turned toward me, drifting her eyes across my face and torso, then shrugged. "I suppose." If I wasn't a nice person, I'd probably called her a few choice words, but it wasn't worth it.

"You suppose?" Drew scoffed. "She's gorgeous, and hopefully mine in the near future."

Heat crept across my face from his admittance. He pushed all the right buttons and tossed the right words for a woman to swoon over. The thing about it was, he seemed one hundred percent genuine.

With a tight-lipped smile, the waitress turned her attention to me this time. "Enjoy."

"I'm sure I will," I beamed as she headed into the kitchen before quiet laughter engulfed the both of us.

My eyes dropped to the plate he scooted over to me. "Avocado toast with tomato and turkey shavings?" He nodded. I quickly lifted the sandwich and took a giant bite. "Mmm…"

"Yet again, I knew you'd like it."

"How did you know?" I spoke around a mouth full of food.

He shrugged. "I'm just that good."

I swallowed. "Oh, come on now! Don't give yourself a big head. You got lucky."

"Luck happens once. I've managed to order food that you like —no love—twice. That's not luck, that's being damn good at reading someone." He held two fingers in the air.

"Really? Damn good at reading someone, huh?"

"What can I say?"

I sat back and crossed my arms over my chest. "Okay, Mister Damn-Good-at-Reading-People, what else can you read about me?"

"That you really want to go on a date with me, but you're afraid of the feelings associated with taking that step."

My throat constricted as a chill crept across my skin. Drew was dead on with his observation. I wanted to spend more time with him, categorizing it as a date made it feel a bit more intense. Was I afraid of the feelings associated with him? Absolutely.

I diverted my attention to finishing the sandwich and the cup of fresh fruit that had accompanied it. Drew had drifted into a topic that might have seemed ordinary to others but was heavy for myself. From the way he let the conversation end, I knew he'd realized he was treading shallow water.

Numerous times I tried to come up with a topic to talk about to break the barrier that had been lifted, but I failed every single time. Not that Drew was saying anything either. I reached for the check, our hands bumping one another as he retrieved it before I could. "Hey…" I extended my hand, palm up and wiggled my fingers, "give me that."

"It's on me."

"I didn't ask you to lunch so you'd pay for mine."

"And I didn't agree to lunch so we could go Dutch." He stood, adjusting his burgundy suit jacket.

He really was a man who made a suit look good.

I removed the napkin from my lap and placed it on the table, covering our stacked empty plates. "Thank you." I slipped between his arms and hugged him tightly, inhaling the woodsy, clean scent of his cologne. "You smell really good." His chuckle vibrated my head against his chest, a feeling I was becoming accustomed to. "Did I say that out loud?"

"You did." Amusement laced his words.

Stepping back, I hooked my hands into my back pockets. "I'll be outside." I hooked my thumb toward the door.

Drew held the ticket in the air. "Give me a minute before you decide to run off."

"Ouch," I gripped my chest, "that was a low blow."

A pointed look pierced through me as he grinned. "Not as big of a low blow as the first nickname you gave me. What was it? Mr. Stick-up-his-ass I believe."

"Touché." I fake saluted him and exited Liberty Diner.

The sun beamed from a slice in a large cloud, instantly increasing the cool body temperature I'd had in the diner. I slapped my shoulder, trying to kill a gnarly looking bug that had landed on me, but ended up only hurting myself. A sharp sting pulsed through my shoulder. "Ah!" The sudden singe of pain startled me. Pulling the thick strap of my tank top to the side I gasped, my creamy pale skin was officially the shade of rare meat. "Shit," I groaned.

"What?"

Drew's voice caused me to jump. "Dammit!" I swatted his arm. "Don't do that."

"You scare too easily," he beamed with amusement. "What were you cussing about?" I yanked my tank top to the side and pursed my lips. "Someone forgot her sunscreen today."

"You think?"

His phone sprang to life before he could rattle off another snarky comment. "I've got to go." Drew stepped forward and kissed me deeply. "Now that I have your number, expect to hear from me." He shook his cell phone in the air on his retreat toward his vehicle.

"I'll be waiting," I called out, not trying to hide the giant smile adorning my face.

CHAPTER TWELVE

Music poured out of *Side Street Drafts* as I opened the door, one of my favorite eighties tunes instantly putting me in a good mood. "Let's Go Crazy" by Prince and the Revolution was one of those songs you couldn't help but get pumped up about.

The place was jam-packed, which meant Gabby was working her ass off and totally loving it. I maneuvered my way through the heavy crowd, slipping against the wall to my usual spot, which was surprisingly left open. Why no one liked that spot of the bar was lost on me. It was the perfect area to get a full view of the madness throughout the place. Yeah, it was a bit cramped against the brick wall, but size didn't always matter...at least in some scenarios it didn't.

"Look who actually showed up." Izzy's smiling face appeared before me. She had the entire eighties theme going on. Frizzed out hair, vibrant makeup, off-the-shoulder crop top, with neon green leggings. It put my outfit to shame. Since it was last minute before Gabby talked me into attending, I had settled on simplicity. Black fishnets beneath a tattered pair of skinny jeans, oversized white t-shirt with the neck cut out of it so it hung off one shoulder, and a pair of hot pink high-top Chuck Taylors. Everything that could been found in my closet. Fishnets included.

"Hey, it's weird to see you behind the bar."

"Not my usual cup of tea, but as you can see," she waved her hand toward the still growing crowd, "It's going to be an extremely busy night. Plus, I had the shift off from the hospital."

"That's nice of you."

"Anything for my girl." She handed a man some change. "What ya drinking?"

"Hadn't really thought about it yet."

Izzy laughed. "You have to think about your drink options? Most people have a go-to or rattle off whatever comes to mind."

I shrugged. "I like to be different."

"So, I've heard."

"So, you've heard, what?" I raised a suspicious eyebrow.

"Just that you're an over thinker."

"I definitely can't deny that."

"You going to chit-chat all night or take orders?" a drunken redhead scowled from three people down.

Izzy held her index finger in the air between us. "There're four other bartenders working tonight. If I'm not fast enough for you, move along." Her words were stern but executed so unbelievably nice the redhead's scowl faded and she nodded in return. The perfect example of killing someone with kindness.

"Damn, I need a few pages out of your book." I did my best to conceal the laughter threatening to spew so I wouldn't rile the redhead up.

Izzy confined her laughter to a snort. "Part of being a nurse. If you're an asshole to your patients, it never ends well. With that being said," She leaned her shoulder against the wall, "there are ways to get the point across nicely."

"So, I've noticed."

"Ever decide on your poison of choice?"

"Just give me a beer, anything will do. I'm not picky."

Confusion washed across Izzy's eyes. "The fact that you're not picky is hard to grasp since you're an over thinker."

"Most people would take offense to that."

She popped the top on an IPA I hadn't heard of before and placed it on the bar. "Good thing you're not most people." I raised the beer bottle and grinned as it touched my lips. "I'll catch you later, need to check on Gabby. She sliced her finger and went to clean it up before you came in."

"Ouch." I cringed. "Hope she's okay."

"I'm sure she is. That girl's pain tolerance is unbelievable."

Izzy disappeared in the back, leaving me with the entertainment of the bar goers. Drunk people always made for a good show. There were the happy drunks who loved to have a good time. The sloppy drunks who spilled shit everywhere, including on others. And then there were the angry drunks that started a fight over the simplest things. You look at them the wrong way, it's on. You smile in their direction, it's on. You offer to buy them a drink, it's on. Those type of drunks were the worst kind.

The music was so loud you couldn't hear the bell above the door, but something pulled my eyes to it as a couple stepped inside. My attention was pulled to the woman first, dressed as Sandy from *Grease* in tight leather pants, black off-the-shoulders crop top, and stilettos I'd most likely break my neck in. She looked absolutely gorgeous. The man smiled widely at something she was saying before tossing his head back and erupting with laughter. Instant jealousy rolled through me. The gorgeous woman had walked inside with none other than a Top Gun version of Drew Cabot himself.

I shrunk back against the wall, hoping like hell his eyes didn't sweep in my direction. He was out with another woman after everything he'd said to me. Maybe he was tired of my back and forth whiplash? Or maybe he was the type of man that liked more than one woman at a time? I shook the second thoughts from my head. Drew came across as a lot of things, but a womanizer wasn't one of them. Although, I'd been warned before that some men had a way with women that rarely got them caught in a scandal. *Come on now....* My inner self berated me. *If he was into someone else, do you honestly think he'd take her to the bar he knows you frequent?* The only thing I was sure of, was he'd shown up with a beautiful woman on his arm, and I hadn't heard a peep out of him since we'd gone to lunch two days ago.

Watching them was like watching a train wreck happen and not being able to look away. My eyes were glued in their direction as his hand landed on the small of her back and they slipped through the crowd, headed to the middle of the bar. I knew he could easily see me when he made it to the front of the line to order drinks, but my body wouldn't move for me to run. Just call me Runaway from Life, instead of Runaway Bride.

I chugged my beer and leaned over the bar to toss it into the trashcan I knew was there when Drew's eyes swung in my direction. *Son of a...* My thoughts scattered and I froze with my body mid-across the bar. His eyes dropped to my chest, which was most likely on display from my shirt ballooning toward the bar top. I silently thanked the heavens I'd tossed on a black push-up bra.

"Are you trying out for a contest to see how long you can stay in one position?"

My eyes turned to Gabby's entertained face. "What?"

"You've been in that same position for a good two minutes." I glanced down at myself and realized how ridiculous I must've looked. Without directing my attention back to Drew, I lowered my feet to the floor and motioned for Gabby to step closer. "I need something stronger than beer, Drew's here with another woman."

"I saw that." The smirk on her face pissed me off. There was nothing funny or amusing about him showing up with another woman. Even if we weren't officially dating, only random kissing partners.

Gabby's face never left mine as she tossed together some whiskey concoction. "Here, this should do the trick." Her annoying ass smirk was still wide as could be.

My eyes narrowed as I lifted the glass, stopping just before it reached my mouth. "Okay, what's so funny?"

She nodded. "Incoming."

"What?" I turned just in time to catch Drew moving around the group of guys blocking me. "Hey..." I plastered on a happy smile as he reached me.

"Surprised to see you here."

"I always come here." The ice in my glass clanked against the side as I chugged a large gulp. "Maybe I should ask you why you're here."

Drew's body went rigid as he shook his head, crossing his arms over his chest. "It's the girl, isn't it?"

I scoffed. "Excuse me?"

He towered over me and caged me in with his hands on the bar. From others' perspective it would've seemed as if things were getting intimate between the two of us, but the look on his face was anything but. "You know what I'm implying, Terra."

"No, I think you need to elaborate." I inched my chin upward to let him know he wasn't affecting me.

His eyes closed momentarily, and when they re-opened the fire blazing within them took my breath. "Remember the conversation we had about women trying too hard?" I nodded. "Don't play games right now."

"It sure feels like you're the one playing games, *Drew Cabot*." His name dripped from my mouth in a smart-ass tone I hadn't used since high school, and I instantly regretted it.

"When you get your shit in check, come find me." Drew shoved off the bar and disappeared, leaving me sitting there with my mouth gaped open like a fish out of water.

"Someone's insecurities are showing."

I whipped my head in the direction of the comment, ready to

verbally attack the perpetrator but calmed when I realized it was only Gabby. "I'm not being insecure." *Big fat liar.*

Her arms folded over her chest as her eyebrows rose. "You sure about that?"

"Uh!" I tossed my hands in the air and dropped my upper body against the bar. "How bad was that?"

"At least a nine, maybe even a nine point five, on the Richter scale."

"Shit." I face-palmed.

"So, is the problem that pretty little blonde shadowing him tonight?"

An exuberated sigh deflated me. "I shouldn't care."

"But you do," Izzy added her two cents as she grabbed a couple beers from the cooler and left before anything else was said.

Gabby hooked a thumb in Izzy's direction. "What she said."

They were both right. I did care. I cared, more than I wanted to admit, that Drew had shown up at the only bar I'd ventured into while living in Philadelphia with some gorgeous blonde in tow. I cared as I watched them toss back a round of shots at a table across the room, his eyes staying on her as she cringed from the taste of whatever was in the glass. Jealousy wasn't a feeling I'd been used to, or would grow fondly of, and the last thing I wanted to do was spend the night experiencing it when I should've been having fun.

I tossed some cash into the tip jar and turned away from the bar, trying to gauge which route to the front door was the best. "Where are you going?" Gabby's hand gripped my bicep.

"Let go." I narrowed my eyes.

"Not until you tell me where you think you're going, and only then I'll let go if you don't say you're leaving." Her stern stare pinned me where I stood.

"Come on now! I showed up, had a couple drinks, now I want to go home. I really don't feel like spending my night watching *them* have a kick ass time while I drink myself into a blubbering stupor."

Gabby dropped her head against her neck and scrubbed her hands down her face before focusing back on me. "You really need a swift kick in the ass, huh?"

"I'd prefer not."

"Drew comes here from time-to-time, on theme nights mainly. He has for years." She paused, eyeing them across the room, probably debating on what to say next. "They aren't together in the sense you're thinking. I'm pretty positive they work together and nothing more."

"What makes you think that?"

She nudged her head in the direction of their table, my line of vision followed. The woman was locking lips with a man who'd taken a seat directly beside her. I instantly regretted allowing jealousy to get the best of me.

"What's he drinking?"

"I've got you." Gabby went about fixing whatever Drew had been drinking and slipped from behind the bar to take it to him, which I hadn't meant for her to do.

My teeth grated against my bottom lip as I watched Gabby hand Drew the drink. Surprise filling is features, his eyes drifted to mine. A small wave was all I could muster up, that and a closed lip smile. I felt like a giant pile of shit that had sat in the hot sun all day for the way I'd treated him. Jealousy was an ugly trait that I'd fallen victim to.

Drew lifted from his chair and I from my stool. His head jerked toward the front door and I nodded to let him know that was fine. I made it outside before him and propped myself against the building a few feet down from the door.

Laughter caught my attention down near my building. A couple embraced as they laughed, happiness in full bloom between them. I smiled watching their interaction, knowing how euphoric that felt. I'd had that once in life, and even if I didn't want to admit it, I wanted to feel that again. Life was hard enough, being lonely only made it harder.

"Hey," Drew's soft voice pulled me from the couple.

"I'm sorry." The words were spoken on a heavy breath deflating my chest and I dropped my arms to my sides.

He shook his head and closed the gap between us, his hands threading deep into my hair, pulling my mouth to his. The sharp taste of whiskey was on his tongue as it delved against my own. Drew swallowed my moan as the passion between us ignited stronger than ever before. My knees threatened to buckle as the fluttering in my core erupted. He was going to be my undoing. The tips of my fingers curled into his biceps, holding on in case my traitorous legs did give out. He pulled back and rested his forehead against mine. Our labored breaths filled the small space between us. "We have to stop pushing against this current, Terra. I know you feel it, you know I feel it." His head rocked against mine. "Just let me in, sweet girl. I don't want to replace anyone, but I do want a portion of your heart to call my own. If you can't give me that I'll walk away now. But you have to tell me."

Overcome with emotions, my bottom lip quivered as I choked back the tears. "I'm afraid." My admittance was barely a whisper.

He cupped my face with one hand, the other still intertwined deep in my hair. "I am, too."

Those three words filled my heart with joy. It was good to know I wasn't the only one afraid. Surprising, as well. Drew seemed so confident in every move he took.

My aching heart thumped like a frantic animal. A part of me lingered toward guilt, while the other part felt elated at the thought of possibly loving someone again. How could your heart and soul be torn between two realities? I didn't understand it, but I'd hate myself if I didn't try.

"What are you thinking?" His eyes searched mine.

"How this can work." I placed a hand on his chest, just above his heart, and he covered it with his.

"Do you feel that? That rapid pace. It's only a fraction of what I feel for you and I barely know a thing about you. Don't overthink us, just let it playout how it's intended to."

For the first time since arriving in Philadelphia, I let out a heavy breath that wasn't laced with devastation. "I can try."

"That's all I'm asking."

Drew lifted his forehead away from mine and linked our hands together. "Care to have a few drinks and relive the eighties?"

"Sounds like a perfect night to me."

Somehow, the bar had gotten even more crowded in the short time we'd been outside. My usual spot had been taken over by a handsy couple while "Sunglasses at Night" by Corey Hart pumped through the room. Drew dropped the aviators that were resting on his head down to cover his eyes as he began to move to the beat, lip-syncing every word as he pulled me into the dancing crowd. Laughter bubbled up my throat at the sight of him. Such a carefree, fun filled version of his usual suit-and-tie self.

I hadn't danced in forever, so I knew I looked more than a little rusty bobbing along with him. Izzy appeared out of nowhere extending drinks in our direction. "Thought you two might want these." She gave me a wink and disappeared into the crowd.

"Talk about service." Drew brought his drink to his lips, slipping his aviators back atop his head.

"The best around."

"Definitely."

One song turned into two, three, four, and so on until my feet were killing me. "I've got to sit down." I flopped in a chair off to the side of the dance floor and lifted my sweaty hair off my neck.

"You okay?" Drew shouted above the music as he knelt and draped an arm across the back of the chair.

"Fantastic." The smile on my face stretched so widely my cheeks ached. "You're a really good dancer."

He tucked his chin to hide his smile and looked up at me from beneath his thick dark lashes, "Can I tell you a secret?"

"Ohhh, is it a dirty little secret?" I clapped my hands together quickly in anticipation. "Are you a male dancer, like Magic Mike?"

Drew's head fell back on his neck as he bellowed with full belly laughter, clutching his abdomen and gripping the back of the chair to hold himself upright. "No." He tried to catch his breath and stop his laughter. "I'm not a male dancer, or Magic Mike."

"A girl can dream, right?"

He shook his head in amusement. "I took dance classes throughout my childhood. My father was big in theater and wanted me and my sister to be fluent in many things. Dancing, playing piano, singing—which I'm horrible at."

"For some reason I highly doubt that you're horrible at singing."

"I've had deaf people tell me they've heard better."

I gasped. "Drew!" I playfully slapped his shoulder stifling a giggle.

He scrunched his face. "That was bad, wasn't it?"

"Unbelievably so."

"Note to self, easy on the jokes."

"Probably for the best." My hand smoothed down his arm until my hand covered his resting on my thigh. "You want to get out of here?"

A closed lip smile sat on his face as my question hung in the air. The insecurity of asking if he wanted to leave was building heavily with each passing second that he didn't answer. I swallowed the lump forming in my throat, hoping like hell he'd say something—anything and fast.

"Where would you like to go?" He squeezed my thigh.

I nibbled my bottom lip, thinking that he answered with a question in hopes I wouldn't say my place or his. That being an assumption. "How about the rooftop?"

Drew stood and extended his hand. "Where it all began."

I placed my hand in his and stood. "Not exactly."

"What do you mean not exactly?" He held the door open for me to exit first. The night air blew across my heated skin, much cooler than inside *Side Street Drafts*.

"If I remember correctly, it all started the day you ran into me while I was leaving Magnolia's."

"Ha! I ran into you...I'm pretty sure if you weren't daydreaming up at the sky you would've seen a man trying to enter the place. But, your face was in the clouds."

"Okay, you may be right, but the attitude you threw at me. Gah! It was brutal." I cleared my throat and dropped my voice a few octaves in an attempt to impersonate him. "Who needs that many pens anyway?" I twisted my face to mimic the smug look he wore the day he said those exact words to me.

Drew frowned as we climbed the stairs. "I really am sorry for being an ass."

"Why were you an ass?" I shoved through the door that led out onto the rooftop. When I realized he hadn't replied, I spun around to see why. He stood in the doorway with his eyes directed at the concrete below his feet.

"Drew?"

He shook away whatever thoughts were clouding his head. "I shouldn't have taken my anger out on you that day." He crossed the roof to where I stood. "But I can tell you, the thought of how adorably flustered you were hung with me until I saw you sitting in the window with Gabby days later."

"Seriously?"

"One hundred percent." He took a seat in the lone chair usually designated for myself and patted his knee. "Sit."

Skepticism pulled my eyebrows together. "Not sure that old thing will hold the two of us."

He patted his leg once again. "Sure, it will. Now come here, woman."

Gently lowering myself onto his knee, I cringed as I awaited the chair to buckle beneath us. To my surprise, it didn't. We sat in silence, taking in the view I'd grown to love, while watching some of the drunks frolic about near *Side Street Drafts*. I hadn't spent much quality time on the rooftop since the night I'd saved Drew from getting ran over. The rooftop was a place I needed to add back into my routine.

Drew lazily traced patterns with his fingertips against my bare arm, causing chills to crawl across my skin. It felt nice. A piece of comfort that I'd been missing. "This really is a prime spot to people watch."

I smiled. "Right? There are some dull moments when the bar is closed, or it's early in the day, but the view is enough for it to be peaceful during those times."

"What made you come up here for the first time?"

I inhaled deeply, then let the large breath out slowly as I nibbled my bottom lip. *Now's the time to let him in.* "One of the first nights after I moved in, a panic attack knocked me off my feet. The best thing I could do was find fresh air. Since the rooftop was the closest to me, I hoped like hell it would open. Even though there was a sign posted telling me not to enter, I tried the door, and it was unlocked. I got close to the ledge there," I motioned directly in front of us, "but not too close, wrapped my arms around myself and cried until my sobs turned silent and the tears slowly faded. That view helped put me at ease, so I've been coming up here almost nightly ever since."

"Anxiety is a heavy burden." Drew's hand moved from my arm to my back beneath my shirt as he rubbed soothing circles up and down my spine.

"Isn't that the truth."

"Have you talked to anyone about it?"

"No, I'm pretty much self-diagnosed."

"Have you thought about it at least?" His eyes were soft as he took me in.

"Yeah," the thought of having a therapist invaded my mind, "for some reason I can't get on board with the thought of someone, who doesn't truly know me and what I've gone through, analyzing me. Telling me that medication, or even meditation, would be beneficial for my wellbeing. How would they know what's beneficial since they don't truly know me? You know? I get they've been taught by books and professors on how to handle people with all kinds of issues, but I don't understand how those teachings can help pinpoint each individual's needs. Everyone is different, even if we're similar in numerous ways." A humorless laugh left me. "And maybe I'm overthinking it like I do everything else."

Drew maneuvered my legs so that I was facing him. "Why are you so hard on yourself? I know your husband died, but is that the only reason?" His voice was soft and full of concern.

The question was one I didn't really know how to answer, mainly because I hadn't realized I was being hard on myself. "Honestly," I licked my lips, trying to figure out the correct way to say what I was feeling without sounding completely insane. "I guess I've gotten used to being hard on myself. Liam's death..." Saying his name to Drew was a first, and it hit me like a ton of bricks when I realized it had left my mouth. Like a punch to the gut, it knocked the air out of me. I took a moment to collect myself. "It was unexpected. One second he was there and the next he was gone. I—" My voice broke as I stooped forward, covering my face with my hands.

Drew pulled me against his chest. "It's okay..." He gently rocked me as I gathered my composure.

"I'm sorry..." I sat back, our eyes locking as silent tears rolled down my cheeks.

His thumbs smoothed across my face, catching each tear. "One thing you need to start doing is quit apologizing. If you want to cry, then cry. If you want to scream, then scream. If you want to cuss as loud as possible, then do it. But don't feel obligated to apologize for feeling something. It's your life to live, and others have no idea the shit you've been through. Only you do."

"How did you become so wise?" My hands rested against his neck.

"Life gave me no choice."

The tightness in my chest began to subside as I stared at the man before me. Something about his words was like a balm covering the wounds I'd been battling. His choice of words, fitting whatever situation was at hand. Almost like he'd lived through some pretty hard times himself and managed to come out the other end unscathed. It was inspiring. In the future, I could only hope to have a grip on life much like Drew's.

CHAPTER THIRTEEN

M y eyes fluttered open to find the sun peeking through the gaps in the half-mast shades. Probably normal for most people who slept in, but an odd sight first thing in the morning for me. I stretched my arms over my head, my back popping as I twisted from side-to-side. For once I actually felt rested. Which was another odd thing to cross my mind after just waking up. Catching a glimpse of the time, I quickly rolled out of bed and slipped into the pair of striped pajama pants I'd left bedside it on the floor. *Was it really almost ten?* I hurried into the living room and found the blanket I'd given Drew for the night folded neatly on the couch, with the pillow resting on top. He was nowhere in sight.

A pang of disappointment hit me as I scanned the room a second time, thinking I could've missed him sitting at the table or something, when I knew deep down he'd already gone. I hurried down the hallway to retrieve my phone in case he'd sent a text message. I swiped the screen and deflated at the sight of no new messages. I thought our night had turned out pretty damn good myself, so why had he left without so much of a thank you for letting him stay?

The sound of a door shutting echoed through the quiet apartment. "What the hell?" I jumped from my seated position on the bed and edged toward the doorway, peeking out into the hall as Drew walked into the kitchen carrying a large brown paper bag. "You scared the crap out of me!"

He spun, almost dropping the bag in the process. "Well, you just retaliated." He shook his head and sat the bag on the counter. "I tried sneaking around so I didn't wake you."

"You didn't wake me." I leaned my forearms against the counter and watched him pull items from the bag to make breakfast. "I was getting annoyed, though, at the fact of the couch being empty and zero texts from you."

A slow smile spread widely across his face. "Dually noted. Leave Terra a goodbye message if I sneak out in the mornings."

My cheeks heated. "Who said you would be staying over again?"

He shrugged, discarding the paper bag in the trash. "You'll beg me to be around more once I cook you breakfast."

"Ah, trying to win me over through my belly, huh?"

With a wink, he turned his back to me and started cooking. "It's just a fraction of what I'm good at."

"I'll have to see how good this breakfast really is."

Retrieving my laptop, I opened my email, afraid of what might be staring back at me since I'd missed checking my emails for a couple days. I was ahead on a few of the freelance projects I'd taken on, but new arrivals didn't stop rolling in. Good news for my pocketbook and career, bad news if I wanted to have more of a social life. It wasn't like I had to accept each one that was offered, but I didn't like passing on any, either.

"What are you up to?" Drew cracked eggs into a glass bowl.

"Catching up on work stuff." I watched him look around the kitchen. "If you're in search of a whisk, top drawer by the sink."

He nodded. "Appreciate that." The whisk clanked against the

inside of the bowl as he beat the eggs until the yolks mixed together. "So, what do you do for work?"

"Freelance writing."

"That's interesting."

I glanced over the computer screen. "It can be. But it can also be very boring. Depends on the job."

"Can't you pick and choose?"

"Yeah, but it's not always that simple. Sometimes you get the boring jobs in abundance, while the fun jobs are scarce."

Bacon sizzled on the griddle as Drew poured the beaten eggs into the skillet. Multitasking was something I'd like to say I was mediocre at, but he handled it like a pro. The smell of delicious breakfast had my stomach roaring. Home cooking rarely happened in my apartment since I'd moved in. Ordering takeout or making something quick and easy was my go-to, mainly because cooking for one kind of sucked. "That smells so good." I tilted the laptop screen down and watched Drew cook.

"Good thing you're hungry, I tend to overcook." Drew's heart stopping smile beamed over his shoulder.

I re-opened the screen and dove into replying to job bids. I had a good handful waiting for me to start within the next week. No, I wasn't hurting for money. That was the only good thing I was left with after Liam's death, the fact that I wouldn't hurt for money for a very long time, if ever. But I'd give the money away tenfold to have him with me again. My eyes lifted to Drew as thoughts of Liam enveloped me. Sadness filled my chest for a brief moment before my ringing cell phone pulled my thoughts to it.

"I'll get it." Drew grabbed my phone from the counter and stared at the screen before turning it so I could see.

Janet – MIL in bold white letters flashed at me. "Here." I motioned for him to hand me the phone, confused when he hesitated. Once it sat firmly in my hand, I pushed the side button to silence the ringer.

"Not going to answer?"

I shook my head, diverting my attention back to the computer screen, hoping he'd let it go. No sooner than the missed call icon popped up, she called again. My hand slapped the screen, swiping to ignore the call and sending her directly to voicemail. She hadn't replied to my email, so I knew the conversation would be one I wasn't ready for. I was sure the voicemail she'd be leaving was going to be more than enough to make me feel like a giant turd. The last thing I needed on top of that was battling out why I ignored her calls to Drew.

Drew plated the bacon, scrambled eggs, sautéed spinach, and fresh fruit for the both of us and carried them to the table. "Come eat while it's hot."

I closed my laptop and left it sitting on the counter. My table was very small, shoved up against the wall with three chairs. It had come with four, but the lack of space made it hard to have all four in the room. So, I repurposed the fourth one and put it in my bedroom by my vanity. I took a seat beside him and kept my eyes zeroed in on the plate. It looked phenomenal, and I was beyond hungry.

Minutes ticked by as we ate in silence. The food was too good to ruin it with small talk, at least to me it was. I could see the outline of Drew's face turned toward mine out of the corner of my eye. "Go ahead."

"What do you mean?"

A puff of air passed my lips as I lowered my fork to the plate and sat back. "You're dying to question me, so go ahead."

Drew wiped his mouth with a napkin. "I don't want to push you."

"I'm giving you the green light here, so go ahead before I change my mind."

He glanced out the window, then down at his plate, ate the last piece of bacon, and finished off his glass of milk as I sat there bouncing my leg, awaiting his questioning. I wasn't sure if he had any clue how bad he was messing with my nerves by waiting. Drew cleared his throat. "That was your mother in-law, right?"

"Yes."

"Do you avoid her calls often?"

"Every single one since the funeral."

Drew's eyes widened. I'm sure he was thinking how horrible of a person I was, but he hadn't walked a mile in my shoes. He hadn't lost who he thought was the love of his life without any indication that it was going to happen. So, if he was going to judge me, he could go ahead. It would put him in the same category as everyone else who gave me crap for grieving the only way I knew how.

"Do you miss her?" He cleared his throat again. "Your mother in-law."

"Of course I miss her." The conviction in my voice rose as the onset of tears pricked my eyes.

Drew laid his hand across the table, palm up, and I wrapped my hand around his. "Pushing people away is the easiest thing to do when grieving. It makes you believe that life didn't exist. Not all of the time, but a portion of it at least. It's like severing all ties with those that linked you with the lost loved one makes the loss seem like a nightmare you had and attempted to block from memory." He squeezed my hand. "Just keep in mind that whatever feelings you run from usually catch up with you at one point or another."

Thick emotions clogged my throat, making it hard to catch a good breath. Drew was right, the longer you run from something the more exhausted you become, and in the end, it will catch up to you. But that didn't mean I was ready to stop running.

"What if you're not ready to let it catch you? That diving in head first and accepting those emotions aren't something you're strong enough to face?"

He raked his fingers through his hair. "Everyone's stronger than they know."

"How are you so sure?"

"Because, much like you, I've struggled with my own grief. For the most part, I've overcome it."

One side of my closed mouth tipped upward. "I admire you, you know."

His bashful laugh had me smiling even wider. "I appreciate that, but there's no need to admire me. Everything I've learned has been by trial and error, or something I've read over the years. I never liked therapists either. In fact, I avoided them at all costs. But I did find a happy medium in reading the words of others dealing with similar issues. It's the one plus side to technology, it's a hell of a lot easier to find someone else who has coped with the heartaches of life. There's something therapeutic about reading the words of another person who's been through what you've been through. Seeing how they handled it, and how life changed after the fact. It gives you a spark of hope you might not have had before."

Our breakfast topic was a heavy one. Maybe it was a portion of the reason I was drawn to Drew. He didn't sugarcoat life, or the hardships I faced, he wanted to help me along the way. Help me reach a sense of peace within myself. I adored him for that and could only wish I'd become as mentally strong as he'd become with each day that passed.

"Maybe I'll give it a try." I took our dishes to the sink and ran some water. Once the sink was full enough I placed the dishes and my hands into the soapy mixture.

"I find it interesting that you'd rather hand wash dishes than use your dishwasher."

"There's something therapeutic about it." Admitting that out loud made me feel a bit insecure. "I don't know, maybe I'm weird."

"I like to say all the best people are." Drew pulled a couple drawers open before finding what he was looking for, a hand towel. I finished washing the first plate and he extended his hand to take it, stepping directly beside me so he could rinse and dry before putting it away. We repeated the motions until the sink was empty and I pulled the drain. "What are your plans for the day?" He leaned against the counter and dipped his hand into a soap pile I hadn't rinsed from the sink yet. I eyed him, knowing he had ulterior motives for lifting that soap pile into his hand.

"What are you doing?" I stepped back with the sprayer in tow, ready to fire any given second.

"You wouldn't dare," he beamed.

"Oh, I totally would." I extended it a little higher. Surprisingly, he stuck his hand under the faucet and rinsed the soap suds away. I placed the sprayer back where it belonged and dried my hands. "I don't have any plans today, really. Actually, I never have plans." I laughed at how pathetic my life had gotten since moving to Philly. My usual routine was wake up, grab a quick breakfast, grab coffee, and find my office for the day. Then, if I was feeling froggy, I'd stop by *Side Street Drafts*, but that was only a recent place I liked to venture, since Gabby had become my closest friend. The thought of her made me realize I needed to check in on how things went for the eighties party. We'd left before closing and I was dying to know all the juicy stories she had to tell. Her stories were in abundance on a regular night, I could only imagine what dressing up a bunch of drunks in eighties attire brought out in people.

"I have to catch up on a few things, but maybe we could spend some time together later?" Drew's arms snaked around my midriff and pulled me in close.

I rolled my eyes side-to-side as if I was thinking really hard about his proposition, when in reality my answer was a given. "I should be able to pencil you in my busy schedule."

He bellowed with laughter. "It would be much obliged." His lips pressed softly to mine and pulled away far too quickly. I gripped the back of his head and pulled him back down to me, not ready to let the moment end. He smiled against my lips as I giggled. "Someone's needy this morning."

"You have no idea." My admittance was spoken between kisses before I finally let him go.

Drew collected his things and headed to the door. "Happiness looks good on you, always remember that." He winked, a growing staple of his affection toward me. Trying to hide my smile, I tucked my bottom lip into my mouth as the door clicked shut behind him.

* * *

Gabby shook her head laughing.

"You're kidding?" I tossed my head back and erupted with full blown belly laughter that didn't want to subside until I was clutching my side in pain. "Who would do that?"

"My thoughts exactly!" Izzy shook her head and blew on her piping hot coffee.

"I'm talking about a handful of condoms on the floor. Not one, not two, but like…twenty." Gabby's face was full of disgust as she laughed at the thought. "And I have no clue why I'm laughing." Her hands covered her face on a groan.

"I'm laughing, even though it's completely gross." I leaned back in the lounge chair.

Gabby and Izzy had been working their asses off to make a patio area in the courtyard out back of the bar. A courtyard I didn't even know existed until they'd drug me out into it. Beautiful manicured bushes outlined the brick walls with colorful flowers of all arrays decorating the greenery. Cabanas stretched one section while cast-iron table and chairs filled the center. They'd done a remarkable job.

"You think we're the only people who drink hot ass coffee on a day like today?" Izzy continued blowing on her cup as steam bellowed from within.

"Nah." I sipped my own delicious dark roast. "Who was tasked with cleaning up Condom Gate?"

Izzy clamped a hand over her mouth to keep from spewing coffee everywhere. "That," she cackled, "is the best description *ever.*"

"Sadly, we were the only two left when I found the mess in the basement." Gabby gagged. "I was more than thankful for elbow length cleaning gloves though."

I doubled over with laughter. "Just remember next time you're planning a theme night that the eighties brought orgies to this bar."

"I could've sworn those started a few decades back," Izzy rattled off as Gabby narrowed her eyes at the two of us.

Gabby motioned between me and Izzy. "I'm going to have to separate the two of you."

With my hands raised, I suppressed my laughter. "No more out of me."

"Oh, come on!" Izzy giggled. "She intimidated you that easily?" Shaking her head, Gabby went inside without a word. "Don't worry about her, it's time to prep the kitchen." Izzy waved a dismissive hand. "She laughed the majority of the night about it, after cleaning it up of course."

I crossed my ankles and pulled my sunglasses over my eyes; the sun had made its appearance from behind the clouds and looked as if it was going to stay. "You two are good together."

"Thanks, I like to think we are too." She stretched out on her stomach. "You know, I'd never dated a woman before Gabby."

"Really?"

"Really." She chuckled. "I had an attraction to a few, but deep down I hid who I truly was by being what society classifies as normal." She made air quotations as she spoke. "I really can't stand that word. Normal is like a box that confines you. Why would anyone want to fall into such a category?" Izzy rolled onto her back and stared up at the sky. "Anyway, our first encounter was here at the bar. I was on a horrible date with a guy who looked as if he'd stepped out of GQ magazine. Totally into himself—not saying all of those sharp dressed men are—but he definitely was. He'd gone to bathroom and Gabby brought over the drinks we'd ordered. She'd cracked a joke about how I looked so thrilled to be there, which made me laugh louder than ever before. And there was just *something* about the way she spoke, the way she moved, that made me want to know her. So, when my date was over I scribbled my name and number on a drink napkin and handed it to her at the bar before leaving. The rest just kind of fell into place."

"The best love usually happens when it's unexpected."

Izzy rolled on her side to face me. "Speaking of love..." Her chin dropped as a knowing look pierced right through me. I knew exactly where the conversation was about to go. *Drew.*

"I'm going to stop you right there." I lowered my glasses and peered at her over the top. "I'm not in love with him. I've had one epic love in my life, and that's the man I lost."

"Doesn't mean you *won't* love me though." Drew's voice came from behind my lounger.

Izzy's eyes widened and she quickly lifted from the seat, leaving the two of us alone.

My face scrunched. "How long were you standing there?"

"Long enough to hear you don't love me," he sat on the lounger Izzy had vacated, an amused smirk on his lips, "which would probably make it awkward if I wasn't okay with that." His hands came to rest on my bare thigh. "Like I've told you before, I'm not here to replace anyone."

I barreled into his lap and took his lips with my own. His chest rumbled with laughter as he laid back on the cushion, holding me at the waist. I sat upright, smiling down at him. His eyes drug down my body to my legs, my shorts riding high on my thighs, exposing an abundance of flesh. Drew tucked an arm behind his head, still grinning widely. "What?" I fingered through my hair and pulled it to rest over my shoulder.

"Just admiring your beauty is all."

I leaned forward and took his lips once more. My hair curtained around us like a privacy wall. "Using words like that isn't fair to a broken girl."

Drew's hands smoothed up my legs and rested on my thighs. "Good thing you're not a broken girl."

"Okay, lovebirds." Gabby's voice filled the courtyard. "I've made lunch, so get in here and eat before we open the doors."

I shot upright and saluted her. "Yes ma'am." As I slipped from Drew's lap, he groaned.

"Thanks for the interruption, Gabby." He draped an arm over his eyes.

Gabby shook her head as the two of us snickered, leaving Drew outside with his pity party.

CHAPTER FOURTEEN

Beautiful trees stretched high in the sky that lined the driveway we'd turned into. "Wow." I touched the window. "I've never seen such a gorgeous place."

Drew's laughter filled the car. "Chesterbrook is a nice area."

"To say the least," I breathed. "Maybe one day when I start a family I'll move out here."

His hand squeezed my leg. "Sounds like a good plan to have." My eyes connected with his over my shoulder. Happiness settled on his freshly trimmed face.

"I can't get over your hair being so short."

"It's not short." He chuckled. "It's only an inch or two difference."

"That's a lot in some cases." I giggled at my own joke as he pushed the gear shift into park.

"Never a dull moment." His head rocked side-to-side.

"Hang around me too long and there will be plenty of dull moments." I shut the passenger door. "I promise you that."

Drew leaned his forearms against the doorframe. "You don't even realize how intoxicating you are."

My face heated and my eyes dropped to the open toe blush

heels I'd paired with my favorite navy wrap dress. He rounded the vehicle and extended his hand for me to take and we headed for the front door.

The two-story home stretched a large portion of the front yard. Its colonial style layout was breathtaking. Something I remembered seeing in movies growing up. I absolutely loved it and I hadn't even seen the inside yet.

We ascended the stairs and Drew pressed the doorbell, looking down at me with a sly smile as we waited for someone to come to the door. "Well, hello gorgeous people," Izzy beamed as she opened the door wide enough for us to slip inside, hugging each of us as we passed.

"Thank you for having us." Drew walked deeper into the sitting area.

"This place is stunning." My eyes scanned every inch.

"Gabby wants to sell it, if you're interested."

"What!" My mouth fell open. "Why would anyone sell such a beautiful home?"

"Too much space and ready for a change." Izzy shrugged, her heels tapping against the hardwood as we followed in the direction Drew had gone.

"Don't you want kids?" I felt bad for prying, but the question had come out before I could stop it.

"Of course we do, but we also want a life together. Gabby's had this house for many years, and if she feels it isn't the best fit for us. I'm okay with that."

The idea of purchasing it filled my head. Yes, I wanted a place I owned once again, but the sorrow of the one I used to have weighed heavy with the thought. *Everything changes,* my inner voice reminded me. Boy, wasn't that the truth. Like the seasons that come and go, everything indeed changes.

"There you two are." Gabby stood on the other side of a giant island in the center of the kitchen, chopping fresh vegetables as Drew stood at the sink rinsing even more.

"Terra was admiring the house." Izzy lifted a half-filled wine-glass from the island and took a sip. "Potential buyer." She faked a whisper and winked.

"Maybe in another life. I have no need for such a big place." Gabby pointed the knife at me as she spoke. "You never know what life can bring. I'm just ready for something a bit newer, and closer to work. Something Izzy and I can start our forever in."

"Aw," Izzy's eyes glassed over as she placed a gentle kiss to Gabby's cheek, "you're the sweetest."

"I love you too, Iz." Gabby sat the knife on the counter and kissed her deeply.

My eyes swept to Drew standing at the sink with a closed lip smile and unspoken words swimming in his eyes. Locking eyes with someone was intimate, especially if it lasted for more than a brief moment. To me, it was as if you could see into their emotions, grab onto a piece of who they truly were. Whether that be good or bad, happy or sad, or even content. My heart flopped like a fish out of water as neither of us broke eye contact. Something about him evoked an enormous amount of intensity within me that I didn't know whether to breathe or hold my breath until it passed.

"Okay, lovebirds." Gabby's voice broke the moment.

I narrowed my eyes in her direction, cocking a questioning eyebrow. "Talking about yourself in third person, huh?" Laughter filled the room as Gabby tossed chunks of carrots at my face. "I'd be warned, I've been known to embark on some pretty severe food fights during my childhood."

"Oh, no!" Izzy ushered the two of us toward the French doors. "No food fight in this kitchen. You two work on things outside, while Drew and I finish up in here."

The clicking of the doors closing behind me barely registered as I took in the lavish backyard, pretty sure an audible gasp passed my lips about a dozen times. The grass was so green and thick, I wanted to lay on it, knowing it would cushion me as good as a top of the line mattress might. A brick patio stretched the entire back of the house, with four-foot pillars lining the end that had black posts stretching into the sky, illuminated with white globes. The overhead uncovered so beautiful nights like the one upon us could easily be enjoyed.

"This place…" Words failed me as I stepped to the edge of the patio. Large trees lined the property, making a perfect border.

"I've always loved how peaceful it is back here. The perfect place to close out the world and relax." My eyes followed the path of Gabby's to the right of the property.

I'd been so enthralled I hadn't noticed the stone path that stretched between a break in the trees. "Where does that lead?"

The broadest smile I'd ever seen stretched across Gabby's face. "Come on, I'll show you."

I followed off to her side as we stepped between the canopy of tree branches. Lights were strung just above our head, stretching from tree to tree, illuminating the path toward a building that resembled a greenhouse on steroids. The glass frame frosted over, making it so no one could see inside. Gabby typed a code into the keypad beside the door and proceeded to enter. Chlorine filled the air as I stepped inside. It wasn't a greenhouse, but instead, a very nice pool house.

"Watch your step," Gabby warned as we took the slate grey steps onto the tiled floor below. Swirls of white and grey, much like marble, covered each square. The pool seemed to stretch on forever, longer than I'd noticed the building to be from the outside. It was simple, yet remarkable at the same time.

I slipped from my heels and dipped my foot into the water. Of course, it was the perfect temperature. "You seriously want to sell this place?" My mouth was slack with shock as she nodded.

"It's too much work. Especially with the bar. I'd settle for a smaller place in town where the pool, if we even want one, is handled by a maintenance person."

My laugh echoed against the glass walls. "You sound like you'd rather live in a retirement home."

Gabby thought over my statement and cackled. "It does sound like that, doesn't it?"

"Definitely." I took a seat on the edge and slipped my legs into the water. The water lapped against my calves as I gently swirled my feet in circles.

She sat beside me but kept her feet out of the water. "You know, when you start over in a certain aspect of your life, you want it to be different. As much as I adore this place, I feel I wouldn't be fully moving forward unless I let it go. Izzy thinks I'm crazy, obviously you do too, but it's not personal items that I need to enjoy life. Izzy's love and support are more than enough. To me, I'd be stupid to hold onto a beautiful home that ties every past relationship I've had to myself, when I could let it go and start fresh with the girl who has captured a piece of my heart the rest never had."

What she'd said made perfect sense, and hearing it was like a switch being flipped on inside of me. I'd done something similar when I'd sold our home in Ann Arbor and gotten rid of the majority of our things, but since I'd moved to Philadelphia I'd burdened myself with the thoughts of whether or not the life I'd chosen to embark on was one Liam would approve of. I'd been constantly comparing instances of my new life to the life I had with him, and that wasn't fair to those around me. That wasn't fair to one particular man.

"What are you thinking about?"

I focused on the water lapping against my legs. "How I moved here to live, but yet I've constantly burdened myself with comparing my current life to the life I had with Liam. I've pushed people away, missed out on opportunities, and wallowed in my own heartache because of it. I loved Liam with all of my heart, and always will, but I need to learn to love myself again." My eyes lifted to Gabby's.

"Sounds like you know what you need to do to live again."

"It's a sobering feeling."

"It sure is." She squeezed my hand resting between us. "Before I met Izzy I was in a relationship that was toxic as hell. We constantly fought—it even became physical on both ends. I'm not proud of it—neither was she—and when the time to end things came, it was the most sobering feeling I'd ever had. Like a calm and realization washed over me at the same time."

"What did you do?"

"I walked into the house, found her in the kitchen, and told her we needed to end our relationship. To my surprise, she agreed. She knew just as much as I did that we were both miserable. We'd been that way for half a year but neither one of us took the initial step to end things. There was no anger, no hurt, and no violence between us. She packed a bag, said she'd come back that weekend with a moving truck for her things, and left."

"That had to be hard."

"It was. Leaving someone that you live with isn't easy, but it isn't impossible either. That's one instance of the memories this home holds for me. One reason why I want to move on to something better. Izzy is that something better, I feel it just as strongly as I felt that sobering feeling that day."

"How did I know you two would venture to this place?" Izzy's heels echoed as she walked down the steps.

"Terra found another part of the property she loves." Gabby lifted to her feet.

"Still trying to convince her to purchase, huh?" Izzy grinned and placed a soft kiss against the back of Gabby's hand.

"Only if she wants to."

"You never know." I lifted from the poolside.

"Well, that's enough talk about selling this place. The vegetables are cooking, and Drew is keeping an eye on the grill. We should get back before he thinks we invited them over so he could cook for us women." Izzy winked.

My heels hung from my hand as I followed them to the house. Drew's back was to us with the grill open, the air filled with that charbroiled aroma that you couldn't help but inhale and smile about. One of the best things about nice weather was grilling with loved ones.

"Look at you." I smiled at the sight of his sleeves still cuffed halfway up his forearms, exposing his tan skin.

He cocked an eyebrow. "Didn't think I could cook?" A sly grin tipped his mouth as he closed the grill.

I sat my shoes on the concrete and stepped into them, lifting my hands in surrender. "I didn't say that." An unexpected squeal escaped my lungs as he pulled me into his chest. Hesitation swam in his eyes, but I didn't allow it to stay but a brief moment as my hands circled his neck and my lips found his. The slow steady movements of our kiss had me weak in the knees. Every stroke of his tongue, press of his lips, and trace of his hands caused my knees to wobble. I was afraid that any moment they'd buckle and I'd look like a fawn learning to walk for the first time.

I sighed against his mouth as our kiss came to an end. My teeth dug into the plump flesh of my lower lip as I attempted to hide the smile wanting to make its appearance and lifted my eyes. Drew stared back at me, specs of forest green mixed with hues of browns exposing just how much he felt the electricity between us. Like a smooth bourbon warming my gut, Drew's passion was warming my icy heart.

His hand slid down my arm and linked with mine as Izzy announced she was taking over the grill. Which I'd thought Drew might've argued about, but he hadn't. He led us over to the far end of the patio where a gazebo housed a giant bed swing. It was one you'd see in a home magazine. Pallet wood for the frame, thick rope looping through heavy duty hooks plunged deep into the gazebo's rafters for a firm hold. Coral and cream cushions that matched the cushions for the iron chairs that wrapped around the grand table in the center of the patio. Every single inch of the property looked like a Pinterest expert had put their knowledge to good use.

Drew sat on the bed swing and motioned for me to join him. Maneuvering onto the bed size cushion was a task. I did my best not to give him a peep show, which he found ever-so amusing by the look on his face. "What?"

"You." He pulled me into his side and gazed down at me.

"Am I really that amusing?"

"You haven't the slightest idea." His fingertips threaded into my hair, massaging my scalp as they pushed deeper.

My eyes fluttered close and a moan feel from my lips. "You're going to put me to sleep if you keep doing that."

He chuckled. "I always wondered what it would be like to have long hair, but I couldn't get much past the ears without it driving me batshit crazy."

"I can't picture you with Fabio hair."

"Who's Fabio?"

I hastily sat up. "Oh, come on!" My mouth fell open. Everyone knew Fabio, right? "The guy on all of your mother's romance novels." His head rocked back and forth. "Blond, barbarian with silky smoothe hair halfway down his back?"

"Nothing."

"Seriously?" I laughed.

"Seriously." He ran a hand over his mouth. "Probably because my mom wasn't much of a reader. She wasn't much of a mother either if I'm being honest."

Sadness filled my heart. "I'm sorry."

"Don't be." He took my hand in his. "Life isn't perfect for anyone."

"Isn't that the truth?"

He pulled me back to his side and placed a kiss against my hair. "You smell nice."

"That wasn't creepy at all."

Our laughter filled the air.

"I didn't mean to sound creepy."

I playfully slapped his chest. "I was only kidding." He raised my hand to his lips. "And thank you. I did wash my hair this morning."

My body shook as he chuckled. "Good to know."

"Wine anyone?" Gabby waved a bottle from side-to-side and I raised my hand.

She poured two glasses and brought them to where we sat, the crimson liquid filled just over half of each. Gabby winked as she handed me the last glass and left us to join Izzy as she plated the table in preparation for the food to finish.

But our conversation faded away as Drew swung us, one arm draped around me while he held the wineglass in the other. I closed my eyes and enjoyed the peacefulness of being so close to him without the usual storm going off in my head. The wine was a delicious fruity blend with a hint of burn as it went down. Exactly the flavor I loved when it came to a good red. A gentle breeze rolled around us as I snuggled a little closer to his chest. His woodsy scent, with just a hint of citrus, filled my lungs as I inhaled deeply, a soothing aroma that I could easily fall asleep with cradling me.

Drew lazily rubbed my arm as the swing slowed. My eyes fluttered open to find him watching me, a relaxed appearance to him with a closed lip smile as his eyes roamed my face. His head dipped closer to my ear. "You're beautiful." His barely audible words caused bumps to rise across my flesh as my eyes searched his. Drew's hand gently smoothed across my cheek as he brought his wine-soaked lips to mine. The sweet taste mixed with just a hint of lingering mint. His forehead rested against mine, but his hand stayed lightly pressed against my cheek as the swing came to a stop and the rumble of thunder sounded in the distance.

"It's not supposed to rain, is it?" The thought of it ruining our dinner crossed my mind.

"I didn't think so." Izzy's face lifted toward the night sky, but the darkness made it hard to tell if storm clouds were closing in on us or not.

Gabby waved off the thought. "We'll be fine. That might not have been thunder anyway."

Izzy gave me a look that said Gabby had lost her mind, and I stifled my laugh as we made our way to the table. With all of the food lining the center and the plates placed at four of the eight spots, Drew took a seat directly beside me. A playful grin caused the light from the strung bulbs above us to dance within his eyes, making him seem like a younger version of himself.

He squeezed my thigh beneath the table, sending a hot flash throughout my limbs. "More wine?" Izzy motioned toward the bottle in her hand. The only response I could muster up with his hand high on my thigh was a nod.

"Yes, please." She filled not only Drew's glass, but mine as well.

"You don't have to do that." My stomach rumbled as Izzy plated our food for us.

Gabby held a hand in the air. "She won't take no for an answer."

Izzy shrugged. "I grew up the oldest of six with a single mother. I helped out whenever I could. That included working at a diner. So not only did I plate all of my sibling's food, I did the same thing at the diner. It's a habit that stuck with me I guess."

A nice helping of roasted veggies and salmon on a bed of rice filled the plate, looking as delicious as ever. "Do you help cook at *Side Street?*"

Izzy eyed me from beneath her lashes. "Heck no!"

Gabby almost spewed her wine across the table as she laughed. "She doesn't like to cook for large groups anymore. It's more of a *"when I want"* to type thing."

Izzy nodded. "I don't mind cooking for large parties every so often. Like an event, but cooking for seven people growing up, and spending more than my fair share of time in the food industry burnt me out. I like to make dishes for a small group to enjoy. Like the four of us."

The first bite slid off my fork into my mouth and a moan instantly erupted from the flavors taking over my taste buds. "Izzy..." I took another big bit, my eyes wide as saucers. "This is the best salmon I've ever had."

She waived a dismissive hand at me, and I could've sworn her cheeks reddened under the string lights. "Oh, stop it."

"I'm not kidding." I glanced over at Drew, who chewed with his eyes closed. Motioning my fork in his direction I swung my eyes back to her. "See, even Drew's in his own euphoric food moment."

The three of us laughed as he opened his eyes and shrugged. "She's right, it's the best." He spoke between bites. "Did you mix lime and lemon in the sauce?"

Izzy beamed. "You can tell?"

He nodded while swallowing. "It's a little trick I've used. It's a nice blend."

My fork clanked against the plate. "Is there anything you can't do?"

Drew covered his mouth with a napkin as he laughed. "All kinds of things."

"Right now, I highly doubt that."

Drew squeezed my thigh and kissed my cheek. "In a few years, we'll see how you feel."

Gabby and Izzy were swooning from the other side of the table while my heart raced wildly from his words. *In a few years we'll see how you feel.* Drew had laid it out there that he expected a future. Panic tried to rear its ugly head, but I kept the smile on my face and inhaled deeply through my nose. "We will have to see then, won't we?"

The remainder of our dinner conversation was light. We each told embarrassing moments of our lives and funny things that had happened to us. Izzy and Gabby had taken the food inside to put the leftovers away while Drew and I offered to clean up the dishes. Of course, Izzy argued that guests weren't supposed to do that, but thankfully Gabby had put a stop to the argument, allowing us to lend a helping hand.

I stacked the last dish on the end of the patio table as Drew's hands gripped my hips and pulled me into an embrace. "I hope my comments earlier didn't bother you."

Confusion knitted my eyebrows. "What comments are you talking about?"

His eyes softened. "The ones about a few years from now."

My tongue rolled over my lips and I nibbled my bottom one as I remembered what he'd said. "It's fine." I shook my head and dropped my eyes to the stone floor.

Drew lifted my chin, a sad smile slowly spreading across his closed mouth. "That wasn't very convincing." He let go of my chin. "Sometimes, I forget how careful I need to be with you. I don't mean to push you or cause any heartache by wanting a future for us. You know that, right?"

"I know." I stepped as close as possible to him. "You don't have to be careful with me." My lips found his with a heated kiss. My teeth grated against his bottom lip, pulling a moan from Drew's chest. The rumbling of it caused me to sigh as I pressed my body further into his. An abundance of wine flowed through my veins, making me a bit more confident than my usual self.

One of Drew's hands threaded deep into my hair, holding the back of my head as the world around us faded away. His other smoothed down the curve of my side, around to my lower back, his fingertips curling into the top of my backside. From the feel of *him* against me, I knew he craved more. I'd be lying if I said I didn't as well. I gripped at the back of his shirt. His mouth trailed across my jaw to the sensitive spot behind my ear. How he knew that spot was my weakness, I didn't know. But the longer he nipped and kissed that spot, my eyes rolled back in my head and my mouth hung slack. Drew was turning me on hotter than a blazing inferno, and I didn't give a shit if there was a drop of water in sight.

Lightning flashed through the sky, illuminating our surroundings for a split second, sending me stumbling back as a clap of thunder followed quickly behind it. Drew grabbed my waist to ensure I wouldn't fall as he shoved off the table. "We need to get inside." A second round of lightning crawled across the sky like veins beneath skin.

We hurried to collect the dishes as heavy rain pelted down from above. I cried out as the cold drops soaked us before we could reach the doors. Once inside I quickly shut the doors and rested my back against them. Gabby took the dishes from my hands as Drew carried his to the sink. All I could do was laugh as I took in my drenched self. The navy wrap dress looked more black than blue and clung to every curve of my body. A chill rolled through me from the change in temperature. "Here." Izzy handed me a towel.

"I didn't think it was going to rain." Gabby took the other towel from Izzy and handed it to Drew.

Drew's eyes turned to me, water dripping down his face. "That was *fun*." His heated gaze drug the length of my body, his statement meaning more than Izzy and Gabby realized.

"Head upstairs to the bathroom just down the hall on the right. There are a couple robes hanging on the door, get changed and I'll dry your clothes."

"Thank you." I patted myself as dry as possible to avoid dripping water all over their beautiful wood floors.

"We appreciate it." Drew stepped into the mudroom connected to the kitchen and kicked off his dress shoes before removing his socks and dropping them into the washing machine I hadn't noticed.

I stepped out of my heels and padded through the living room, feeling Drew's presence behind me as I ascended the stairs. Flipping the light on in the bathroom, I paused to take in its beauty.

Dark rectangle tiles with light grey grout covered the floor, but my eyes were drawn to the bathtub of my dreams. "Are you going to step inside?" Drew's whispered words broke my swooning.

"Oh, hush." I shoved his shoulder and entered the bathroom.

"I'll let you change first." He went to close the door but I grabbed the frame.

"It's fine." My heart slammed in my chest. "There's no need for you to stay in those while I change."

Drew stepped inside and closed the door. The bathroom was far from small, but something about his tall frame standing with his back against the door made it seem as if the walls were pushing me closer to him. I swallowed the lump in my throat and pulled the tie of my wrap dress. Unlike in the movies, the damn thing wouldn't come untied. The rain had knotted it into a sopping mess.

"Here," Drew stepped forward and attempted to undo the knot, "let me help you." His skilled fingers loosened the material. His eyes lifted to mine as he pulled the tie from its secure hold.

His eyes didn't waver from mine as he dropped the tie causing the front of my dress to gap open just enough to show a small portion of flesh. My breathing hitched as his warm hands slid against the curve of my sides. There was questioning in his eyes as he paused. I curled my fingers around the collar of my dress and slipped it from my shoulders, the slap of it hitting the floor echoed. The bob of his Adam's apple caught my attention as his eyes roamed down my chest, to my stomach, and legs before lifting back to mine.

"Terra..." Drew closed his eyes as my name fell from his lips on a strangled whisper. His eyebrows pulled low in the center and the realization of my attempt at seducing him washed over me like a bucket of ice water.

I reached behind him and snatched one of the robes, slipping it onto my body and turning away from him. Even though his eyes were closed, I didn't want to risk showing him every inch of me as

I discarded my panties and bra before securing the robe tightly against my body. "I'm decent." Drew slowly opened his eyes, the pained expression adorning his face faded away, but before he could say anything else I gently moved him to the side and exited the bathroom. Not only leaving him behind, but my pride as well.

When I reached the stairs, I stepped off the first one and leaned against the wall, careful not to send anything crashing to the floor. Willing back tears, I exhaled a shaky breath and quickly gained my composure. Technically he hadn't turned me down, but the sight of him struggling on what the right thing to do was made my heart ache. Was I pushing us too hard? The alcohol clouded my mind. I knew better than to make any life changing decisions while under the influence, but apparently, I'd forgotten in the haste of being caught up in Drew.

"Hey." His voice caused me to jump, sending a picture tumbling toward the floor. Drew quickly grabbed it and hung it back where it had been. "Why are you standing here?" With his wet clothes in one hand, he smoothed the other through his damp hair.

"I was—umm…" My gaze dropped to the stair where I stood.

"Any other time I would've jumped on the chance to strip you down," Drew lifted my chin, his face a few inches from mine, "but you've had quite a bit more to drink than me, and I didn't want to step over that line without knowing one hundred percent that you're ready."

I sighed. "Sorry for that back there. I don't know what got into me."

"There you go apologizing again." He slyly grinned.

"About that." I couldn't help but to smile. "I'm totally failing, huh?"

He chuckled. "You're not failing so long as you're trying. Now let's get these clothes dried, shall we?"

CHAPTER FIFTEEN

"Sweetheart." Someone was shaking me awake. My eyes fluttered open and Drew's face came into view. "Hey, sleepyhead."

I rubbed the sleep from my eyes, hoping like hell I didn't look like a zombie from smearing my makeup. "I didn't mean to fall asleep." He helped me from the car.

Confusion hit me like a ton of bricks as I took in my surroundings, trying to shake the sleepy haze from my head. As we stepped into the building I realized exactly where we were, Drew's penthouse.

The elevator dinged opened and we stepped inside. I swayed and latched onto the bar attached to the wall. "Damn, I can't wake up." A cold chill hit me. After the rainstorm I hadn't fully gotten warm again. Not even two bottles of wine later could I shake the chill in my bones.

Drew's arms circled my waist and I leaned against him. Warmth radiated from his body, making me snuggle deeper into his side. We exited onto his floor and curved around the hallway before his door came into view. The walk had woken me up a bit, but not fully. Something about drinking wine exhausted me, but I was a glutton for punishment and continued to drink it, anyway.

The foyer came to life as he flipped the switch just inside the door. It was the second time I'd been to his place, and the entryway was just as breathtaking as the first time. My hand skimmed across the decorative table as I entered the living area. My heart stuttered as my eyes landed on the view outside of the two-story windows that wrapped around the living room. The lights from the city twinkled, giving just enough illumination. "If this was mine I'd always be in this room."

"You haven't seen anything yet."

I turned with a curious tilt of my head. Drew had retrieved a couple bottles of water from the refrigerator and extended one to me. "Thank you." I took a large pull from the plastic bottle. "I probably should've asked you if you were fine to drive before we left Gabby's."

"I stopped drinking after the second glass." He tapped two fingers against his temple. "I would never intentionally put you in danger."

"That puts my mind at ease." A shiver rolled down my spine. The water I was drinking had intensified just how cold I still was. "I don't know why, but I can't get warm."

"I'm a little cold myself."

I wrapped a hand around his forearm. "Not as cold as me. Your arm feels good." I closed my eyes as he yelped from my frozen touch.

"Why don't I run you a hot bath? That should help warm you up."

I rolled my bottom lip back and forth between my teeth as I thought about taking a bath. The offer was appealing, but was it smart? I knew Drew would be a gentleman and give me privacy, but did I want to make myself that cozy at his place? A second chill caused the bumps to rise even farther on my arms. "That would be amazing." I finished off the water and he took the empty bottle from me to discard.

"I'll get the bath water going." He pointed toward the couch facing the windows. "You have a seat and relax while you wait."

I nodded and watched him leave the room. The sound of the faucet turning on made me smile as I made myself comfortable on the couch. I could see why he didn't have a television in the room, the view alone was more than enough to keep me occupied. Peaceful, and full of beauty. If I had a good book, I could curl up with a cozy blanket for hours and never move.

"I hope you like your water pretty warm." I turned my body so I could see over the back of the couch. Drew stood in the doorway unbuttoning his shirt. My eyes watched as each button slipped through its eyelet. He truly was a handsome man. Inside and out. But why was he single? I couldn't shake that one simple question, which obviously wasn't so simple.

"If it turns my skin red, it's perfect." His eyes lifted to mine and a lopsided grin tipped one corner of his mouth.

"It's ready when you are." He winked, his shirt hung open exposing a snug grey tank top tucked into the waist of his slacks. A pang of disappointment hit me from him not being bare beneath it, but I quickly shook the thought away and lifted from the couch.

I took his hand in mine and placed my other over his heart. "Thank you for everything."

His lips grazed mine. "You don't have to thank me."

I lifted on my tiptoes and deepened the kiss. He tasted like a new journey my soul wanted to embark on, but my mind was still lingering at the crossroads trying like hell to catch up. Forcing the dilemma from my head, I pulled his tank from the waist of his slacks and slipped a hand beneath it. My hand explored his warm defined abs as he hissed from the temperature of my palm.

"My God." He spoke through gritted teeth as he pulled my hand away. "Get your ass in that tub before I dump you in it. Those things are close to frost bit." Giggles bubbled up my throat as I stepped around him in search of the bathroom. "To your right," he called out.

My mouth fell open at the sight before me. Without glancing back at him I stepped into the bathroom, shut the door, and sunk back against it in awe. Candles lined the sides and back of the biggest Jacuzzi tub I'd ever laid eyes on. So big that someone Drew's height, well over six feet, could easily relax in it. I couldn't discard my clothes fast enough at the thought of all the space to stretch out in. I stepped into the water and moaned from the perfect temperature enveloping my body as I lowered myself down. The scent of lavender filled my lungs as I realized the water had a faint purple hue to it. He'd gone the extra mile to make my bath as relaxing as possible. My heart squeezed in my chest in awe of him. All of that wasn't the best part either, the tub sat back in an arched-out part of the room, with windows stretching the entire back side, giving that gorgeous view of the city in the living room a run for its money. I never wanted to leave the comfort of the tub.

My head rested against a curved spot of the tub that perfectly cradled it. There wasn't a single aspect of comfort missed in its design. I needed one of them for myself. There was nothing more soothing than a hot bath with peace and quiet. It pushed the stress out of your body, relaxed your muscles and bones. I loved lying in them until the water turned cool, and I planned to do just that in the lavish bath Drew had drawn. With my eyes closed my mind began to drift to a memory I hadn't thought of since my teenage years.

The first day of summer break after fifth grade.

I'd hurried down the steps not long after the sun had risen to grab a bite to eat and get over to Shelley's house before her parents could give her a list of things to do. We'd planned to spend the day down at the creek. Fishing, basking in the sun, and floating on inner tubes. It had become our yearly first day of summer ritual, and what I looked forward to the most.

The carton of milk I'd pulled from the fridge barely had any in it, and as I lifted it to my nose I gagged on the smell of death wafting from inside. No cereal for me. I rummaged through the cabinets in search of anything quick I could munch on during the short bike ride to Shelley's but came up empty handed yet again. Mom hadn't been to the grocery in close to a month, leaving me to fend for myself while my father spent his dinners out on the town with whatever fling he was hooking up with that day. Definitely someone I wanted to look up to...Not.

Careful not to wake mom, who was out of it on the couch, I quietly made my way back up the stairs to change. I'd learned at a young age to do my own laundry, otherwise it would sit in the hamper until hell froze over. I wasn't sure what had happened to my mom along the way. Faint memories of her being a loving mother crept in every so often, but I was to the point of wondering whether my subconscious had made them up or if they were actually real. My father on the other hand, he'd always been in and out of the picture. They never got divorced, but he'd done his fair share of cheating. Every time my mom got tired of it, he was out the door, then a month or so later he'd be back. It was the same song and dance. One they never got tired of, but I sure did.

Once I was changed I hurried back down the stairs and through the kitchen to the door that led out back where my bike was waiting. But before I could hook a leg over it my body went flying to the gravel below. "Where the hell do you think you're running off to?" The palms of my hands burned, along with the side of my face. Both had hit the gravel pretty hard. A shadow blocked the sun from my eyes as I stared up at a very angry version of my mother. Bloodshot eyes, sores on her face, and ratted hair. She looked like death, and someone Jonesing for a fix. I had to get out of there before she put another bruise on my body.

"I was running to the store to get some milk." I rummaged in my pocket and pulled out the couple bucks I had, that I was actually going to use on something to eat for myself.

She snatched the cash from my grasp. "You selfish little shit! Where *did you get this?" She shook the money at me and I flinched.*

"I helped Ms. Margaret carry groceries in last week." My bottom lip quivered, afraid she was going to hurt me, or keep the only money I had. Sadly, I would take a beating where I could leave after than to lose that little bit of cash. The thought made my stomach churn in hunger.

She tossed the cash at my face. "Well, hurry back, and grab some chicken noodle soup while you're at it. I feel like I'm coming down with something." The screen door slammed behind her. Tears welled in my eyes as I quickly got to my feet and took off down the driveway on my bike. She'd be mad when I did make it back home, but I was going to ensure that wasn't until the wee hours of the morning when she'd be good and passed out.

I sloshed water over the edge of the tub as I frantically sat up. Pounding came from the other side of the bathroom door. "Terra, are you okay in there?"

My heart hammered. "Yeah." The word came out muffled from the thick emotions clogging my throat.

"Are you sure?" He didn't sound convinced.

I lifted from the water and toweled off before wrapping it firmly around my body and unlocking the door. A shirtless Drew leaned against the frame with his eyes directed to the floor. "I must've fallen asleep." I shook my head. "Woke up flapping like someone drowning from a nightmare."

He took a step forward and smoothed the back of his hand down my cheek. "I thought I heard you cry out."

My fingers wrapped around his wrist. "I might have, I'm really not sure."

"Liam?" Drew's eyes softened as my deceased husband's name left him.

"No," a heavy sigh deflated my chest, "my mother." Drew had previously mentioned the hardships of having a crappy mom, but the way he was looking at me was full of pain and understanding. My heart ached at the sight. Having crappy mothers was another common ground we shared.

He pulled me against his chest and kissed the top of my head. "Sorry you had to deal with that."

"I should say the same to you." My fingers roamed his toned back as I laid my cheek against his chest. The warmth from the bath began to fade but was being replaced by the warmth of his body.

I unexpectedly yawned, exhaustion washing over me from everything the night had brought. "I have a spare bedroom if you'd rather stay, it's pretty late." Drew's offer caught me by surprise.

"What time is it?" I hadn't even noticed since we'd arrived at his place. Hell, I couldn't remember the last time I checked a clock since we'd arrived at Gabby's.

"Last I checked, it was creeping toward three."

I rolled my head around my neck. "No wonder I'm running on fumes." I towel dried my hair with a second towel, realizing I was only wearing the one I'd wrapped around my body to let Drew into the bathroom. "Umm..." I glanced down at myself. "I didn't bring any other clothes."

His eyes lowered to my bare legs. "I'm sure I have something you could sleep in." We left the bathroom and took a quick turn into a bedroom.

Everything was sleek, yet simple. The same monotone color pallet throughout. Very fitting for Drew. "Is this where the magic happens?" I smoothed a hand across the olive-green comforter.

The lack of response to my witty question had my eyes lifting to his. Drew grasped a shirt in one hand as the other ran over his mouth. The heat in his eyes could be felt where I stood as they roamed down my towel clad body. A tremor rolled through me as he shoved the drawer closed and stalked around the bed. I sucked my bottom lip between my teeth as he towered over me. The rise and fall of his chest beckoned me to run my hands over every inch of flesh, but I stood frozen as his eyes bored into mine.

Unspoken words hung between us as the temperature in the

room spiked. My heart fluttered within its cage, pouring anticipation throughout my veins. Our eyes searched one another's for any indication that we weren't feeling the same fire scorching the room. But, boy, were we feeling those flames. The tension was so thick it stole the air straight from my lungs as the shirt dropped from his hand and he reached for the piece of towel tucked at the center of my chest to hold it in place. I gasped as his knuckles grazed my skin and he pulled the piece from its secure hold. Holding my breath, I let it fall from my body, but Drew's eyes never wavered from mine until I slowly nodded, giving him permission to take in every inch of my bare flesh.

His hand snaked around my lower back, leaving goose bumps in its wake as he claimed my mouth with his own. Pure need shot through my body as he devoured me, my knees buckling but his arms keeping me upright. My mind overloaded by the warmth of his hands tracing my bare back, his lips trailing down the column of my throat to my collarbone, and then to the valley between my breasts.

He backed us toward the bed until my legs knocked against the mattress. My body lowered to the comforter as his tongue circled my nipple, his mouth closing over the pert bud as he palmed the other. My body came alive beneath his touch, like a spark before a flame. Something I hadn't felt in quite some time. His hand gripped my hip as he descended down my sternum, to my navel, stopping as he reached the invisible line where my panties usually laid.

I sucked in a sharp breath as his tongue ran across the invisible line and his hands smoothed up the curve of my hips, gripping the flesh of my sides. His hot breath trailed lower, causing my thighs to jerk inward. He was driving me absolutely mad, and I loved every second of it.

"Drew…" His name was a panted breath falling from my lips as his mouth latched on to that one spot that made patterns dance behind my eyelids. My fingers threaded into his hair as his tongue lapped against me, causing my grip to tighten. He was pushing me higher and higher toward that release my body craved, and then like the drop of a hat...he was gone.

My head snapped up from the mattress, ready to question why he'd stopped, but all words failed me as he stepped out of his jogging pants. His body was one that put Greek gods to shame. All fine lines and chiseled abs. One you wouldn't believe was real unless you'd seen it with your own two eyes.

Drew crawled up my body creating a path of peppered kisses against my flushed skin. His eyes reached mine and he paused. "You take my breath away." The flakes of green shined brighter than ever.

No snarky comment, or declaration of admiration, could explain how Drew made me feel. The only response I could form was to crash my lips against his. To show him how deeply I felt his presence in my bones. How much he made me want to live again when I thought a life full of hope and love wasn't going to happen a second time around. It hadn't been long since we'd met, but this man had come into my life like a hurricane, stirring up the false calm I'd created for myself, forcing me to feel every ounce of pain and sorrow my soul was baring. I wasn't through healing, but I was steadily on my way to being able to breathe again.

"Are you sure about this?" Drew's husky words made me smile as I nodded the confirmation I was ready.

He reached into the nightstand and pulled out a condom, something that hadn't crossed my mind in the heated moment. I watched as he rolled it on and positioned himself back between my thighs. With his head resting against mine, I gripped his back as he slowly pushed inside of me. Tremors quaked throughout my body from the intensity of us coming together as one.

Our labored breaths filled the room as we poured our feelings into every stroke of flesh on flesh, into every press of lips, and every exploration of hands, creating a beautiful moment between us that wouldn't soon be forgotten. The moment would forever mark a piece of my heart, tying me to him for all eternity. My soul had officially been divided into three pieces; one for myself, one for Liam, and the last for Drew.

* * *

"Tell me that is cookie dough, and I'll never leave." I sat up with the blanket wrapped around my chest.

Drew cocked an eyebrow as he crossed the room and sat on the edge of the bed. "Maybe it is, maybe it's not." He quickly shoved a spoonful into his mouth.

I narrowed my eyes, trying my best to investigate the container he so sneakily covered with a paper towel. "Give me a bite then." My mouth hung wide open as I awaited a spoonful.

Laughter bubbled up my throat as he flew the spoon through the air, mimicking airplane noises that one would make for an infant who couldn't yet feed their self. "Incomiiiiiing…" The airplane spoon landed in my mouth, dumping the plain-Jane vanilla onto my tongue.

"Aw…man…" I groaned around the mouthful of ice cream. "What is this?"

"Looks like you won't be staying forever." An over exaggerated frown settled on his face. "And that is vanilla."

Taking the spoon from his grasp I pouted as I scooped another nice helping into my mouth. "I know what it is…uh…brain freeze." My eyes squeezed shut as I opened and closed my mouth, trying to swallow the freezing lump as quickly as possible.

Drew chuckled, taking the spoon away from me. "That's what happens when you're being a glutton."

I massaged my temples, hoping it would help push along the dreadful brain freeze pulsing through my head. "No. You. Didn't…" My eyes narrowed in his direction.

"Yes. I. Did," Drew mocked in his best Valley Girl tone.

His playful side made my heart flutter. A content smile played on my lips as I watched him lift another helping to his mouth when it hit me. I was falling for someone who wasn't my husband. The thought didn't terrify me like I'd anticipated. Did my heart ache? Hell yes. It ached because I knew things were changing inside me. Things I'd been so desperately trying to keep the same, as if Liam was still alive. I knew in my core he wouldn't have wanted me to be lonely for the rest of my life. He would've wanted me to fly on my own, learn how to find love again, and be happy. Liam strived to find happiness while he was alive. He quit a shitty job in search of a dream career, and he made that dream career happen. Without his ambition and heart of gold, I wouldn't have ditched my own nine to five in search of my dreams. No, I hadn't found them yet, but not everyone's journey was the same.

"What has you smiling like that?" Drew's hand drifted across my shoulder.

"Just thinking about life, and how tragically beautiful it is."

Drew's eyebrows lifted. "I couldn't have said that better myself." He traced lazy patterns down my collarbone and back up to my shoulder over and over again. "Life is truly a tragedy if you think about it. Everyone dies in the end, ninety percent of people never find their happy ever after, but still...there's something absolutely beautiful about living."

"Making it tragically beautiful," I added.

He cupped my face. "Exactly." The sweet taste of vanilla lingered on his lips as they pressed against mine. "We should probably get some sleep before the sun makes an appearance."

Drew discarded his jogging pants and slipped beneath the comforter, pulling me into his chest. A smile settled on my lips as I hooked a leg over one of his. "Night."

"Goodnight."

Falling asleep in his arms was unexpected, but exactly where I wanted to be.

CHAPTER SIXTEEN

"You know I love you, right?" Liam's lazy smile sent my heart into a fluttering mess.

"Until the sun no longer shines." I pressed my lips to his chest above where his heart laid.

"And the moon can no longer rise." He quickly flipped us, causing me to squeal as the mattress cradled my body.

I spoke between soft kisses. "There will always be a you and I."

"Even after one of us dies." His last word was barely a whisper.

I shot up from the mattress gasping for air, reaching for the warm body beside me. But that body didn't belong to Liam...

My head rocked side-to-side. "This can't be happening..."

My lungs burned like the air I'd taken in was spreading poison throughout their lobes. Uncontrollable tears shot down my face as gut wrenching sobs ripped from my body, Liam's words echoing in my ears. *You know I love you, right?*

I loved him too, yet I was lying beside another man.

You care about this man too.

My internal thoughts being the voice of reason.

"Hey..." Drew sat up, sadness swimming in his eyes. "Come here." His arms outstretched welcoming me.

I shook my head, unable to control the sobs, my throat raw from my cries. With a hand covering my mouth I stared back at him. "I. Can't." My voice broke as I folded forward, burrowing my face into the blanket.

"You can." Drew's voice was at my ear as he pulled me upright and into his arms, holding me tightly against his bare chest. My arms snaked around his neck as I gripped onto his back like my life depended on it. His warmth, his embrace, my soul needed them both. "You can talk to me." Every inch of my body shook even harder than before.

"I. Can't." The words were heartbreaking to my own ears.

"Baby, you can." His voice was a little louder as he smoothed hair from my face, taking in the mess I'd become. "Maybe not today, maybe not tomorrow, but you can talk about these feelings that are crippling you. You're strong. You need to remember that."

The tears slowed and my sobs morphed into hiccups, but the hollow ache in my chest was so intense I felt it would cave my sternum in. A part of me wanted it to so I'd no longer have to feel.

"I—I had..." I paused and removed myself from his embrace. The tightening in my throat rendered me speechless. The thought of explaining what I'd dreamt, and how it made me feel, was heightening my anxiety.

"Shh..." Drew took my hand, gently tugging at it so I'd return back to his arms. "Lay with me." The tone of his voice was soothing. I closed my eyes and snuggled against him as the soft hum of an unfamiliar song vibrated between us. Whatever song he was humming helped ease the hollowness burrowed deep in my chest.

The amount of time that passed as we laid there in one another's arms didn't matter. All that mattered was that Drew was slowly healing my aching heart. He'd been able to pull me from the sorrow I'd woken to, and as one hummed tune turned into another, and another, I knew choosing him was the only decision I could make. Pushing him away would send myself deeper into despair when I'd been trying to crawl my way out of it. I'd always heard when one door closes another one opens, but never in my life did I think that would apply to finding a tomorrow with someone after you've lost the love of your life.

* * *

Drew had somehow gotten me calm enough to fall back asleep after the chaos I'd awoken to. But no matter how many hours had passed since, sorrow still lingered within me. A feeling that was hard to shake.

I towel dried my hair and slipped back into my dress. My eyes caught my reflection in the long bathroom mirror. Despite how I felt, I looked happier than I'd been in quite some time. A faint blush filled my cheeks, most likely from what had transpired with Drew. The night replayed in my mind, causing my heart to flutter and my thighs to squeeze together. Remembering the way his hand felt against my skin had me craving more. I dabbed my face with cool water from the faucet and let out a slow breath as I stared at myself once more. "Get yourself together." A chuckle fell from my lips as I shook my head. *Had I really just talked to myself in the mirror?*

Before I exited the bathroom, I made sure everything was as clean as it had been when I'd entered. Nothing irked me more than someone leaving a mess in your home when it was clean before they came. Silence filled the air as I left the bathroom in search of Drew. He was still in bed when I'd gone to take a bath but promised he would get up in a few. As I reached his bedroom door, I noticed it was slightly closed. Knowing I'd left it completely open, curiosity washed over me. Drew's voice came from inside the bedroom and I stopped dead in my tracks. I knew it was wrong to eavesdrop on someone, but I couldn't make myself take the extra few steps to alert him I was there.

"I'm not sure that's what she would have wanted." I'd never heard him sound so annoyed. Not even the day we'd first met outside of Magnolia's. His heavy sigh let me know that whatever the person on the other end of the line was saying didn't sit well with him. "Yeah, I can be there some time tomorrow probably. Just give me a little more time and I'll make it happen. I'll email you the information later today. Bear with me, I've been working on this for years now, failing's not an option."

I pushed through the door with a smile on my face, hoping he didn't know I was listening in on his conversation, surprised to find him sitting shirtless on the edge of the bed cradling his head. "You okay?"

His eyes lifted to mine and as if all the worry that had been weighing him down didn't exist, his face morphed into pure happiness. "Feel better?"

The fact that he didn't answer my question didn't go unnoticed, I decided to leave it be. I understood all too well not wanting to talk about things, the difference between him and I was that I didn't push someone to let out whatever was bothering them. "If I could kidnap that bathtub, I totally would."

His laughter crinkled the corners of his tired eyes. "It's yours whenever you want to use it."

"Don't make offers like that, I may just take you up on it." I winked. "So, are you planning on taking me home in a pair of boxers and no shirt?" Drew glanced down at himself and lifted from the bed. "Not that I'm complaining about the view, but society tends to frown upon the showing of excess skin in certain situations."

"A business call threw me off." He tossed his phone on the bed. "I'll take a quick shower and get changed, then we can grab a bite to eat on the way to your place. Sound good?"

"That works for me." I kissed his lips. "I'm ahead of schedule with my jobs, so no rush here."

"Thank you for understanding." He kissed me and headed into his bathroom.

The sound of the shower turning on filled the room as I

glanced around at his belongings. There wasn't much décor wise, only a couple picture frames sat on the dresser. One filled with a photograph of a young boy with an older man holding baseball gloves, most likely Drew and his father. The other was Drew with a beautiful brunette standing on a cliff in hiking gear. If the frame itself didn't say world's best brother, it would've still been easy to tell she was his sister from the identical hazel eyes and same smile as his.

Even with the two personal photos, the lack of décor made me sad. It didn't seem like he'd just moved in, but he hadn't said he hadn't either. The furniture was top of the line, beautiful and sleek, like a photograph you'd see in an advertisement to purchase a penthouse. Even the solid color comforter, towels in the bathroom, and throw pillows on the couch in the living room screamed impersonal. Even men who hated decorating had more to their place than Drew had. There would be items placed throughout that told who they were, but the two picture frames were all I'd noticed.

I laid back on the bed and stared up at the ceiling. I'd spent a lot of time telling Drew about my life, but he hadn't shared much of his own. The shower turned off and a few minutes passed before Drew came out of the bathroom with a towel around his waist. My elbows dipped into the mattress as I sat up and watched him cross the room to the dress. The towel slipped from his waist, exposing his firm backside. I swallowed as I took in every inch of him from behind, his body a beautiful sight that was soon covered by a pair of boxer briefs and an undershirt. Drew faced me, a sly grin tipping one corner of his lips. "Are you watching me?"

I nodded. "A girl could do this all day."

He towered over me as his hands sunk into the mattress, his arms caged me in as his lips found mine. I moaned as he deepened the kiss, pushing one hand into my damp hair. His lips left mine. "And I could do that all day."

"No argument from me." Drew chuckled as he left me sitting in a heaping mess of hormones so he could finish dressing.

My mouth fell open as he stepped from the closet in navy slacks paired with a crisp white button down rolled to his elbows, a camel colored belt with matching dress shoes. No matter if he wore a pair of boxer briefs, jeans with a plain-Jane shirt, or was dressed to the nines in a tailored suit, Drew was a sight to behold.

"Your trap's open."

I gasped. "You shithead."

His laughter filled the room as he buckled a large face watch onto his wrist. "I'm ready when you are." My head fell back on my neck. "What's wrong?"

I lifted my head and watched as he tied a navy tie with tiny white polka dots around his neck. "You look like that," I waved a hand at him, "while I look as if I'm doing the walk of shame after a one-night stand."

His eyes drug down my body on a shrug. "If the shoe fits."

"Drew, I don't know your middle name, Cabot! I will personally kick your ass for that." I lunged to slap his chest but his hand caught mine before I could reach him.

"I was only kidding." His lips pressed against mine. "You look just as beautiful as you did last night."

"You're such a sweet talker." I slipped my hand into his as we made our way into the kitchen, collected our things, and headed down to the parking garage.

The breeze blew in through the cracked windows as we drove through downtown. Traffic was at a steady pace, making the trip from his penthouse to my apartment quicker than usual. Classic rock played softly on the radio as I sang along to just about every word of each song that poured out of the speakers, the occasional smiling glance from Drew as I bobbed my head to the beat, followed by a nice little harmonizing part. The sorrow that weighed me down first thing in the morning had subsided, happiness settling firmly in its place. I couldn't remember the last time

I'd felt so carefree and weightless...actually I could, it was many months back with Liam, but I wasn't going to let myself feel guilty for enjoying the day. I was embracing the now and really breathing for the first time in forever.

"What happened to my personal concert?"

His statement pulled me from my thoughts. "I hadn't realized I'd stopped singing."

His eyebrows dipped low, but the smile on his face never faltered. "Must've been deep in thought."

"I was."

"Want to talk about it?"

I rested my head against the headrest with my face still turned toward him. "Are you sure you're not secretly a therapist?"

Drew's deep laughter made me smile even wider. "If I had a quarter for every time I've heard that."

"I'm just saying, you'd be decent at it."

"Decent?" He scoffed. "That's it?"

I nodded with laughter.

He smoothed a hand over his mouth. "I guess that's better than saying I'd be shitty at it."

"At least I didn't say don't quit your day job."

"True." The light turned green and we ascended down the street.

"Speaking of..." I paused. "What do you do?"

"What do you mean?" He cocked on eyebrow, his eyes focused on the road ahead.

"What do you do for a job? We've talked about mine, but we've never talked about yours. As fancy as you look day in and day out, I'm going with something corporate."

We pulled up to the curb outside my building and Drew turned in the driver's seat to face me. With one arm resting on the steering wheel, he removed his aviators from his eyes. "Well," he paused for a brief moment as his eyes scanned my face, "why don't you see for yourself instead?"

"Okay." My fingers nervously drummed against my thigh.

"What does your schedule look like for the rest of the day and into late tomorrow night?"

I quickly ran through everything I had on my plate and what I'd already accomplished in my mind. "I need to check my planner, but I'm pretty sure I could make whatever you have planned happen."

"Good." Drew put the car back in drive and pulled around to the parking lot designated for my building. He exited the vehicle and rounded it to the passenger side as I watched in confusion as he opened my door and extended his hand for me to take.

"What are you doing?" I lifted from the vehicle and he shut the door, my feet crying out with each step I took. I wasn't used to wearing heels for more than a few hours at a time.

"If you're schedule works out, you'll need to pack an overnight bag."

"Where are we going?"

A sly grin filled his face. "It's a surprise."

My heart fluttered from the excitement dancing in his eyes. We were officially going out of town together. Even if it was only for a night. I couldn't help the excitement and nerves hitting me at the same time.

CHAPTER SEVENTEEN

"I still can't believe you didn't tell me your birthday's next week." Drew hadn't let go the fact that I'd kept my birthday quiet. No one in Philly knew the day I was born, and I was hoping to let this year's birthday pass without so much as a thought of it being anything than just another day. But stupid me had written it down in fancy-schmancy bubble letters in my planner. The same planner everything else was listed in. So, when I'd checked my schedule for the next couple weeks, like a hawk, Drew's eyes had zeroed in on my birthday.

"It's really no big deal."

His head whipped in my direction. "No big deal!" A humorless laugh puffed his chest. "It's a huge deal."

"No," I shook my head and crossed my arms over my chest, sinking further in the seat, "it really isn't."

"Terra..."

"Drew..."

"Stop acting like that."

"Seriously, I don't want anything spectacular. No cake, no party, not even a happy fucking birthday." My voice rose with each passing word. "Understand? The day's going to be hard enough, I don't need anything from anyone to make it worse."

He leveled me with his eyes. "I can't promise you that."

"Please..." I gritted my teeth, mentally punching myself for allowing him to come up to my apartment while I packed.

"You need to stop running from the things you should be celebrating. I'm sure Liam wouldn't want you to live that way."

Like a knife to the heart Drew had sliced me open. Tears pricked my eyes from the truth he'd handed me. Liam wouldn't have wanted me living the way I'd been for months. He wouldn't want me to run away from the days that always brought me joy simply because he wasn't here to celebrate them with me. "Okay, we can do something small." Drew's face lit up like a kid on Christmas morning. "When I say small, I mean it."

"Okay." His sheepish grin gave me all the affirmation I needed that he wasn't going to heed my warning.

Classic rock filled the car as I reached for the radio to end all conversation. A long driveway came into view as we topped the hill. Vast land stretched before my eyes, the grass was a vibrant green, with large trees providing shade periodically throughout the property. It was crazy to think we were merely a couple hours outside of the city.

I seriously needed to get out more.

"That place is beautiful." I pointed out the window.

"I have to agree." The car turned into the driveway, and my mouth fell open as my head whipped in Drew's direction.

"We're going there?" I sat up straighter in the seat.

He nodded.

"Do you know the owners?"

Drew was beaming from the driver's seat. "You could say that."

"Do you work here?" My voice sounded like a child experiencing Disneyland for the first time.

"Something like that."

Words failed me as I sat back in the seat to take in every inch of the establishment. The drive circled around a large water fountain that sat a few hundred feet away from a giant colonial home. I was almost positive it wasn't used to house people overnight any longer, but when it did, I could imagine extremely wealthy goers spending weekends on the property. The only thing missing was a sign that told exactly what business was housed in the home.

Drew rounded the fountain and pulled into a covered unloading area off to the side. That's when the full size of the back part of the property came into view. It stretched for what seemed like miles of almost flat land with giant shade trees, much like the front of the property. Four other buildings were scattered throughout, a paved walkway leading to each.

As we reached the side door, Drew pulled a set of keys from his pocket and unlocked three locks so we could enter. The cool air felt nice as we stepped inside the silent room. Hardwood floors stretched from one wall to the next, ones you'd think would groan from their age as you walked about them, but they managed not to make a sound as I followed him deeper into the room. To my surprise, the majority of the room was empty except a long counter with barrel staves covering the face.

"What is this place?" I turned slowly, taking in every inch as Drew continued on.

He stopped just before he reached the counter and turned to face me, pride beaming across his features. "Cabot's Cellar."

"As in..." My mind was firing off an array of scenarios. I couldn't focus on just one.

"As in, a winery." Drew held his arms out wide. "It's set to open in October. The property was up for purchase when the last owner passed away. The same buddy of mine that pushed me to purchase the penthouse ran across this. I've owned it for a little while now and have been slowly renovating it over the years."

I squealed with disbelief. "Are you serious?"

"Absolutely." He chuckled as I crossed the room and tossed

myself into his arms. "It needed more work than anticipated when I purchased it, but it's almost time to open the doors."

"This is unbelievably amazing, Drew. You have to show me the rest of the property."

Drew linked our hands. "Shall we, then?"

The place was gorgeous. Ceilings that stretched to the heavens with windows that took my breath away. Sitting areas not only inside, but outside as well. The cellar in the basement was naturally chilled, with rows of barrels full of delicious wine, and empty ones ready to be filled. The size of Cabot's Cellar put Gabby's beautiful home to shame, and that was saying a lot.

We stepped into the yard and ventured from the paved path to one of the shade trees. Drew sat down, leaning his back against the tree and motioned for me to join him. "Be careful, that crisp white shirt won't be so white."

Drew waved a dismissive hand at me. "I'm not worried about this shirt, now get your fine ass down here with me."

I giggled as I lowered to the grass and settled between his legs, resting my back against his front. Beneath the tree the temperature was a good five degrees cooler, and the gentle breeze made it absolutely perfect. I closed my eyes as his arms circled my waist and he placed a kiss to the side of my neck, just above the thick strap of my top. His lips lingered a bit longer than a sweet kiss would. A closed lip smile settled on my face as I relaxed.

"I rented a log cabin a few miles from here for the night."

I twisted and looked up at him. "You did?"

"I did." He smiled and pressed his lips to mine. "It's the only one within miles too, so we can be as loud as our hearts desire."

My stomach flipped with anticipation. I wanted so badly to jump up and demand he take me there as quickly as possible, but I didn't. The night would be upon us before we knew it, so enjoying Cabot's Cellar before anyone was my main focus.

"I'm looking forward to it."

Drew's chest rumbled with a growl as he lifted my hair from

my neck and peppered kisses down to the curved hem of my top. "Want to have a tasting?"

"A tasting of what?"

He laughed against my skin. "Of the wine, but I can continue my own tasting if you'd like." His hand slipped beneath my shirt, giving my breast a gentle squeeze.

I groaned. "Of course I want to taste your wine."

His teeth grated my ear. "We can finish this later."

Drew guided me to the building just down from where we sat. The inside was more modern than the main house, and still tied in nicely with the barrel staves and antique hardwood floors. Metal mixed throughout the décor, with a large mirror behind the bar that read Cabot's Cellar in white sophisticated print. The bar was at standing height with a few high-rise chairs lining it. I took a seat in one of the chairs as Drew rounded the bar and retrieved a pair of empty wineglasses. He ran the glasses under water and dried them before pulling four bottles from beneath the bar. I bounced with excitement as he popped the cork from the first and poured a nice helping into each glass.

"Let's see how good your palate is." Drew cocked an eyebrow and grinned.

The first was a deep red. "Mmm..." I took a sip and swooshed it around in my mouth. "It has a nice bright taste, which I like. Blackberry or raspberry, maybe?"

"Raspberry." His smile grew wider as I patted myself on the back.

"Next." I bounced in my seat.

"Okay, let me try something a bit harder." His beaming smile morphed into a wicked grin as he rubbed his hands together.

I watched as Drew pulled a bottle from below the bar, popped the cork, and poured a small amount in my glass. The color alone threw me for a loop. Lifting the glass to my lips, I narrowed my eyes at him before taking a sip. "Oh," I paused to take another sip, "this has a hint of..." I sniffed the glass and took an even larger sip the third time. "I swear it has a bourbon feel to it."

Drew shook his head in disbelief. "That's because it's brandy."

"Ha!" I sat the glass on the counter and clapped my hands. "Maybe I should hire you since you know the flavors pretty damn well."

I shrugged. "I'm a girl who enjoys wine in all varieties." I leaned a little closer. "Even if I favor tart and sweet over the rest."

Drew placed a hand over his heart and opened his mouth in fake shock. "That's a secret I won't repeat."

Laughter passed between us as I finished off the brandy. "What's up next?"

He leaned his forearms on the bar. "You said tart and sweet are your favorites. Want a floral or fruity?"

"Surprise me."

"You're one of the only women I've met that actually likes surprises. That asks for them." He chuckled as he pulled another mystery bottle from beneath the bar.

"I kind of feel like you're aiming to get me drunk."

Drew looked like a deer in headlights as he paused holding the bottle mid-pour. "Damn, you caught me."

"You know," I leaned over the bar and wrapped my hand around his tie, pulling him closer to me, "there's no need to get me drunk."

"Is that so?"

"It's so."

Drew closed the distance between us, his lips finding mine as his tongue ran across the seam begging for entrance. This kiss was all consuming. One you felt deep in your chest, ripping open your heart and embedding itself in your soul. His hand gripped the back of my neck as he held me in place, forcing me to crawl on top of the bar. My hands threaded deep into his hair as I maneuvered my body around so that I was sitting, instead of kneeling, on the bar top. His free hand slipped up my thigh, his fingertips tracing the hem of my shorts, pulling a sigh from me every time they rolled over the sensitive flesh of my inner thigh. My body was alive, pulsing with need as he groaned against my lips, provoking my heart to thump even harder than its already frantic rhythm.

"Mmm..." Drew moaned as I pulled back. "That mixture," he motioned toward my swollen lips, "would be a damn good wine in itself. I could even name it Terra." My face heated as I tried to suppress the smile spreading across my face. "Although," Drew took my lips once again, "I wouldn't want to share that taste with anyone but myself."

Once again, I wrapped his tie around my hand and pulled him closer. "If you keep that up, we won't make it to the cabin."

His heated gaze searched mine. "Did I mention I own this place?"

"You might have." I smiled against his lips.

"As much as I'd love to break in this bar," he checked the time on his watch and dropped his head into my lap, "I have a few things to take care of business wise." He glanced up at me. "You might want to freshen up a bit beforehand."

Drew ran his hands through his hair, attempting to smooth the mess I'd created away then helped me down. "You can come with me or I can take you to the cabin. It's up to you."

"Definitely coming with. There are far too many horror movies about a girl alone at a cabin in the woods. I don't want to be another statistic."

Drew tossed his head back and bellowed with laughter. My own uncontrollable laughter soon followed. I clutched my stomach as tears pricked my eyes. "You. Think. I'm. Kidding?"

He nodded and wiped beneath his eyes. "That was the funniest thing I've heard in a while."

My laughter slowed as I steadied my breathing, still clutching my aching belly. "You can't say I'm wrong."

"That's the kicker," he chuckled, "it's the truth."

"Right!" We continued to laugh as we headed for the car.

* * *

Drew was on his third phone call since we'd left the winery. I was surprised the amount of time he'd spent on the phone since I'd met him wasn't more than it was. He mouthed an apology at me before returning his eyes to the road. I covered his hand on the center console and gave it a reassuring squeeze. He'd told me at least a hundred times not to apologize, which is exactly what he needed to consider for himself. The man was building his dreams, apologizing for having to work to do so was insane.

"I'll be there in half an hour at the latest." I turned the volume down on the radio, so it wouldn't disrupt him. "There will be someone with me. You'll get to meet her, I promise. Yeah, yeah, you better not. I'll see you in a little while."

"Not to be nosey or anything..."

"It was my sister, she's a business partner of mine. Who is also dying to meet the girl I've been spending quite a bit of time with." He turned his hand over and threaded his finger between mine.

I was getting ready to meet the one living person he cared about more than anything in the world. His sister. My heart slammed rapidly within its cage, a wave of nausea washed over me at the thought of meeting her. This would take our relationship quickly to another level. I couldn't help the thoughts from filling my head of whether or not I was ready for that.

My peripheral vision darkened as tunnel vision took over. The radio muffled as my pulse thumped loudly in my ears. "Terra?" Rapid breaths left my lungs as I lifted my free hand to my heart.

"Terra?" The sound of my name pierced through the panic attack. Drew turned my head toward him, his hands cupping my face. "Breathe. You need to breathe."

"Okay," I choked out and began counting slow steady breaths. *One. Inhale. Two. Exhale. Three. Inhale. Four. Exhale.*

Blinking a few times to clear my vision, I realized the car was parked on the side of the interstate. "Oh, God." I dropped my head into my hands and groaned. Drew rubbed soothing circles across my back. "This is embarrassing."

"Don't be embarrassed. I've battled my fair share of panic attacks over the years. I know how easily they sneak up on you."

I lifted my eyes. "Always the voice of reason."

His lips pressed softly against the back of my hand. "Just trying to help make healing a little bit easier for others than it was for me."

It was the perfect chance to ask him what he'd gone through over the years that caused him so much grief and heartache, but before I could open my mouth his phone sprung to life. A sad smile faded from his face as he answered the call and I sat back in my seat.

"Drew Cabot." Hearing him announce himself as he answered the phone made me smile. Full of confidence, yet firm at the same time. A long pause filled the car as I directed my eyes to the road ahead. "That's fine. The initial order will work just fine. Yes, Friday afternoon is perfect. I'll talk to James to ensure he'll be there for the arrival and let Eden know the change. I appreciate the call. Talk to you soon."

Drew deflated as he exhaled a heavy breath. "That bad?" I rolled my head in his direction.

He gripped the steering wheel with both hands. "Just a change in a few plans." We turned onto a gravel drive and the car bounced from the uneven ground. "I have to get used to the unexpected changes that happen. That's one of my downfalls. I think every-thing has to unfold a certain way, and when it doesn't I struggle with going with the flow of things. Letting it unravel and work itself out. A lot of times it isn't something major, but I still get the sense of it being a mountain instead of a hill, you know?"

"I get it. I really do." I squeezed his hand. "I haven't had to handle something of the magnitude of opening my own business, but I understand completely how it feels to not have full control over something when that's exactly what you need. You've come to terms with the fact that it isn't healthy to feel that way, so you've taken the first step."

"Yeah, I'm working on it."

"That's all you can do."

We wound further down the gravel drive as the fields turned into heavy trees lining the road, our intense conversation falling away as the radio station filled with static. We were officially off the grid.

The gravel road morphed into a large wooden bridge that stretched a few miles. "I hope you know where we're going."

Drew's eyes shifted my way. "I'm taking you back in the woods to murder you and easily dump your body." The fact that his voice was void of all amusement and laughter made my heart rate spike.

"Umm..." We came to a stop beside the most beautiful cabin I'd ever laid eyes on and the realization of where we were caused full belly laughter to bubble up my throat.

"Told you I was bringing you here to murder you." He winked before exiting the vehicle.

I shook my head, grinning, and got out of the passenger side before he reached my door. "I thought we were meeting your sister." My eyes scanned the property. An array of colorful flowers outlined the porch, with tall trees shielding the cabin from the afternoon sun.

Drew strapped my bag over his shoulder and carried his much smaller one in his hand. "The keys should be beneath the mat." He nodded toward the door.

I took off up the steps and easily found the set of keys exactly where he said they'd be. Drew reached me as I pushed the door open and stepped aside so he could enter first since he was carrying the bags. "This place..." I stood in awe as I gazed at the back of the cabin. Glass stretched as tall and wide as the room we were in. A rustic version of his place. The sun beamed through the trees, cascading a beautiful rainbow onto the wood floors. Every place I'd entered with Drew took my breath away, this one included.

"You like?" From behind me, he wrapped his arms around my waist and rested his chin on my shoulder.

"I do."

"Good." He kissed my neck. "There's a bathroom in the master bedroom, and one right down the hall, first door on the right, if you want to freshen up before we head out to meet Eden."

"Eden's your sister then?" I turned in his arms.

"Yeah." He grinned down at me.

Suddenly I felt insecure about the way I looked, afraid I wouldn't seem good enough in his sister's eyes. Which was absolutely ridiculous considering the fact I'd never met her and had no idea the type of person she was. If Drew was any indication of how she'd be, then she wasn't going to care whether or not I was dressed to the nines or drove an expensive car. She would only care about the type of person I was and how I treated her brother. I glanced down at my flowy tank top and khaki shorts. "Should I change?"

Drew's eyes scanned my body. "I don't see why you need to."

"Are you sure?"

"Yes," he pulled me in closer, "why do you feel like you need to?"

I shrugged. "You look business ready, while I'm everyday casual, and we're handling business related stuff today, right?"

"Yeah, but don't feel obligated to change because of that. If there was a dress code I would've told you before we left your place." His fingers slipped beneath the strap of my tank top. "Plus," his lips pressed against the curve where my neck and shoulder met, "I like being able to do this." He made a path of kisses down my shoulder and onto my chest, stopping at the swell of my breasts where the neckline of my tank top laid.

"If you keep doing that we won't be meeting your sister." My breathless warning made him laugh against my skin.

"She'll kill me if we're a no-show." He stepped back, holding both of my hands. "Are you sure you're up to this?"

My heart galloped like wild horses from the anxiety of what was to come, but backing out would only delay the inevitable if things between us continued to work. I had no choice but to dive in head first. "I'm sure." A hesitant smile adorned my face, one I hoped like hell he didn't notice.

CHAPTER EIGHTEEN

My body shook as we ascended the steps of the Fork & Spoon Market. A catchy name for a restaurant if I ever did hear one. Nervous as all get out, I brushed my clammy hands down the front of my shorts. Drew's eyes softened as he watched the anxiety rolling through me like a tidal wave.

"Hey," his hand slipped into mine as we paused just outside the door, "she's not cutthroat. I know meeting family for the first time is nerve-wracking and I didn't mean for it to unfold like this, but take a deep breath. It'll be fine, I promise."

I inhaled a deep lung burning breath and let it out slowly. "Let's do this." A tight-lipped smile settled on my lips as he pulled the door open.

Thankfully the place wasn't jam-packed with patrons since the normal lunch hour had long passed. No sooner than we crossed the threshold, my eyes zeroed in on the beautiful brunette from the picture in his bedroom. A wide smile stretched across her face as she stood from her seat, arms wide as Drew hurried over to her with me closely in tow. Eden squealed as he lifted her into the air and spun a full circle before sitting her back down.

"I swear you've gotten even taller." Her voice was as sweet and loving as the happiness dancing across her face at the sight of her brother.

"Or you've gotten shorter." His laughter filled the air as she playfully swatted his arm.

Their interaction made me smile. Exactly what a brother and sister duo that got along should be. "Oh hush, just because you got the better genes doesn't mean I can't kick your ass."

"Only because I wouldn't hit a woman."

Eden rolled her eyes before focusing on me. "Oh!" She perked up, standing a good inch taller in her high heels. "You must be the girlfriend."

"She has a name." Drew rolled his eyes, making me chuckle.

"Terra." I extended my hand that Eden bypassed and pulled me into a hug.

Personal space didn't exist with this family, which was something I hadn't quite gotten used to. "I'm Eden, this shithead's sister."

"Very nice to meet you."

Eden held me at arm's length, taking in every inch of my body. Normally I would've cringed as my very self-conscious thoughts clouded my head, but instead, a heated blush crept across my face before she let go and gave her brother the thumbs-up.

Drew shook his head. "Ignore her." He pulled the chair out for me to sit before planting himself to my left. His arm circled my shoulder and his fingertips traced an invisible pattern across my skin, causing chills to roll through me.

Eden sat directly across from me, smiling ear-to-ear as her eyes lingered on Drew's fingertips before clearing her throat. "So," she clasped her hands together, "did you go by the winery?"

"We did."

"Well," she paused, "what do you think?"

"It's coming together nicely." His fingers grazed the side of my throat, making me shiver. "Do you feel that we're on track for a fall opening?"

"Late fall is totally doable." Eden pulled her planner from a large black bag sitting in the chair beside her and flipped a few pages into it. "We could aim for mid to late October."

"Halloween!" I blurted out. Both of their attention swung to me and I sunk down in the chair, embarrassed by my sudden outburst, but unable to stop my mouth from unloading a round of information diarrhea. "Opening night could be a Halloween party. There could be wine named after silly poisons and spells, a costume contest, and even have people bob for apples. If the weather's nice, lights could be strung from tree to tree and pumpkins carved with faces to light the walkways."

Drew's hand dropped from my body as the two of them stared at me with open mouths. "That's brilliant!" He laughed and pulled my mouth to his.

Eden clapped. "Why the hell didn't I think of that? Terra, we're going to need your help getting this idea off the ground."

"What!" I shook my head. "No way. I won't be any good at it."

"Are you kidding?" Eden scoffed. "The ideas you just rambled off are better than anything I have written down for months, and you just heard the possible opening date. You have to help us." She turned to Drew. "She has to help us, Drew."

"I would love her help," he sat back and crossed his arms over his chest, "but that's one hundred percent up to Terra."

"Guys," I looked between the two of them and pointed at myself, "I'm right here."

Eden's eyes swung back to mine. "Is that a yes then?" Her eyes narrowed and her face pinched with anticipation of me saying exactly what she wanted to hear.

"Okay, I'll help you guys."

"Yes!" Eden high fived me.

Drew kissed me so deeply I almost forgot Eden was watching us. "If you'd said no, I would've never heard the end of it."

"Oh, hush." Eden waved a dismissive hand.

The entire time we were with Eden I felt at ease. She had an infectious personality that made it hard to feel anything but comfortable around her. I couldn't imagine seeing an angry side to the girl. The love she and Drew shared was inspiring. A brother and sister bond so strong, nothing could break it. One could only wish for such a relationship in life. Drew had told me a little of their upbringing, which made seeing their relationship that much better.

When we'd said our goodbyes, Eden hugged me tightly and said to get her number from Drew when we had a free moment. That she'd enjoyed meeting me and was happy her brother had finally found someone to fill the portion of his heart that had been shattered years ago. I wasn't sure the story behind that, but the bit of the conversation he had heard didn't seem to sit well with him. His mood had changed as we headed to the car. There was a distance between us that made me wonder if I'd done something wrong, but deep down I had a feeling it was because of what Eden had said to me. One of those subjects that you felt you shouldn't touch base on unless the party it revolved around wanted to, so I slipped into the passenger seat without a word and kept my eyes focused straight ahead as we pulled onto the interstate.

As the silence lingered between us, my nerves picked up. I reached for the radio and slowly turned the volume up just enough to drown out the hollowness. Drew's eyes never left the road ahead as we left the interstate, engulfed by the beauty of the surrounding trees once again. I nibbled my thumbnail, a nervous habit I caught myself doing over the years, but only when the most awkward situations reared their head. Enduring a car ride without any form of conversation with Drew was slowly becoming one of the most awkward moments I'd experienced in quite some time.

The car bounced as we turned onto the gravel road that led back to the cabin, still not a single word uttered between us. My heart rate spiked as we came to a stop and he quickly exited the car. I stayed in the passenger seat as I watched him hurry up the front steps and paused just outside the door. He turned and dropped his head like he just realized I was there waiting in the vehicle with confusion written all over my face. He started in my direction, but before he reached the car I got out and stalked past him.

"Terra," he called after me as I hurriedly opened the door, thankful he'd already unlocked it, and snatched my bag from where he'd placed it when we first arrived. Not sure what the hell I was doing, I headed directly toward the sliding glass doors. "Where are you going?" His voice boomed, forcing me to stop my insane departure.

I spun to face him and dropped my bag to the floor. "I have no idea." I shook my head and tossed my hands into the air. "Did I do something?"

Drew scrubbed his face with his hands, stopping just short of being in my personal bubble. "It wasn't you."

"You heard what Eden said about you."

His lips flattened as he nodded the confirmation I'd already known. There was a heartache lingering in Drew's life. What exactly it was, I didn't know. But, Eden had said enough to throw a warning flag. Combined with the way he was acting only made my internal warning even louder. "Sometimes, she says things without thinking."

"Do you want to talk about what she meant?"

"Maybe another time." He took my hands in his. I wanted so desperately to jerk them away and storm off from his lack of information. A different version of me probably would have, but I knew doing that would only hinder what was happening between us. Whatever the story was, it was his to tell when he was ready. If I had to wait to know the depth of Drew Cabot, I would, because the heart does fickle things when you care for someone.

"Okay."

I squealed as he scooped me into his arms and held me against his chest. "What I really want to do is give every inch of your body the attention it deserves."

My breath caught as my stomach fluttered from his words. "Then by all means." A shy smile crept across my face that soon exploded into a full one as he took off deeper into the cabin, my laughter floating through the air as he shoved open a half-closed door to what I assumed was the bedroom.

Drew carried me to the bed and gently sat me on the edge, his eyes never leaving mine as he discarded his crisp white dress shirt. He reached behind his head and grabbed the collar of his undershirt, his gaze disappearing for the quick moment it took to pull the shirt over his head and drop it to the floor. I couldn't pull my eyes from him as removed his belt and kicked his shoes off. My mouth was suddenly dry as he shoved his slacks to the floor and stepped out of them. It wasn't the first time I'd laid eyes on his beautiful body, but just like then, my heart stuttered at the sight before me.

His fingertips slipped beneath the bottom hem of my tank and lifted it over my head. Our lips found one another as his hands snaked around the dip in my waist, one stopped its path as the other smoothed up my spine. His deft fingers unlatched the clasp of my bra and pushed it out of the path of his hand. My eyes closed as his fingertips threaded beneath my hair, lightly scratching my scalp, awakening chills across my flesh. With each sensational kiss, my body was winding tightly, in search of the release only Drew could give me.

With impatience rolling through me like a tidal wave, I unfastened the button fly on my shorts and slipped them from my body, careful not to break our connection. I shimmied out of my bra and Drew's hands quickly found my breasts. A breathy moan passed my lips as my head fell back against my neck and his mouth trailed down the column of my throat, leaving hot wet kisses over the swell of my breasts, while descending the plump flesh in search of the pale peak awaiting his lips.

Drew pulled his mouth from my flesh and stepped out of his boxer briefs. "Scoot back." I followed his husky demand as he retrieved a condom from his wallet and slid it on.

His eyes swam with such intensity I could feel it deep in my bones as he crawled onto the bed, wrapped his fingers into the top of my panties and pulled them from my legs. A trail of nips and kisses started at my knee and curved around to my inner thigh, he didn't stop until the last one pressed gently against the apex of my inner thigh. His wet tongue drew a line in the crease of my inner thigh and over to my center. A whimpered cry jutted from my lips as he kissed the most sensitive spot my body had to offer. I gripped the sheets with one had as the other threaded into his hair, quickly replacing the styled locks with disarray as I pulled on a handful and clutched the back of his skull. Bright spots danced behind my eyelids as my lower body lifted from the mattress, his strong arms holding my pelvis at the perfect angle to intensify the euphoric feeling pulsing through every inch of my being. With one last flick of his tongue I convulsed with pleasure as a heavy wave of relief washed throughout my body. My chest heaved with panted breaths as his lips found my lower abdomen and trailed their way up to mine.

"I'm so thankful you ran into me that day." His whispered words brushed against my lips as he rolled his hips forward, making us one.

Labored breaths filled the room as our bodies rocked against one another, finding that delicious rhythm only the two of us knew. Flesh against flesh, lips against lips, as we explored every inch of one another. Drew was a skilled lover, very attune to what my body was telling him. Never taking for granted a single moment of the pleasure building between the two of us. Giving his all to ensure the experience was just as euphoric and memo-rable to me as it was for him. It was good to find someone who wasn't so caught up in their own pleasure that they didn't help you reach yours. I'd been lucky to find two men in my life like that.

I rocked my hips to the side and rolled us so I was seated atop him. Drew's hooded eyes sparkled with surprise as I began to move, finding a sultry slow pace to drive him wild. His fingers curled into my hip bones, my hands were flat on his smooth chest that was slick with sweat. I caressed his skin, picking up the pace just enough for a groan to escape his slack mouth and his eyes to close. Long lashes splayed against his lower eyelids, a faint cluster of freckles adorned his right temple. I smiled from the sight of them. My nose and cheeks were dusted with many more than Drew had, and the thought of how much I loathed them growing up crossed my mind.

His hand caressed my face as he lifted upright, bringing us eye-to-eye, those hazel orbs full of passion with a hint of sorrow buried deep within them. I continued to move as that familiar burning deep in my core ignited, my breaths became short staccato sounds as everything around me faded away except four words that singed their selves onto my heart as they left his mouth. "I love you, Terra."

I tucked my knees a little tighter against my chest as the porch swing barely swung. The night's air was cool enough to be comfortable with a warm cup of coffee in my hands, resting on top of my knee. Drew was sound asleep when I'd slipped from the bed with my mind going a million miles a minute. He'd told me he loved me and I didn't say it back.

Hell, I didn't say much of anything besides a few good moans followed by some kissing.

Afraid I couldn't trust my voice to be strong enough after having someone else confess their love for me since I'd lost Liam.

I thought I'd feel guilty.

I thought I'd be stricken with heartache and sorrow.

None of that made an appearance.

Only confusion.

After we'd made love, Drew snuggled against me and quickly fell asleep, but my mind wouldn't allow sleep to find me. So, I made my way to the coffee machine, made a pot, and brought myself out to the peaceful surroundings of nature with a piping hot cup in hand. I'd never lived in a place where the closest neighbor was miles away, the peacefulness of it was unbelievable. I'd always wanted a little bit of land, trees blocking off my property, and a large patio with a swing. It had been my dream since I'd flipped through home magazines as a teen, something Liam and myself were working on for the future.

A future we'd never get to share together.

Sorrow pinched my heart as the thoughts of making a new future with Drew crept their way in. A smile settled on my face, the sorrow dulling within my chest as happiness bloomed in its place. I could easily have a life with Drew, a happy one at that. But some tiny little part of me was holding back. Why? I couldn't quite put my finger on it yet.

I lifted the mug to my lips and blew on the steaming liquid before taking a sip of the darkest brew in the land. I wasn't usually a coffee drinker, much less black, but like everything else, times were changing...and it had become my staple since making Philadelphia home.

My head rested against the plush cushion as I gazed at the stars. The night sky was full of them, lit up like a city skyline. It was breathtakingly beautiful. I continued to swing as I watched the stars twinkle. Some disappeared behind clouds I couldn't see, while others seemed as if they were burning brighter with each passing minute. A gasp fell from my lips and I almost toppled the coffee mug onto the ground as a shooting star raced across the sky, the first I'd ever seen. "Wow!" I hastily closed my eyes and rattled off a wish with a closed lip smile.

"Let's see who gets the wish." I gripped one end of the wishbone and Liam wrapped his fingers around the other.

Narrowing his eyes, he lifted his free hand and counted down from three. We both pulled, breaking the bone almost directly in half, except he had just a fraction of a longer piece than me, "Ohhh...." His laughter filled the room as I swatted his chest.

"You cheated," I wiped my hands down the front of my apron, "that's the only thing that makes sense."

"Don't be a sore loser." He pulled me into his arms and peppered wet kisses all over my face as I squealed for him to stop. "If that bird tastes anything like you do, it's going to be delicious."

"You're such a perv." I playfully shoved his chest. "Well, what did you wish for?"

He lifted a shoulder and dropped it back down. "I have everything I want and need."

"Even though that's the sweetest thing I've ever heard, you still need to make a wish. It's a law or something."

"Is that so?" A playful grin danced across his face.

"Yep." I popped the p on the end. "If you don't make a wish, bad luck will come your way. Kind of like breaking a mirror."

His index finger tapped against his chin. "I feel like you're bullshitting me, but I'll make a wish if it makes you happy."

Liam closed his eyes.

A long howl startled me back to reality, jarring me forward enough to slosh coffee over the rim of the mug and onto my bare legs. I hissed from the hot liquid rolling across my skin and quickly pulled my tank top off to soak up the liquid. Once my legs were dry I shoved my shirt into the mug and headed back inside.

The moon illuminated the living room and kitchen of the cabin so I didn't bother turning on any lights as I padded over to the sink and ran some water to soak my top in. I placed the empty mug beside the sink and caught a glimpse of my reflection in the stainless-steel microwave beside where I stood.

My hair was knotted against the base of my head, my face was void of makeup. The skewed reflection reminded me of a much younger girl who chased after love, who wanted everything out of life. A girl who was always searching for tomorrow. I longed to be that girl again.

"Couldn't sleep?" Drew's gruff voice sent my heart into a raging thunder.

"Shit." I spun around and clamped a hand over my chest.

He blinked a couple times as he took me in. I could only imagine the thoughts running through his head at the sight of me standing in the kitchen, staring at the microwave, clothed in nothing but my bra and panties.

"I haven't been to bed yet." My eyes slipped down his chest, stopping on the floor between us.

He yawned. "It's like four in the morning."

"I know." I smiled. "I've been outside for a while, it's peaceful out there."

Drew crossed the room and I wrapped my arms around his body, resting my face against his chest. "Good thing there aren't any neighbors around, because that outfit is for my eyes only." His hand slipped down my backside and gently squeezed.

"Well," I lifted my head, "I spilt coffee all over myself so I had to make quick do of something to clean it up with." I nodded toward the sink. "Hence the soaking tank top."

"Ah." He slowly lifted his head in understanding. "Did you burn yourself?"

I lowered my eyes to my thigh. "I have a few red spots, but all is well."

"Are you going back outside or coming to bed?"

"I haven't decided yet. I probably need to sleep, but I can't seem to turn my mind off."

"Need a listening ear?"

"No," I kissed his lips, "but I'd love a firm shoulder and warm body to snuggle with out on the swing if you're available."

He glanced down at his wrist. "I've got some time, but only if you stay the way you are."

I rolled my eyes with a smile firm in place. "Since that's my only choice."

Drew grabbed a blanket from the back of the couch as we headed for the porch. He took a seat on the swing and draped an arm along the back. I snuggled against his side and tucked my legs onto the swing. His hand came down to rest on my hip as he gently swung us. A soothing breeze picked up since I'd gone in, the longer we swung the more I found the need for sleep creeping into my bones.

"What's your favorite book?" Drew lazily drew an invisible pattern against my leg.

"Even though a question like that shouldn't be asked, simply because a well-read woman doesn't like to pick her favorites, but...." I paused as numerous books played out behind my eyes. "Classic would be *Little Women* or *Jane Eyre*, children's book is *Where the Wild Things Are*, and most recent book would be *From Sand and Ash*. Yours?"

"You can't ask such questions, what's wrong with you?"

"Seriously?" I narrowed my eyes at him over my shoulder. Full belly laughter shook my body as I smiled at his goofiness. "Okay then, how about..." I drummed my fingers against his leg. "Favorite eighties movie."

"What!" He jerked us forward. "That's even worse than favorite book."

I giggled. "Payback's a bitch."

"Can you narrow it down, give me options maybe?"

"Sheesh, I didn't get the luxury of options, but I suppose I can." Drew dipped his head and kissed the soft spot behind my ear. "*Breakfast Club, The Goonies,* or *The Outsiders.*"

"Son of a bitch." He ran a hand over his mouth. "I thought options would make it easier...but that's a joke."

"The clock is ticking." I tapped my wrist with a grin.

"The Outsiders."

I placed a hand over my chest and gasped. "No one puts *The Goonies* in a corner!"

"Wrong movie." He ruffled my hair as we fell into a fit of laughter.

"I know that." I pulled my hair loose and smoothed out the mess he'd made. "It's called being funny, ha ha."

"Never a dull moment." He squeezed me tightly. I turned my head so his lips could reach mine. As the kiss grew hot and heavy, I turned in his hold, placing one leg on the outside of his so I was straddling his lap. His hands smoothed over the globes of my backside and stopped on the narrow part of my waist. "Did I step over a line earlier?" Drew's eyes searched mine as I sat fully on top of him.

The conversation I'd hoped wouldn't make an appearance was well on its way. "No," I shook my head and dropped my eyes to my folded hands, "you didn't step over any line." He lifted my chin for me to look at him. "Everything's so new, so different than what I was used to. I have deep feelings for you, Drew, I honestly do. I hope you don't think otherwise."

His knuckles grazed my cheek as he pushed thick strands of hair behind my ear. "I know you do. I just needed to make sure I didn't hurt you in anyway by loving you."

I gently kissed his lips and moved from his lap to snuggle back against his side. With my head resting against the front of his shoulder, he wrapped his arm around my side and pulled me into him as close as possible. A comfortable silence blanketed us as the swing moved slowly. Each loving word that passed Drew's lips was like a stitch sewing together my broken heart. I didn't know why our paths had crossed, whether or not fate had played a part, or the stars had aligned. Either way, a future with Drew became clearer with each moment we shared.

CHAPTER NINETEEN

I t was officially my birthday.

No sooner than my eyes had opened I'd blocked a handful of numbers from calling me. Definitely a shitty thing to do, but my heart wasn't in the right place to listen to voicemails and read texts from the people who filled my life with Liam. The day was going to be hard enough being the first birthday without him, if I could avoid any form of added sorrow, I would go above and beyond to ensure that.

My laptop stayed on the coffee table unopened as I went about my morning routine. I giggled as Drew's text message from the night before came to mind. He'd made it a point to inform me that he'd be at my place no later than two so we could celebrate my day of birth together. Even though I'd told him time and time again I wasn't up to the task of celebrating, he wouldn't take no for an answer. A part of me knew he had something up his sleeve, most likely a get together with the few people I called friends in Philly, or at least that's the extent of a celebration I was hoping for.

Avoiding my laptop like the plague was a daunting task. Every morning I'd open the thing and rummage about in my emails to see what jobs awaited a decision, or what jobs were coming due. But checking my email had gotten placed on the "can't do" list for the day, knowing damn good and well there would most likely be a dozen from Janet waiting for me to read them. Especially after she realized I'd blocked her from being able to call me for the time being.

I felt like an asshole for doing so, which was enough of an indicator that blocking her was wrong. To have just an inkling of happiness, my mind needed the peace. The toaster dinged as my bagel lifted to the top, a quick and easy breakfast I'd grown to love. I slathered the cinnamon swirl circle with cream cheese and devoured a nice little chunk. "Happy birthday to me," I said aloud to no one.

Knocking echoed from the front door as I swallowed the giant bite and padded over to the door, cursing for the lack of a peephole. Hoping it was merely the delivery man, I cracked the door open. "What are you doing here?"

Drew stood before me with a bouquet of wild flowers extended. "Happy birthday!" he beamed as I took the flowers from him and he planted a kiss against my cheek as I let him in.

"Thank you." A blush heated my face. "But, you are *extremely* early."

"I know." He plopped down on the couch and crossed his ankles on the coffee table. "I couldn't let you spend your birthday morning alone, now could I?"

Happiness bloomed in my chest as I shook my head with a smile. "What's on the agenda?" I pulled a vase from a lower cabinet and filled it with water. The wild flowers looked gorgeous sitting in the center of the island.

He dropped his chin and stared at me through thick eyelashes. "I already told you there's a surprise, that's all you're getting out of me."

I groaned as I left the living room to get ready for the day.

* * *

The process of picking out a birthday outfit wasn't as hard at it had been in the years past. Maybe because Drew had shown up in dark jeans and a wine-colored polo tucked in at the waist. Which meant I could pull off a somewhat casual look for the day and be okay. I'd settled on my favorite pair of boyfriend jeans, the kind that weren't skin tight but weren't overly baggy either, with distressed markings down the front of each medium washed leg. I cuffed the bottom hem of each leg so they'd rest just above the ankle and slipped my feet into a pair of tan chunky heels that never failed me in the comfort department. To round out my birthday ensemble I pulled on a slouchy off-the-shoulder blush top, allowing it to fall off my left shoulder and clasped a thin silver bracelet around my wrist. I wasn't much on jewelry, but I needed something that reminded me of Liam to feel complete. He might not have been alive to celebrate my day, but he could be with me in spirit.

I lifted the wooden top of my jewelry box and retrieved the diamond studs he'd given me as an anniversary gift. Seeing them made me smile. I placed one in each earlobe and examined myself in the mirror. Swiping on a couple layers of mascara, I smoothed my hands down the front of my thighs and grabbed my wristlet off the dresser.

By the time I finished getting ready it was well past two. Drew had made himself comfortable on the couch, watching some cooking show I'd never seen. I couldn't help the laugh that bubbled inside of me from the sight of him stretched across my small sofa while the man on the show taught the audience how to make the perfect soufflé.

"Sorry it took so long." I pulled my heavy hair over one shoulder as I rounded the couch into his line of vision.

Drew's eyebrows rose as he dropped his feet to the floor and stood. "You look absolutely stunning, Birthday Girl." His arms wrapped around my waist and he pulled me in for a deep core burning kiss.

"Happy birthday to me." I rubbed my lips together.

He chuckled. "That's just a taste of what's to come." His lips gently pressed to my cheek before he let go of my waist and checked his watch for the time. "Is there anything you want to do today, before the surprise that is?"

"What time *is* the surprise?" I nibbled my bottom lip, hoping he'd give me some inkling of information.

He wiggled an index finger at me. "Nice try, but I cannot divulge such information. If there's something you want to do though, just let me know what it is and I'll see if I can work it into the schedule." A lopsided grin tipped the corner of his mouth.

An exuberated sigh deflated my chest. "Surprises are the devil." My comment pulled full belly laughter from him as we headed toward the door.

I locked it behind me and Drew extended a hand to take my keys, knowing they wouldn't fit in the tiny wristlet I'd settled on carrying. He dropped them into his front pocket as I pushed the down button for the elevator, surprised that it was already waiting. Maybe it knew my birthday was upon us? I silently laughed at the ridiculous thought.

"Well?" He cocked an eyebrow as we stepped inside and hit the button designated for the lobby.

"What?" I tilted my head and slipped my hand into his.

"Is there anything you want to do today? It is *your* birthday after all."

"As long as it's a good day, I'm fine with whatever we do."

The elevator doors opened and arguing voices from an older couple quickly hit us as we stepped into the lobby. My attention was drawn to the pair. The silver haired woman tossed her hands into the air as a round of cuss words that would make the cheeks of mouthed bikers blush came barreling off her tongue. Drew cleared his throat to alert the couple they had company, but it didn't seem to matter. The man flipped her the bird as he hurried toward the exit, but from the looks of things he wasn't getting away from her that easily. I cringed as the scene unfolded before our eyes. One minute they were on the verge of killing one another and the next she whipped him around to face her and smashed her mouth against his. I covered my mouth as we passed them just outside the door to stifle the laugh threatening to escape, my eyes lifting to Drew's. An amused smirk played on his lips.

Once we were far out of earshot I leaned into his side. "Well, that was interesting."

"To say the least." He chuckled.

"I bet they have some intense makeup sex."

Drew's steps faltered. "Thanks for that image." I giggled, realizing exactly where we were headed, *Side Street Drafts.*

Or so I thought. Instead of stopping at the front door, Drew paused at the curb before taking a left down the alley. Just past the bar, a tall iron door with a keypad caught my attention. Beautiful vines with tiny colorful flowers framed two thirds of the doorway. To my surprise, we stopped in front of it. Drew dropped my hand to enter a code I had no idea he knew. The door clicked and he pulled it open, announcing it was us before entering the patio area. My eyes light up as I took in the changes Gabby and Izzy had made since I'd last been out there.

The same seating arrangement, but even more rustic décor laced with beautiful flowers stretched throughout. Izzy came bouncing out of the building and tossed her arms open wide. "Happy birthday!" her voice echoed loudly through the enclosed space.

"Thank you." She enveloped me and I squeezed her tightly. Izzy was one of kind, always beaming with happiness and full of enthusiasm. The perfect yin to Gabby's yang.

Izzy directed us to a cabana toward the far back of the patio. "This one is set up for the two of you." We stepped inside, the wink she passed to Drew caught my eye as I took a seat, pretending to be oblivious to the hushed conversation transpiring between the two of them. I was in awe of the birthday streamers strung throughout, and the crown sitting on the table.

"A crown!" I snatched it up and placed it on my head.

Izzy bounced on the balls of her feet. "I knew you'd like that. Every girl wants to feel like a princess, or queen, on her birthday."

"Isn't that the truth." Drew cozied up beside me as Izzy drew the privacy curtain on her way out. "Is this the surprise?"

He leveled me with a gaze and laughed. "I have better surprises than the bar you frequent."

"There's nothing wrong with bringing me here," I quickly back pedaled, not realizing my question had come across in a negative way. "I love this place."

Drew squeezed my thigh as voices carried out onto the patio, the usual lunch time rush. I was thankful that Izzy had closed the privacy curtain. "They've made it a very welcoming place compared to the past owners."

"So, you've frequented here a lot?"

He nodded. "The name was different before—actually everything except the skeleton of the building has been changed. The man who ran it years back wasn't the friendliest. Always seemed pissed off at the world the majority of the time. It was no surprise when it went up on the market."

The thought of someone other than Gabby owning it crossed my mind. What a different life I'd probably be living if that was the case. Every instance snowballed into the next. Meaning, if Gabby didn't own *Side Street Drafts,* I most likely wouldn't have become a regular and in return, might not have met Drew or Izzy in the process. "I'm glad Gabby ended up purchasing it."

"Me too." Drew slid from the cushion and extended his hand to help me up. "How about we grab some drinks?"

"That sounds perfect."

He gripped the curtain and paused, a sly smile spreading

across his face, making my heart flop in my chest. As he pulled the curtain back and motioned for me to step forward, a handful of people erupted, "Happy birthday, Terra!"

The surprise of their smiling faces knocked the wind out of me. My hand flew to my chest as tears welled in my eyes. Gabby, Izzy, Eden, and the rest of the gang from *Side Street Drafts* stood before us. Gabby stepped forward with a beautiful floral cake that read *Happy Birthday Terra!* in bright pink letters.

Drew draped an arm around my shoulders, pulling me into his side. He kissed the top of my head. "Happy birthday, beautiful girl."

"Thank you all!" I choked out as Gabby sat the cake on the table beside where everyone stood.

"Do you want us to sing happy birthday?" Leon from the kitchen spoke up.

"Oh, no!" I covered my face with my hands. "Something about that song embarrasses the hell out of me."

"Oh, come on!" Drew knocked his shoulder into mine.

"Please, no." I slowly dropped my hands.

"Okay," Izzy placed her hands on her hips, "since it's your birthday we'll give you that as your one pass." She leaned forward, pretending to whisper, "And because we all know the majority of us can't sing worth a lick."

Laughter filled the air.

Eden groaned. "Birthdays are about embarrassing those we're celebrating." She moved around the small group and pulled me into a tight hug.

"How'd you know it was my birthday?" I squeezed her.

"One thing you'll learn is Drew doesn't let certain days go uncelebrated. He might not go to elaborate ends, but he'll make it clear that it's a special day. Especially for those he loves."

My cheeks heated and her grin widened. "He's a good man." I gazed at him laughing with some of the guys who worked in the kitchen.

"He's the best man I've ever known." The pride in Eden's voice made my heart swell.

From what I knew about Drew, there wasn't a bad bone in his body. Which was a vast difference than my initial view of him after our first encounter. I silently laughed at the thought of just how much I loathed the guy. I'd even given him a nickname before I'd known his actual name. That version of Drew seemed the polar opposite of his true self. I'd never uncovered why he'd been so verbally angry that day, and when the question had come up he'd danced around an answer. People had bad days, I was one who knew that better than anyone, but since that day I hadn't really experienced Drew having another bad one. Either he rarely had them, or he was a master at hiding those emotions.

The patio buzzed with chatter as Izzy went about cutting the cake and handing out pieces to everyone. Beautifully wrapped gifts sat on the table beside the remainder of the cake. I couldn't believe anyone had gotten me anything. I wasn't expecting a cake, let alone gifts. To be honest, I was expecting to spend the day curled up in bed with a pint of rocky road and an aching heart. But Drew had other plans.

With each bite of my slice of heaven, a satisfied groan passed my lips. "If you don't stop making those noises I'm going to have to cut this party short for the both of us." His nose brushed my ear as whispered words sent a chill across my heated skin.

"It's seriously that good, though."

His teeth grazed my ear. "You'll be saying that about me later." A knowing look passed between us, his buzzing cell phone breaking the trance. "I'll be right back."

"I'll be here." He kissed my lips and headed inside.

Eden rambled on with stories of their childhood as movement caught my eye in the doorway to the bar. The voices around me faded away as I watched Liam's parents—my in-laws—pass the threshold onto the patio. My heart stopped as I blinked a couple times, hoping like hell my eyes were playing tricks on me. But that wasn't the case. The roaring thump of my pulse blocked all sound around me.

I couldn't look away as Janet's eyes locked with mine and Brad shook Drew's hand. The realization of what was happening washed over me like a tidal wave. Drew had invited them. Without my consent, without my knowledge, he'd gone behind my back and invited the two people who could remove the stitches holding my fragile heart together to town for my birthday. Scenarios of how he'd gotten in contact with them quickly played out in my mind as Janet's beaming smile began to fade the closer they stepped toward me. Knowing the look on my face wasn't a happy one, I choked back the building emotions flooding through my veins and plastered on the best smile I could muster up.

"Terra." Janet's voice wavered as my name rolled off her tongue, piercing my heart like an arrow.

"Hi." My voice was small as she pulled me into a hug, the familiar citrus infused perfume that always filled their home engulfed my senses. I narrowed my eyes over her shoulder at Drew, the happiness adorning his face disappearing.

"It's good to see you, Terra." Janet's arms were replaced by Brad's.

I tried to swallow the lump in my throat, but it was far too large. My mouth opened and closed, words failing me as I attempted to say something—anything that wouldn't stir up heartache and pain between the three of us. But the only thing flashing through my mind was the fact that Liam had his father's eyes, his mother's smile, and my chest was caving in with each passing second.

"Excuse me." Before they could utter a response, I took off into the bar, bypassing Drew on the way, and went directly into the bathroom. My hands gripped the sink and my head hung between my shoulders. Inhaling deeply, I tried to calm my erratic heart beat but was interrupted when the door swung open and Janet stepped inside.

"Why are you running from us?" She blocked the door so I had nowhere to run, crossing her arms over her chest.

I squeezed my eyes shut and took a deep breath, letting it out slowly. I was on the brink of losing my shit. None of what was happening was Janet's fault, it was the cruel ways of life, and my own internal battle of learning to heal. But deep down in my bones I couldn't find the strength to endure the heartache of constantly being reminded of Liam by having a relationship with his parents. It was completely selfish, I knew that, but a part of me wasn't able to see past him when it came to them.

"Janet, I—" My brain couldn't produce a good reason that wouldn't rip the band aid from both our hearts.

"Don't you dare give me some shitty excuse, Terra. We love you..." Her voice cracked on the end, her shaky hand covered her mouth as she tried to gain her composure. "We love you like our own daughter, but you want nothing to do with us. Losing Liam made us lose you as well, it's not right, and we don't understand why you've pushed us away."

My body shook as nausea churned my gut and tears blurred my vision. "I can't do this." I shoved past her and yanked the bathroom door open, but she grabbed my arm before I could fully clear the doorway.

"Liam knew he was sick. That's what I've been trying to tell you for months now." Her voice was void of emotion as the world seemed to slow around me. *Liam knew he was sick?*

"No, he didn't." I frantically shook my head.

"He did, dammit." Her eyes softened. "He'd been diagnosed with a brain aneurysm a week before his death, the same type his father had surgery on decades ago."

"He didn't tell me..." My voice sounded foreign to my own ears.

Janet released her hold on my arm. "He was going to tell you,

Terra, he was…but he wanted more information about what his father had gone through before he broke the news to you. He thought there was more time. If any of us had known he would—"

"You all *knew!*" I stumbled back into a chair. "And no one bothered to tell *me*, his *wife!*" I spat, the words like venom spewing from my mouth. "I deserved to know…" I pounded a hand against my chest as I shoved the chair I'd stumbled into crashing to the floor and took off toward the front door, my name echoing through the empty bar. Nothing was going to stop me from leaving, not even Drew.

I tossed a hand in the air as a cab came into sight. Thanking the heavens, one was even in the area. Drew's voice filled the air behind me and I turned, hastily lifting a hand to stop him. "Don't." Anger vibrated the lone word. "How could you?" My head tilted and my chin quivered as a round of fat tears rolled down my face. I hastily got into the cab and instructed the driver to go as Drew's muffled pleas came from the other side of the window between us.

CHAPTER TWENTY

"What's the meter up to?" I asked the cabbie. He rattled off a number I wasn't expecting, but in reality, I should've expected it. We'd driven around the city for hours with no planned destination. Thankfully he didn't seem to mind since he'd be getting paid no matter what. "Here's fine."

His dark eyes stared at me through the rearview mirror. "You sure?" His eyebrows furrowed.

I shielded my swollen eyes with a pair of sunglasses I'd purchased when we'd stopped at a convenience store to get gas. "Yeah, I'm about out of cash." I extended every ounce of money I had on me and slipped from the cab.

"Have a good day." He shook the cash at me.

I waved as he drove off.

The weather had morphed from its sunny happiness to an overcast as if Mother Nature herself felt the sadness rolling through me. A humorless laugh escaped me as my eyes landed on the entrance to Love Park. "How ironic." I lifted my face toward the sky and closed my eyes for a moment, letting out a slow and steady breath.

Before I allowed the thoughts of how disastrous Drew's

surprise had been to seep in, I entered the park and found an open seat near the fountain. The cloudy sky must've run the usual crowd off due to the scarce amount of people lingering around. I let out a trembling breath as how the day had played out rushed my mind, unable to push the thoughts away.

I choked back a shaky cry as Drew's betrayal weighed heavy on me. *But was it actually a betrayal?* My internal voice made a good point. I'd never told him not to reach out to my in-laws, but I never in my wildest dreams figured he would. Most people don't go running to make friends or be civil with people from their significant other's past life, they avoid all contact. Who was I kidding though? Drew wasn't most people.

My life was in shambles and my mind had never been clearer.

A good majority was my own fault, I wasn't oblivious to that fact. For some damn reason, I couldn't get a grip on my emotions or find the strength to full on deal with the heartache left in the wake of Liam's death. I'd tried on numerous occasions to move forward, but was I truly moving forward? The answer was an easy one, because in fact I wasn't moving forward at all. If anything, with every couple of steps in the right direction, I'd find myself taking three steps back. I'd neglected myself and everyone who cared for me.

Janet's words rang in my ears...*Losing Liam made us lose you as well.*

I hadn't looked at it from her or Brad's perspective. Honestly, I'd only looked at it from my own. They were hurting just as badly as I was, and I'd only made that heartache worse by closing myself off from them. I was a part of their family when he was alive, and his passing didn't change that. Running from those who loved me didn't accomplish anything except causing more pain for everyone involved. I'd gone above and beyond for months trying to avoid them, trying to close them out of my life, when in reality I should've been embracing their love, and leaning on their shoulders when I needed someone who understood what I was feeling.

I'd caused the disastrous mess I called my life, and I was the only person who could make things right.

Being upset with Drew for getting them to Philadelphia didn't help matters either. His heart was bigger than most, and I knew he felt having me come face-to-face with them was the first step in the right direction of being able to heal. Even if him crossing those personal boundaries made me mad as hell.

I pulled my cell phone from my wristlet and powered it on as I flipped the switch on the side to silence it. It felt like eternity as the screen lit up and morphed until it settled on my home screen. Like rapid fire, over a dozen text messages and voicemails vibrated the device in my hand. Before I checked any of them I unblocked my in-law's numbers.

Laura's name popped up on the screen and my heart clenched. She was my closet friend in Ann Arbor, yet another person I'd pushed out of my life since I'd left. If I was going to turn over a new leaf, it needed to start by answering her call.

"Hey." My voice was small as I held the phone to my ear.

Scuffling came from the other end. "I can't believe you answered." The shock in her voice made me sad, letting me know just how much I'd hurt her.

"I'm sorry, Laura." Sorrow weighed heavy on my words.

"You know," she took a breath, "I planned out so much to say to you if I ever had the chance, but I wasn't expecting you to answer. Not today. I expected to leave a short voicemail wishing you a happy birthday and telling you how much I missed you, but you actually answered my call." Her humorless laughed filled my ear. "Then you apologize right off the bat." She scoffed. "I don't want your apology, Terra, I want my best friend back. I want to be able to talk to you about life, love, and everything else. I want to drink wine with you on the porch or at a local bar like we used to do. But losing Liam made you cut everyone out of your life. I never thought you would do that to me...not ever."

"Laura—"

"Let me finish," she spoke over me. "I can't say I understand what you've gone through losing your husband, because I've never had to go through that and pray I never will. I can't tell you how I'd handle any of it. Whether I'd do exactly like you did by running away from the life you had in search of something to fill that void isn't an answer I can give, but I hope like hell I would embrace those who love me. Because losing someone that holds a piece of your heart because they choose to leave is about as hard as losing someone to death."

Hearing the bitter truth of the heartache I'd caused sucked the air from my lungs and filled my eyes with unshed tears. "I never meant to hurt anyone. I honest to God mean that." I cleared my burning throat, not bothering to wipe away the stream of tears dampening my face. "Losing Liam changed me. It made me feel that the only way to heal my heart was to create a life where nothing from my past intertwined with the now. I know that sounds crazy, it sounds crazy to me as I say it, but that's how I rationalized my decisions. I'm sorry, Laura, I really am. You've been the best friend I could ever asked for and I miss you more than words can explain. I know an apology and explanation of why I've done what I've done isn't enough to fix this, but I hope like hell we can be friends again."

The line went silent and I checked the screen, afraid she'd hung up or we'd gotten disconnected but the call was still connected. "We shouldn't have had this conversation on your birthday, Ter."

I laughed. Even still she was thinking about my wellbeing. "This day was ruined before it ever got started."

"I really hate to hear that." She sighed. "Is Philadelphia not treating you well? I, um, know you're there from Janet."

"There's no need to explain. I'm glad she passed on the information. You deserved to know where I moved to just like they did. I've treated every single one of you wrong for my own selfish reasons."

"Don't dwell on it, just make a change. If Philadelphia isn't everything you thought it might be, pack up and move. I'm not saying you should move back here, even though I'd love for you to, I'm just saying you have the ability to find your happiness. You deserve to find happiness again, so don't settle for anything less."

Tears brimmed my barely dry eyes. "Here's the thing." I coughed and wiped my nose on my sleeve. "I've found happiness, but like everything else in my life, I've second guessed it and pushed him away."

"Him."

I exhaled a heavy breath. "I feel so guilty for it, Laura."

"You don't feel guilty because of Liam, do you?"

A hiccupped cry bubbled up my throat. "Of course I do."

"Terra, honey, he wouldn't want you to feel that way. Liam would've wanted you to move on with your life. To find happiness and love again. Not to live each day with the sorrow and loneliness of being without him. You don't need to be so hard on yourself."

"I think I love him." I wiped beneath my eyes.

"There's no thinking you love someone, Terra. Either you do or you don't, and by what you're saying, I feel that you do love him. And I don't even know the guy."

She was right, I loved Drew. I hadn't thought I could love another man, especially after how deeply I loved Liam. Our relationship was one for romance novels, and I wasn't ready to let that go. Loving another man meant making room in my heart for it, could I do that? I'm not sure why I even asked myself the question because, love doesn't give you a choice. It comes in like storm winds, making itself known.

"Life is so damn hard." I dropped my head into my hands.

"If it was easy it wouldn't be worth it."

Laura was the voice of reason when I needed it the most. "You're right."

"Damn straight I'm right."

A giggled rolled up my throat. "Not just about life, but about me loving Drew."

"Drew." I could hear the smile in her voice. "I like that name. Hopefully I'll also like the man who owns it."

"I'm sure you'll love him."

"Just hearing you say that makes me happy." Muffled voices filled the background on Laura's end. "I hope this isn't the last time you answer my calls."

Guilt weighed heavy on my shoulders. "It won't be, I promise."

"It's good to hear your voice again."

"Yours too, Laura."

"Talk to you soon."

I dropped my phone into my lap and stared at the cement. Inhaling the biggest breath I could muster up, I let it out slowly and cracked my neck. Exhaustion beat me down, but without my house keys there was no way to go home. Unless I sucked it up and gave Drew a call, begging him to pick me up and take me home, apologizing for running out like a lunatic. But I couldn't bring myself to call him. Even if he meant well, the fact that he stepped over that line without consulting me first still weighed on me. No one was perfect, but the fact that he'd done it bothered me.

The clouds had moved away just in time for the setting sun to make its appearance. The sky was blazing with beautiful hues of reds, pinks, and blues that stretched like a blaze across the horizon. The gorgeous sight brought back memories of lying in his arms watching the sun set.

The park lights came to life as the sun slowly disappeared. Tears slipped from my eyes as I lifted to my feet, hugging my midriff tightly in an attempt to console myself. My heels clanked against the concrete as I rounded the LOVE statue, glaring at its bold red letters. "Love," I scoffed, "why are you even here."

"It's here because people fought for it be here."

I turned on my heel. "People cared that much about a statue?"

Drew shoved his hands into his front pockets. "In 1976 the statue was first placed here in John F. Kennedy Plaza, and in 1978 it was removed. Over time, more and more people demanded its return and here it is. If you think about it, the removal of the statue was like love leaving the city. The people fought for love and were given it." He closed the distance between us and unraveled my hands from around my waist, taking them in his own. "This is me fighting for love, Terra. I shouldn't have put you in that position." He ran a hand through his disheveled hair. "I thought you needed a push in the right direction. But that push shouldn't have come from me. I had no right, I know that now. Just know that I meant well, even if it was a total disaster."

I pulled my hands from his. "I appreciate your apology, I really do, but you had no right to do that. We barely know one another —actually you know a hell of a lot more about me than I know about you if we're being honest here."

"I—I don't know what to say." His eyes dropped to the cement.

"Tell me something I don't know about you, something personal. More than your favorite color or movie."

His eyes lifted to mine, glassed over with unshed tears. I stood there waiting for him to say something—anything, but the silence continued to hang in the air and my heart began to crack parallel to the break Liam's death caused.

I tossed my arms wide. "You can't even give me a small piece of you, Drew. There's something wrong with that." I turned to walk away hoping he'd stop me but the further I got the more I realized he wasn't going to. A sob ripped from my chest, and I covered my mouth with a shaky hand to try and suppress the next one. My emotions were getting the best of me, so I stopped walking and knelt to the ground, curling in on myself as silent sobs shook my body.

Arms wrapped around me and lifted me to my feet. Drew was silently crying as he held me against his chest. "I lost my fiancée."

His words caused my heart to falter. "Drew..."

He shook his head. "The day you ran into me outside of Magnolia's was the fourth anniversary of her death."

"That's why you were so angry."

A sad smile tipped his mouth. "It's not." My heart bottomed out, not understanding what he was saying. "I was an asshole because—" He laughed. Not a humorless laugh like you'd expect, but a genuine happy laugh that threw me for a loop. "You made me feel something I hadn't felt in many years. I sound like a fool, I know, but it confused me. No one in four years had caused my heart to leap out of my chest like you did by trampling me to the ground and tossing snarky words in my direction." He brushed his hand against my face, wiping away my tears.

"I'm so sorry about your fiancée." I hugged him tightly.

"Can we get out of here?" He rubbed a soothing hand across my back.

I nodded. "Please."

* * *

I bent to unbuckle my shoes just inside the door and yelped as Drew hoisted me into his arms before I could get the first heel off. "What are you doing?" I bubbled with laughter.

He carried me into the kitchen and sat me on the counter. His deft fingers unbuckled each strap around my ankles with ease and slipped them from my feet. I moaned as he lifted one foot into his hands and massaged the aching sole, over the arch, and the soft skin on each side of the Achilles tendon before moving to the next.

My arms snaked around his neck. "Thank you for that."

"I owe you more than a foot rub."

I kissed the tip of his nose. "Yeah, you kind of do."

"I really am sorry."

"I know you are. Thank you for opening up to me."

His eyes searched mine. "I should've done it sooner. You've been pretty open with me since day one."

"Which isn't like me at all." I laughed.

"Well," he pressed his lips to mine, "I'm glad you've been that way with me." Drew rested his forehead against mine and we sat in silence.

I lifted a hand to cup his cheek. "Will you tell me what happened to your fiancée?" My voice was barely above a whisper as the question passed my lips.

Drew's eyes softened and he stepped back from my hold. I was afraid he'd close in on himself, but I needed to hear the story. I needed to know if he would confide in me the parts of life that scarred his heart. Like I'd confided my own scars to him.

"We lived in St. Louis." He turned away and walked over to the windows. "I was out of town at the time, looking at the property that's now Cabot's Cellar." His humorless laugh broke my heart. "I begged her to go with me, but she was studying for The Bar Exam she was scheduled to take the following week. I had all the faith in the world that she'd pass it, but I understood why she felt the need to continue to study up until the day of. Her dream was to have her own law firm, a dream that never got fulfilled." Drew poured himself a drink from the bar cart at the far end of the large windows while I sat on the counter watching him, with sorrow aching my chest. "Everything happened so quickly." He downed the half glass of Scotch and poured another. "I'd spoken to her right after I'd boarded the plane, letting her know I'd call her as soon as we'd landed in Philadelphia, but to my surprise when I powered my phone on, more than a dozen voicemails and urgent text messages awaited me. She'd gone out to pick up Chinese for dinner from her favorite little spot in a sketchy part of town when it happened. Farrah was the type of woman who would stare fear in the eyes and laugh if it tried to intimidate her. Strong willed, bullheaded even, traits I never seemed to mind until that day..." He cleared his throat before taking a nice pull from the glass.

The agony and sorrow in his words sliced through me like a knife. I was frozen in place sitting on the counter as I awaited the horror story I knew was about to come. He kept his back to me as he lifted his free hand and placed it on the window, staring out at the night skyline of the city below. "When I think about that day, every scene unfolds like a slow-motion movie. I'd spotted my bag on the terminal when the first frantic voicemail from her mother began to play. I couldn't make out the words she was saying, only *call me back as soon as you get this* at the end of the message was spoken clear enough through her sobs for me to understand." He dropped his head forward, putting his weight in the hand that was pressed against the glass. "Farrah was killed during a carjacking."

Those six words sent a chill across my flesh. Fat tears relentlessly rolled from my eyelids. I slid from the counter and crossed the room, not stopping until my front pressed against Drew's back and my arms snaked tightly around his waist. I rested my cheek against his spine. "Saying I'm sorry doesn't help anything, I know that firsthand, but I don't know what else to say."

He sat his empty glass on the bar cart and turned to face me. His hands rose to cup my face. "You don't have to say a single word. Life threw me a curveball. One that shattered every dream I had for the future. I'd only been surviving since then, trying to find something to fill the void in my heart from losing Farrah. A ghost of my previous self. Nothing touched that void until I met you." His laughter was music to my ears. "You literally came barreling into my life out of nowhere, Terra."

A sad smile settled on my lips. "Life hasn't been an easy road for either of us."

"No, it hasn't." Drew wrapped his arms around my waist and pulled me in closer. "I have faith that's about to change."

An unexpected yawn escaped me. "I hope you're right."

"Tired?"

"Completely wiped out." I finger combed the tangled ends of my hair.

He took my hand in his and guided us back the short hallway to the bedroom. I sat on the corner edge of the bed as he rummaged through his dresser drawers.

"Here." He tossed a plain white t-shirt at me.

I held it in the air. "What's this for?" I cocked an eyebrow.

He ran a hand through his messy hair, stopping on the back of his neck. "Would you rather go home?"

I discarded my shirt and wiggled out of my jeans. Drew's eyes raked over my bare flesh as I slipped my bra from my body and pulled the white t-shirt over my head. "All I want are some snuggles and sleep."

The corner of his mouth tipped as he crossed the room. "I can help you with both."

"It would be greatly obliged." My arms snaked around his neck as his lips found mine. The rich taste of Scotch lingered on his tongue.

We moved up the mattress and he pulled the comforter back so I could slip beneath on the side I'd designated as my own. Drew kicked his jeans off and yanked the polo over his head and snuggled beneath the comforter with me. Pulling me into his chest, I shoved my arm beneath his pillow so I could get as close as possible to him. I let out a heavy breath in an attempt to push the stress of the day away. Drew's breathing evened out and I laid there with my head on his side, taking in the calming feeling of the rise and fall of his chest.

Just as I thought he'd fallen asleep, his hand glided beneath the oversized shirt and soothingly stroked my spine. "You awake?"

"Mmhmm."

"The main reason I invited your in-laws was because I pushed away those closest to me after Farrah's death. For years, I avoided contact with her family, the friends we'd made together, and even the friends I'd had before her. It's a coping mechanism to push away those who care about you when a tragedy happens, and it isn't healthy. You end up with regrets and lost time. It can even burn bridges that can't be repaired. I didn't want that for you. Sorry doesn't fix what I did, but I hope time will."

I pressed my lips against his bare chest and sighed. "Do you believe in fate?"

Drew readjusted so he could see my face, a storm of emotions brewing deep in his hazel eyes. "I do now."

CHAPTER TWENTY-ONE

S weat coated my palms as I stared up at the building where my in-laws where staying, hoping they hadn't checked out yet. Drew had given me their hotel information without any fuss when I'd asked as soon as his eyes opened. I needed to make amends. Going about life with unneeded bad blood between us wasn't how I wanted to live. Liam wouldn't have wanted it either.

I kept replaying how things unfolded on my birthday. The guilt rearing its head wasn't leaving anytime soon, not until I hashed things out with Janet and Brad. I entered the building and quickly found the elevators as the doors were closing on one headed up. "Hold the elevator!" I ran as fast as my legs would move and slid between the doors. "Thank you." I bent at the waist trying to catch my breath.

The elderly man who had held the door for me nodded. "No problem at all, young lady."

My foot nervously tapped against the tiled floor as we ascended. What should've been a short trip to the twelfth floor felt like an eternity. The elderly man exited on the sixth floor after telling me to have a good day, leaving me alone for the remainder of the ride. No sooner than the doors opened on the twelfth floor, I took off like a bat out of hell. I stopped at the end of the hall to quickly examine the arrows and room numbers posted on the wall so I knew which way to go. I hastily turned left, and hurried down the long corridor catching the room numbers with each passing step. My heart sank as what should've been their room came into view; a cart sat just outside the door with two women inside stripping the bed of linens and collecting used towels.

I didn't bother asking them if they'd seen the room occupants when they'd shown up to clean, because I knew they hadn't. With my head hung low, I started back to the elevator. I pulled my phone from my pocket and typed out a message to Drew, letting him know by the time I'd arrived they were already gone. The last resort was calling Janet, but I didn't want to hash things out over the phone. I'd never liked handling personal matters over the phone if it could be avoided.

The first thing on my mind when I'd woken up at Drew's was finding my in-laws. He wanted to join me, but understood when I declined. It was something I had to do on my own, without an audience of any sorts.

The lobby was buzzing with conversations of people coming and going from the hotel. I didn't pay much attention to any of it as I made my way through the front doors, pulling up the app to request an Uber for the ride to my apartment. The last text I'd received from Drew stated he would meet me there, he knew not finding them would ruin my morning. There weren't enough kind words in the dictionary to explain how thankful I was for him.

The temperature change from stepping outside made me cringe. It was hotter than it had been in days, and that was saying something. The sun casted a glare on the screen of my phone, making it hard to schedule an Uber. I searched for shade and found a sliver of it up against the building.

"Terra?"

My head whipped in the direction of her voice. "I thought you were gone." I closed out of the app and slid my phone back into my pocket.

"What are you doing here?" Janet was standoffish, totally understandable after our last encounter.

"Looking for you."

Her head jerked back with surprise. "Why would you be looking for us?" She crossed her arms over her chest.

"I wanted to talk." My throat bobbed as I tried to swallow the lump forming.

She waved me to follow her. "Come on, I need to see if they found my cell phone."

With a curt nod I followed her back into the hotel and straight to the front desk. A woman in a navy-blue polo smiled as we reached the desk. "Hi, how can I help you?"

"Well," Janet sighed and rested an elbow on the desk, "I seemed to have lost my cell phone. With everything that happened last night with our room, it must've gotten lost in the bustle of things. Do you mind asking the cleaning people if they've found it? Or has anyone turned one in?"

"Of course!" The woman smiled as she typed away on the keyboard in front of her. "I need the first and last name the room's under and we can go from there."

"It should be under Janet Anders."

"Oh," her eyebrows pulled to the center, "I'm sorry you had those issues with your room. If you could give me just a moment I'll be right back." The girl slipped through a door directly behind where she stood.

Janet turned to me and sighed. "This is a very nice hotel, and even though we've had some issues here, they've taken care of everything with ease."

"That's good to know."

Her chin lifted and fell. "Good business."

"Mrs. Anders?"

"Yes?" We simultaneously answered. Janet shot me a confused

look before turning her attention to the woman behind the counter.

"They indeed found your cell phone. It was by the ice machine just down from your old room." She extended the phone to Janet.

"Oh, thank you so very much." She shoved it into her purse with a smile.

"If you need anything else during your stay, feel free to let us know."

"I appreciate that." Janet turned her attention to me. "Come on." I followed her toward the elevators.

"So, you haven't checked out?" I leaned against the wall as we awaited the elevator.

She shook her head. "No, last night our room started leaking around the window seal when that quick storm blew through, so they ended up moving our room."

"That's horrible. I didn't even know it stormed."

"Nothing was ruined, so it wasn't that bad." The elevator dinged and we quickly boarded. "I'm sure you didn't know it stormed if you were spending time with that beautiful man, Drew." She rose a perfectly manicured eyebrow. I could feel the heavy blush wash over my face as I did my best to keep my composure. "You don't have to tell me anything." She waved a dismissive hand as we came to a stop on the fifth floor. "This is us." She motioned for me to go first.

My heart thundered from her words. "Is it weird?"

"Is what weird?"

"Me being with someone else." I followed her around the corner.

Janet stopped and took my hands in hers. "Liam's gone, honey. We all know that. You moving on isn't weird, it's life. We only want you to be happy, Terra." I blinked back the tears filling my eyes. "The last thing I would ever want for you is to look back years from now and wish you'd made other choices."

She was right. Moving on wasn't weird, my insecurities were

pulling those red flags up the flag pole on their own. "I can't shake the feeling that I'm doing something wrong. I know I'm a widow now, but…I don't know…maybe I'm being crazy."

Janet gently touched my arm. You're not being crazy, you're still grieving."

Grieving Liam was something I'd do for the rest of my days. I was sure of that. He played a huge role in my life, he was my first true love. I didn't know if it was possible to ever fully shake that kind of loss, and I wasn't sure I wanted to.

"You know," Janet paused, "I'm surprised you kept the last name."

"Anders? Why does that surprise you?"

She nodded. "Figured you would've taken your maiden name back after the way things have gone."

Guilt washed over me like a hangover. I hated the fact I'd made her think that way. Being selfish of my own journey toward healing was the culprit. I hadn't considered how others who loved Liam were feeling.

She placed the key card against the door handle and shoved it open. "Brad, look what the cat drug in." Janet held the door for me.

Brad peered over the rim of his glasses. "Well, hopefully this goes better than last time."

I deserved that.

"Be nice." She leveled him with her almond hued eyes.

He folded the newspaper he'd been reading and placed it on the end table. "My apologies." He lifted from the chair.

Even though his words stung, I mustered up a smile. "It's fine. I definitely deserved it."

Brad shook his head and removed the readers from his eyes. "No, you didn't deserve that. Nobody deserved anger spat at them when they're hurting too. I just hate seeing my wife cry when there's nothing she, nor I, can do to fix things."

I crossed the room and hugged Brad. Words didn't suffice. He hesitated, but after a few passing moments he wrapped his arms around me and softly squeezed. "I don't know what to say." My words were a gargled mess.

"Coming here says enough."

A round of tears sped down my cheeks and I hastily wiped them away as I stepped from his hold. My in-laws were genuinely good people. I'd been blessed with them. Some wouldn't be as understanding giving the circumstances, but Janet and Brad were. Not to mention Janet was one persistent woman when it came to things she believed in and people she loved.

"I'd like to talk about what Liam knew." Like instinct, my fingers reached for the wedding band that no longer adorned my ring finger. I'd placed it safely in my jewelry box, knowing it was time to remove it. A slight grin settled on my lips from the ping of sadness that hit me in the chest from its absence.

"Okay." Janet's voice was small.

We hadn't gone further into the room than the seating area of the suite, but just from the looks of it, they'd definitely gotten the better end of the deal after the flooding fiasco. Brad motioned for everyone to have a seat as he lowered himself back into the chair he'd been sitting in. Janet sat beside me as I faced the two of them.

Brad cleared his throat. "Liam came to us about a week before his death." He leaned forward and clasped his hands between his knees. "He'd been having headaches, thought they were from everyday stress, but his doctor found a similar aneurysm to the one I had many years ago. He knew I'd had the surgery to repair mine, and the doctor even offered that as an option for his, but he wanted to speak with me first. To see how the recovery and everything was. No, they weren't located in the same spot, so it wouldn't be completely the same procedure and recovery, but it gave him an idea."

Janet wiped beneath her eyes. "Only fifteen percent of people who encounter an aneurysmal subarachnoid hemorrhage die before getting medical treatment. Fifteen percent. A number low enough to give people hope that they won't fall into the bracket, but Liam had."

"Why didn't he tell me?" I whispered, knowing my voice wasn't strong enough to speak much louder.

Janet gave my knee a pat. "He wanted to, he was going to. But he wanted all the information from his test results, and to speak with us first. Liam loved you more than anything, Terra. He was afraid to tell you, but only because he knew how much you'd worry. That's one of the last things he would want to burden you with. He told me that himself."

"We made it very clear that he needed to tell you." Brad sat back in the chair. "Janet warned him that she would tell you if he didn't, but I told her that wasn't our place. Liam agreed once he received his bloodwork results he would sit you down and go over everything. There just wasn't enough time before it claimed his life."

"I'd be lying if I said it didn't hurt hearing that he knew and hadn't told me. But I understand why he chose to wait. I hate that he died beforehand, but hanging on to that resentment will only stain Liam's memory for me. He always tried to do what's best for others, I wish we'd had more time."

"We do too, sweetie." Janet blew her nose on a tissue and extended the box in my direction. "Never could I've imagined I'd bury my son." She lost all composure as those words rolled off her tongue. Brad dropped to his knees and pulled her into an embrace as she cried out the sorrow ailing her heart against his shoulder.

The chance of losing your husband is something you expect to happen when you're old and grey, not in your thirties. But I couldn't imagine the anguish they felt from losing their son. That's something that shouldn't cross a parent's mind, because in most cases the child buries the parent, not the other way around.

As Janet's sobs subsided, Brad sat back in the chair. "That Drew seems like a well put together man." A knowing grin crinkled the skin around his grey eyes.

Hearing Drew's name had my heart flopping like a fish out of water. The feeling took me back to my younger days when I'd had a crush on some boy at school. Except Drew wasn't some boy, he was a man who I'd developed intense feelings for.

"That he does," Janet chimed in with a smile.

I diverted my eyes to a picture of the LOVE statue hanging on the wall behind where Brad sat. "He's a really good man."

Janet tucked a leg beneath her. "If you don't mind me asking," a wide grin spread across her face as she pipped up, "is it getting serious?

"Janet…" Brad scolded. "That's none of our business."

I chuckled and waved a dismissive hand. "It's fine, really." I brought my eyes to Janet's and tucked my bottom lip between my teeth, trying to hide the happiness talking about Drew brought me. "It's kind of serious, I guess."

"Kind of?" Janet arched an eyebrow. "There's no kind of serious, honey. It either is or it isn't."

"Okay," my face heated, "it's getting there. He wants it to be further along than it is, and I'm still pumping the brakes at every turn. I'm pretty sure I'm holding back because of Liam."

Janet's playful smile faded to an understanding grin. "I've never had to deal with losing my husband before, but I do know Liam wouldn't want you to let a good man pass you by. If it feels right, jump in head first. Ninety percent of the time, regrets are harder to swallow than mistakes."

The way Drew made me feel reminded me of Liam. They were similar, yet different all at the same time. I loved Liam with everything I had, and those feelings would forever be there. But if I was going to allow Drew into my life, I had to let go of a fraction of Liam to make room for him in my heart. A portion of me knew I already had, but I needed to convince the other portion of myself that it was okay to do so. I needed to learn how to stop second guessing what the right thing to do was and simply follow my heart…because my heart made it loud and clear exactly how it felt.

* * *

When I'd arrived at my apartment I knew Drew would be waiting, but the sight of his car sitting at the curb just down from the building had me smiling from ear-to-ear. A smile that wouldn't fade as I rode the elevator and stepped into my apartment.

It stretched even further, causing my cheeks to burn, as my eyes landed on him stretched across the small couch fast asleep. I almost didn't want to wake him, but I knew he'd give me the third degree if I didn't. With my hand on his shoulder, I gently rocked him. "Drew." I rocked him again, this time his eyes opened and a sleep filled smirk tipped his lips.

"Hey." His voice was scratchy as he sat up and stretched his arms.

"Hey, sleepyhead."

He fingered through his hair and checked his watch for the time. "I hadn't meant to fall asleep."

"It's fine."

"Is it really seven?"

I confirmed with a nod. "Thank you." His hair felt silky smooth as I ran my hand through it, stopping on his cheek.

"For what?" Confusion swam in his sleep filled eyes.

"For giving me the push I needed to make things right with Liam's parents. I'm not so sure I would've ever convinced myself to do it without you pushing me. Without you bringing the elephant into the room and making me face what was right in front of me."

He squeezed my thigh. "I don't need praise."

"I know you don't."

He leaned forward and pressed his lips against mine. "I'd do anything for you. Whether that be pushing you out of your comfort zone, cooking you breakfast, throwing a birthday get together that blows up in my face," I couldn't stop myself from giggling, "or simply just spending time with you. I'm here. As long as I'm breathing, I'll always be here."

I sat there for a moment gazing into his eyes as his words filled not only my head, but my heart. "I love you."

His eyes glassed over and his hand wrapped around the back of my neck, pulling my mouth to his. No words were spoken as we lost ourselves in one another. I could spend the remainder of my life kissing Drew. It felt natural, like we were two pieces of a puzzle that fit together even with their frayed edges.

With his hands still holding the back of my neck he leaned back just enough to look into my eyes. "I love you, too, Terra. So damn much." He softly kissed my lips and lifted from the couch. "Stay right here."

"Okaaay." Anticipation pulsed throughout my veins as Drew hurried down the hall. A few long minutes passed before I heard a bit of a ruckus behind where I sat on the couch. I twisted to peer over the top and squealed as Drew came walking into the room with arms full of gifts.

With a megawatt smile, he placed the packages on the coffee table. "Thought you might want these."

I jumped to my feet and tossed my arms around his neck. "Thank you! I hadn't even thought about where these were."

With a chuckle, Drew lifted me off the floor. "It was a tiring day." The sadness lacing his words had me hugging him even tighter.

"Where should I start?" I rubbed my hands together as we both took a seat on the couch. He handed me a gift bag with a smile. Opening gifts reminded me of being a child. The excitement pulses through you as anticipation spikes until your eyes lay on the gift inside. On most occasions happiness fills your heart from what those who care about you thought you would enjoy for your birthday, Christmas, and even your wedding day.

We spent the next half hour going through the gifts and making note of who got me what so I could be sure to thank them. Each gift I'd received meant more than words could express. I'd uprooted my life back in Ann Arbor and made a new home in Philadelphia without a single friend around. To my surprise, in the short amount of time I'd called Philly home, I'd been blessed with more love than deserved.

As I gathered the ripped gift wrapping and tissue paper, I hadn't realized Drew had disappeared from the room. "Where'd you go?" Silence answered me. "Drew." I padded back the hallway and almost rammed into him coming out of my bedroom. "What are you doing?" I cocked an eyebrow in question.

"Nothing." His attempt at hiding the guilt written across his face was laughable.

"You're up to something."

He grinned and stepped around me. "Come back in here." I followed him back over to the couch and lowered myself onto a cushion. "This is from Janet and Brad." Drew pulled a small red box from his pocket and handed it to me.

I pulled one end of the silk bow and cracked the lid open. Tears engulfed my eyes as I took in the beautiful necklace staring back at me, the pendant filled with dried flower petals. Janet had preserved some of the rose petals we'd tossed into the water with Liam's ashes. I lifted the necklace from the box, my hands shaking as I held it closer to my eyes to take in its beauty. It was remarkable how the petals looked frozen in time, a reminder of the day I'd said goodbye to my first true love. A trinket I would have for all eternity.

"This is—" I let out a shaky breath.

Drew gave my leg a light squeeze. "It's very thoughtful."

My eyes lifted to his. "It is." I wiped a round of tears from beneath my eyes as he took the necklace and latched it around my neck. My fingers rubbed the cool surface of the charm as I closed my eyes. In that moment I felt closer to Liam than I had since his passing.

"Are you okay?"

I clasped my hand over his resting on my thigh. "Yeah." He pulled his hand from beneath mine and produced yet another small box from his other pocket. "Where else do you have gifts hiding?"

He slyly grinned. "You'll have to search for yourself."

I smoothed my hands up his thighs and skirted them beneath the hem of his shirt. "You know I will."

"That's exactly what I'm hoping for, but first you have to open this gift." He extended the polka dot wrapped box. "It's the last one, I promise."

I hastily tore the wrapping and lifted the top from the box. A single gold bangle perched on white cushioning shined. I lifted the bangle from the box to read the inscription on the outside. Coordinates sat on each side of a date. "This is stunning."

"The coordinates are Magnolia's, while the date is when you first ran into me outside their front door."

My heart overflowed with love. His gift had more than a little thought put into it. Drew had gone above and beyond to find something meaningful, something I'd cherish. He amazed me at every turn.

I slipped it onto my wrist and stared in wonder. "It's perfect."

"Almost as perfect as you." He leaned his forehead against mine.

"You're going to give a girl a giant head."

A lopsided grin tipped the corner of his mouth. "I've got something like that for you." He tackled me backwards as a fit of laughter erupted between us but was quickly cut short as his lips collided with mine.

It's crazy how your heart and soul are searching for something even when you're not aware of their journey. Mine had been looking for tomorrow since I'd lost Liam. Never in my wildest dreams did I imagine finding my tomorrow within the arms of Drew Cabot, but that's exactly where it laid in wait for me.

EPILOGUE

"Life's a fucking roller-coaster, that's for sure." Cora slouched back in the metal folding chair and kicked one leg over the other, her black lace up boots worn so badly on the toes the black had faded to grey.

"As cliché as I'm about to sound, it does get better with time."

Cora scoffed, "It needs to hurry the hell up then."

"Try looking at the good in things for once, Cor," Sidney, Cora's sister, chimed in.

Cora leveled her with a glare so fierce I felt it myself. "Not everyone lives a cookie cutter life."

Sidney's face morphed from optimistic to heartbroken. "Come on now. I know what you're dealing with, I'm trying to help you."

Cora crossed her arms over her chest. "Why don't you try keeping your mouth shut for once, that would be helpful."

"Cora…" I shook my head at her.

Sidney's chair screeched across the floor as she scooted away from the table, hastily collected her things and tossed the straps of her purse onto her shoulder. "I love you, Cora, but I'm not taking your cruel words any longer." When Cora didn't bother to respond, Sidney took off toward the exit.

Cora dropped her head into her hands and groaned.

"You've got to learn how to not push people away. It'll make you feel a hundred times better in the long run."

Cora's tear hazed eyes lifted to mine. "It's like I can't stop myself from being a bitch to her."

I placed a hand on her shoulder. "We'll work on ways for you to cope with the pent-up anger, okay? Give me a minute."

She nodded.

I hurried toward the exit and pushed through the double doors. "Sidney, wait!" I tried to catch her before she reached her vehicle but was too late. Tossing both of my hands in the air waving, I hoped she'd see me in the rearview mirror, but that wasn't the case. My head dropped as I watched her silver sedan disappear around the curve.

"Terra?"

I turned and smiled. "Hey, you."

"Session over early?"

My head rocked side-to-side. "Things got a little intense. I was trying to flag down Sidney."

Drew pulled me into his arms. "If everything in life was easy, there would be nothing to live for."

I smiled against his chest. "You and your wisdom." Stepping back from his arms, I finger combed the ends of my curled hair and hooked a thumb toward the building's entrance. "I need to get back in there and do damage control with Cora."

"Of course." He kissed my lips. "I'll be in the car." He pointed two rows back.

"Hopefully it won't be too much longer."

Drew held a hand up. "Take all the time you need. They can wait on us."

I knew that wasn't true but loved the fact he didn't hurry me along given the circumstances. With my hand on the door handle, I exhaled a heavy breath. Some days were more trying than others, but I wouldn't trade a single one for anything else.

One day, while reading the local paper, I found an ad looking for volunteers to help run a support group for people struggling with an array of sorrows. Something deep in my soul told me to apply. Fast forward two years, and I found myself running my own support group, trying to help others find their tomorrow, much like I'd found mine. It might not be in another person, but tomorrow is out there for everyone. The dawn of a new day, with a breath of fresh air to begin again. Living a life that didn't choke the happiness out of you is attainable. Drew was my first step to finding that, and the support group was the second.

My leg bounced as we turned onto the winding road I'd become all too familiar with. Drew's hand capped my knee and gave it a gentle squeeze. I turned my face away from the window and focused on his neatly groomed face. His tanned skin, from our vacation to the Caribbean a few weeks back, made his hazel eyes standout even more. Those green flakes danced with happiness. "I'm proud of you." He smiled.

I covered his hand with my own. "Where did that come from?"

He lifted my hand to his lips and pressed them against the flesh below my knuckles. "Just thinking about how far you've come. Watching you chase after your dreams has been an inspiration for me." The car came to a stop. "We wouldn't be about to step inside the grand opening of the second location of Cabot's Cellar if it hadn't been for you."

A grin wider than the Grand Canyon stretched my face as I took in our surroundings. Tons of vehicles filled the parking lot already. Drew had a dream of opening a winery, a dream that turned into more than he could've asked for by blessing him with the ability to open a second location just outside of Boston. One location was a huge accomplishment in itself, but two...that was beyond anything he had dreamt of.

Hearing him say that he was proud of *me*, that I was the reason he'd been able to open his second location filled my heart with joy. Drew coming into my life had taken me by surprise. We were a storm cloud raging with thunder and heavy rain at first, but as our heartaches flashed like angry lightening, we became a sunny sky that neither of us had in quite some time. Over time, he'd helped me find the balance of peace, love, and happiness I'd thought I'd lost when Liam left this world.

"We've come a long way in a little over two years."

"Seems like a lifetime already, huh?" He pulled me into his chest and kissed my forehead, his lips lingering a moment longer than usual. His nose brushed mine as he lowered his chin in search of my anticipating lips. The kiss was slow and full of passion as his hand flattened against my lower back, scooting my body further into his.

"It does." My whispered words were quickly swallowed as his tongue danced with mine.

The driver cleared his throat. "I'll give you two some privacy." The driver's door opened and closed, but we didn't miss a beat exploring one another.

That familiar flutter in my abdomen took a furious flight as my fingers deftly unbuttoned the top two buttons on his navy dress shirt. To my surprise, his hand wrapped around mine to stop me. I pulled back and searched his face for any indication that I'd done something wrong, but the only emotion I could find was pure admiration staring back at me. "Not here." His breathy words eased the questioning of my thoughts. "I love you, Terra."

"I love you, too."

He let out a puff of air. "Marry me." His gruff words sent my heart into overdrive as the realization of what he was saying hit me like a freight train.

My hands shook as I brought them to my mouth. Tears blurred my vision as Drew produced a small grey box and popped it open.

I gasped as a single princess cut diamond stared back at me, much larger than any I'd laid eyes on before. I bobbed my head as words failed me. Drew was asking me to spend the rest of my life with him, to be his forever, and without hesitation I'd said yes.

Sobs ripped from my chest as he slid the ring onto my finger. A familiar feeling washed through me. Both happiness and sorrow filled my heart. I loved Drew with my entire being, just as I'd loved Liam. So, I knew that making it official was the right step for us. I felt it deep in my soul, but I'd be lying if I didn't admit that thoughts of Liam proposing washed in.

Drew hugged me tightly. "I didn't mean to make you cry."

"How could you expect me not to?" I laughed through the tears.

He chuckled. "I hate to ruin our moment, but we need to go inside." His voice was barely above a whisper.

I slowed my breathing and wiped beneath my eyes, pulling a mirror from my clutch and inspecting how much damage control my face needed. For once though, I didn't care. My red blotchy face wasn't from the heart shattering parts of life, it was from happiness. The promise of forever with a man I loved more than life itself. "I'm ready." My cheeks burned from the smile still lifting them.

"We can wait if need be."

I shook my head. "I'm beyond fine. Let's go inside and get this shindig started."

Drew opened his door and slipped from the vehicle. He leaned forward and extended a hand for me to take. Getting out of the car was a task in the sweetheart mermaid gown I'd settled on. Simple, yet elegant in its cream blush tone. It paired nicely with Drew's grey suit and navy dress shirt.

With my hand encased in his, he helped me maneuver from the vehicle and fixed the small train behind me. His arm wrapped around my waist, his hand settling low on my hip as we passed through the double doors and into the ballroom. I paused as many familiar faces filled the room.

Drew leaned close to my ear. "I might've lied about this being opening night." He kissed the soft spot just behind my ear, sending a chill across my skin.

Gabby's beaming face with those red glasses perched on her nose filled my sight. "You little shit!" She lifted my hand and directed her narrowed eyes at Drew. "You didn't wait!" she scoffed.

"The moment felt right, I had to go with it."

Gabby slapped his arm and pulled me into a bear hug. "Congratulations, you two deserve all the happiness in the world."

"Is this real life?" I squeezed her tightly and attempted to fight back the tears rushing my eyes.

Gabby laughed, holding me at arm's length. "This is your fairytale, Terra." Her eyes lifted above my shoulder. "Here comes mine."

"Terra, let me see that beautiful ring!" Izzy's voice carried from behind me.

Gabby released her hold on me as Izzy bounced into view, gasping as her eyes landed on my ring finger. "Wow." She was in awe of the diamond sitting atop my finger. "You did good, Mister." She poked Drew's shoulder, making us all laugh. "Were you expecting it?"

"Not at all." I glanced up at Drew.

"Although, he was supposed to wait and propose in front of everyone, I had a good feeling he couldn't last that long." She gave me a wink.

Drew shrugged. "I feel like I should apologize, but on the other hand I'm not sorry for jumping the gun."

"You know I'm only teasing you." Izzy patted him on the back.

He gently knocked his shoulder into hers. "I know."

"I better go grab the hellion before he destroys half this place." Izzy scurried after their toddler son, Jeremy. They'd adopted him not long after Gabby had placed her house on the market. But instead of running from the past, they'd decided on removing the for sale sign from the yard and keeping the house for their growing family.

My eyes drifted around the room. My breath caught at the sight of Janet and Brad heading our way. I wasn't expecting them to be in town, let alone in on the hush hush engagement party.

"Oh, Terra, congratulations." Janet's words lodged in her throat as tears raced down her face. She enveloped me in her arms and every emotion imaginable crashed down on the two of us.

We stood surrounded by people, crying through the heartache and happiness of what me marrying Drew truly meant. Both of us knew this landmark of a step pushed our lives into another direction. She and Brad had been astonishingly welcoming to Drew, accepting him into their family as if he was one of their own. Hell, Brad and Drew had gone on many trips together golfing, fishing, and hiking. It made my heart happy that they'd developed such a relationship, but also made my heart ache for the loss of their true son...my first husband. No matter what, they would be in my life for as long as I lived. We were like pieces of a shattered heart glued together to make it whole again.

I'd come a long way in the two and a half years since Liam's death, and I still had a hell of a long path ahead of me. But there was nowhere else I'd rather be than surrounded by those who truly loved me through the dark times, and into the light. Each and every person around me had impacted my life in one way or another. I was forever grateful for them.

If you opened the book of my life, it would be filled with love, broken pieces, and ugly truths. But it would also be filled with a major comeback, peace in my soul, and a man who saved me from the darkness. Overcoming grief wasn't an easy task. It lingered when you least expected it, but I'd learned that grief was much like an ocean. At times the water was calm, while other times it raged, and all you could do was learn how to keep your head above the water.

"Laura and Mark send their best. It broke her heart that they couldn't make it. But her pregnancy is far too along for her to travel." Janet squeezed my arms.

"I'll give her a call later."

As I stepped from Janet's arms, I went directly into Drew's. His strong hold was like a balm soothing my aching heart. He kissed the top of my head and rubbed circles over my bare upper back. "Marrying me doesn't replace the love you had for Liam. Like I told you those years ago, I don't want to replace anyone. I only want a portion of your heart to call my own. You know that, right?"

My head bobbed up and down as I focused on his face through tear filled eyes. "I truly thought the sun left when Liam died, but you brought it back into my galaxy. You pushed me to find the tomorrow my heart and soul had been searching for. I can't thank you enough for that."

His lips pressed softly to mine. "For the remainder of our lives, we can show one another just how thankful we are for this love."

And, boy, did we ever.

THE END

ACKNOWLEDGMENTS

I honestly can't believe this is the tenth time I've been blessed with writing acknowledgments. Without each and every one of you, I wouldn't be able to share my stories with the world. So, first and foremost, I want to say THANK YOU!

To the ladies who worked their butts off to make Finding Tomorrow the best it could be, Virginia and Traci, I can't thank you enough.

For those that don't already know, this story came to fruition from the heartache of losing my fur-baby Jack, to cancer back in March. I found my outlet for the grief and sorrow by writing Terra's story. Many tears were shed throughout the writing process of Finding Tomorrow, but I'm thankful Jack was able to give me the gift of this beautiful, yet heartbreaking, story to share with my readers. To those that don't understand the bond one can have with a fur-baby, I hope one day one walks into your life and shows you how great their love truly is.

Last, but not least, I want to thank my right-hand-lady, Regina Bartley. Girl, without our crazy chats, plotting messages, and intense laughter, my days would be a lot less fun.

'Til next time. <3

ABOUT THE AUTHOR

From the Most Beautiful Small Town of America & the Bourbon Capital of the World, Bardstown, Kentucky, Savannah Stewart writes Contemporary Romance, New Adult, and Romantic Suspense. She's a Book-a-holic who loves music, tattoos, photography, singing, writing, & laughing. One of her favorite quotes is "Love is the beauty of the soul."

http://www.authorsavannahstewart.com

Email: savannah@authorsavannahstewart.com

42440725R00146

Made in the USA
Middletown, DE
18 April 2019